MINION

MINION

A VAMPIRE
HUNTRESS
LEGEND

L. A. BANKS

 ST. MARTIN'S GRIFFIN 🏛 NEW YORK

www.stmartins.com

Book design by Jonathan Bennett

Library of Congress Cataloging-in-Publication Data

Banks, L. A.
    Minion : a vampire huntress legend / L.A. Banks.—1st ed.
        p.   cm.—(The dark legends begin ; bk. 1)
    ISBN 0-312-31680-1
    1. Women artists—Fiction.   2. Vampires—Fiction.   I. Title.

PS3602.A64M56   2003
813'.6—dc21

                                                            2003042042

First Edition: June 2003

10   9   8   7   6   5   4   3   2   1

DEDICATION AND *SPECIAL* ACKNOWLEDGMENTS

This book is dedicated to those people who believe in things unseen and have walked by faith for so long that it's second nature. All of us know the elders who have that unshakable belief that there's a spiritual plane, and without those individuals holding the line, who knows what shape this world would be in? And yet while predators come in all forms, and have besieged our communities on many levels, there still seems to be a force that keeps a total eclipse of the light at bay. These elders teach, impart quiet wisdom, and ready another generation to take the baton as they pass it.

On the surface it may appear that the battle is a hopeless cause, and that there are no young, strong replacements . . . one could easily buy into "the illusion" that all is lost. Not so, because there are so many young warriors out there whose names we have yet to learn, and so many old guardians still keeping the lantern lit. Some say it's myth, others call it legend—but I have seen these people moving in mysterious ways. Therefore, do not believe in the smallness of things, believe in the light within.

In his inauguration speech, Nelson Mandela said it best: "Our worst fear is not that we are inadequate, our deepest fear is that we are powerful beyond measure. It is our light, not our darkness, that most frightens us. . . . As we are liberated from our own fear our presence automatically liberates others." Keep your lights on!

To my spiritual team of women warriors of light, I thank you: Mom, Aunt Julia, Aunt Hettie, Aunt Ruby, Aunt Ruth, Grandmom Pete, Grandmom Thornton—y'all were awesome while on the planet! Count them . . . there were seven, who have now crossed over into the light . . . and who keep me there in my darkest moments. *Thank you, Father God.*

Special acknowledgments go to: My editor, Monique Patterson— whose creative vision and chutzpah allowed this project to be realized; my agent, Manie Barron of William Morris Agency, Inc.—the crazy man who dreamt up and pitched the concept! To the *Evening Star* writers of Philadelphia: Hilary, Kamal, Karen, Jenice, and Sheila . . . thanks, guys, for guiding me and reading scary stories that nobody wanted to read. To my sister, Liza Peterson, a spoken-word, hip-hop artist/actress extraordinaire! Thanks, sis, for keeping it real. Last, but not least, thanks to my husband and children for putting up with my dark side, my late nights, and total immersion in the realms of otherworldliness while I went into the mind-set and half-turned personae of vampiri in order to create a story about keeping the light.

PROLOGUE

SARAH RICHARDS stood in the middle of her bedroom trying to console her infant who was wailing at the top of her tiny lungs. Yes, she knew what pain was, and wanted to cry out as much as her baby was carrying on right now. Instead, silent tears slid down the sides of her face as she turned her chin up to the ceiling and shut her eyes. How, Lord, was a preacher's wife supposed to deal with the fact that her husband was having an affair?

For months she'd denied the obvious. But now her husband's lies regarding his whereabouts had been found out. He'd even violated the sanctity of their home by bringing this woman to their bed—their marital bed. Evidence, in the form of the marriage-violator's perfume and blood, still clung to the sheets. She'd only been gone an hour on a church errand her husband had contrived for her to do. One hour, and now this?

Sarah covered her mouth and turned away, hastening from the sight and stench of the filth, taking her baby girl to lay her in her crib. With her hands trembling, she left the screaming infant, whose wails intensified as she turned away from her. Shame burned through her. How could she call the church elders, or talk to Mother Stone about something like this? How did a preacher's wife, the first lady of the church, force her lips to say that her husband, the Reverend Richards, had lost his natural black mind?

Amid the now hiccupping bleats from the nursery, Sarah became very still as she heard movement in the small clapboard house below her. There were two voices. One soft, seductive; the other was that of her husband. He'd brought this whore back to his home again! Once was not enough? Did he think she was so foolish as to run another church errand to an elderly neighbor, at night, again, so he could be doing God knows what? Couldn't he hear his own child screaming her lungs out—and wouldn't he know that *his wife* was upstairs? Did he have so little respect for her, or was it that this whore's pull was that strong?

Tears of bitter rage and hurt stung Sarah's eyes, the pain of her acknowledgment almost crushing her rib cage as the muscles around her heart constricted. This woman, this transgressor, had a hold on her husband that not even the Lord could seem to break . . . because, Father God knew, she'd prayed on it from the first inkling of doubt. Now, her husband had brought a violator back into his house? *Her* house. A home designed for a minister, his wife, and children, across the street from hallowed ground? Sarah felt her knees begin to buckle as she envisioned the faces of loyal parishioners who hung on the good Reverend's every word . . . just as she once had. This house was not a home, nor was it a place where she or her child could find peace.

She resisted her first instinct, which was to barrel downstairs to confront her husband and the heifer that had crossed her threshold. But something slithered inside Sarah's soul and gave her pause. The green-eyed monster raised its ugly head. She had to know what this hussy looked like . . . who was this woman that could break up hearth and home using something that all women had? She wanted to spy and know the things her husband said to this home-wrecker. What lies had Armand Richards told?

Silently, like a thief in the night, Sarah Richards crept down the hall, hugging the wall. She knew this house by heart and easily avoided the creaky floorboards. Stretching her body, she clung to the very paint as she peered around the corner of the landing. The baby's cries escalated, her pulse rising along with it. She held her breath as she rounded the corner—and froze.

A tall, handsome, male figure the color of café au lait and dressed in an impeccable black suit, ran a palm across her husband's jaw. The caress was sensuality personified. The sight stole the scream from Sarah's lungs, as her husband closed his eyes and dropped his head back in a display of sheer feminine submission. Sarah took the stairs one by one, clutching the handrail to keep from passing out. She couldn't breathe as she watched in abject horror while this man . . . a man . . . not a woman . . . embraced her husband like a lover and lowered his head to Armand's exposed throat.

When she heard her husband groan, something fragile within her snapped.

Everything became a blur. Her feet flew down the stairs; her screams outstripped her infant daughter's. The words became a chant—"God, no! Not that!" She would crucify this beast, the fouler of her household! There was no rational thought as she hurled herself forward trying to grab hold of his broad shoulders. She wanted blood. A pound of flesh! But the agile intruder simply swept her husband up in his arms as though he were sweeping away his bride, and deftly slipped through the door with him.

Sarah gave chase into the front yard, screaming, crying, hollering behind them, but only the night heard her. She spun in a crazed circle, searching the darkness for them. Where had this lover taken her husband? And so quickly? Sarah fell to her knees in the gravel driveway. The stones cut through her nightgown and pierced her knees. Bloodied, she lay outstretched, sobbing a futile prayer. A man? It was a man. Dear Jesus in Heaven, no! A man, gorgeous, with jet-black, penetrating eyes, a regal carriage, flawless skin, thick, black lashes, onyx curls that would shame any woman . . . a man . . . please no . . . a man that stood six foot two, with a solid frame, and strong enough to lift her husband as if Armand was a baby! No!

She heaved and vomited, wiped her mouth, and clawed the dirt until she could push herself upright. She stared up at the sky and then at the lit window of her daughter's room. Sarah walked slowly back to the house and reached for the telephone. The church matriarch should send her daughter, Marlene, to look after the baby tonight, she heard her inner voice say. Marlene was good with infants. She was a nice young woman.

Right now, Sarah Richards had an errand to run. One that she'd put off all these months. She needed something more than prayer. Her husband was with *a man,* and the church elders didn't know nothing about pain like that. The old lady who lived on the edge of the swamps had potions and such to correct these kinds of abominations. And what Sarah would tell her would stay between her and the old witch.

For three days Sarah sat at the living room window as the church elders held the prayer vigil at her home. Young Marlene had brought them with her when Sarah had hysterically called for a baby-sitter at that odd hour of the night, and had told the girl that her husband was gone. What else had she expected? One didn't call at that hour and think the girl wouldn't have to explain things to a mother, who would then call in church reinforcements—not when there was a problem at the church head's house.

But desperation had kept Sarah from thinking things through that far. If they thought he'd just run off, fine. That had been enough for the old folks to mount a prayer posse—Minister was nowhere to be found, his wife and child had been abandoned. Evil was at work. That was all Sarah would say on the matter.

She slept in the parlor chair while she struggled with her plan, unable to ever go back to her own bed, unable to even lie down on the couch. She refused to eat, barely took a sip of water, didn't move, just stared. Who knew what other piece of furniture had been violated within her home? Each day that passed the black bag she'd hidden in the pantry issued a more urgent call for her to take matters into her own hands. Yet, to do so would be a death of all she'd been brought up to believe in. It would be flying directly in the face of the Lord. Three days, and three long nights, Sarah pondered the seductive choice.

She quietly thanked the praying people that had descended upon her house, never saying so out loud, just in her mind. Their eyes remained lowered and she appreciated their discretion, and she said a prayer of thanks that young Marlene Stone was taking such good care of her child while her nerves took leave.

Sarah Richards knew that she had checked out of life. Her eyes simply watched the point of nothing beyond the window. But on this third night, she also knew what she had to do. The elders, for all their prayers, didn't know where her husband's car had disappeared to, or where the good Reverend was, for that matter. But the old seer had spoken of a mansion—a plantation. Had given her directions and landmarks to follow. And she would arm herself with her spell and a butcher knife to right this wrong as soon as the sun set . . . just as the witch had advised.

Without a word, Sarah stood and feigned illness, leaving the prayer warriors who had murmured without relent since the night she'd seen too much. Sarah went to the bathroom and splashed water on her face, then snuck into the pantry to collect her bag that had been secretly readied. In her bare feet and robe, she slipped from the house and into the night without a sound. She was gonna fetch back her husband, or die trying.

Sarah stood in the center of a circle of weeping willows with tears streaming down her cheeks and stared at the expansive estate. Elaborate ironwork graced the veranda that rimmed the entire second floor of the mansion. Tall white columns created a formidable entrance to the place she'd dared to go. Spanish moss billowed from the trees and nary a cricket sounded. Her husband's car was in the driveway, just as the old woman had prophesized. Sarah's hand clutched the satchel and her feet never consulted her brain as she moved forward, rounding the mansion to the back door that was surprisingly unlocked.

The mansion was eerily quiet as she slipped into the darkness within. Money, power . . . what riches had been promised her husband by this wealthy perversion of a lover, she wondered? How could a man she'd loved with all her heart and soul do this to her? How could he live such a lie, allow her to bear a child for him? How could he do this to his baby girl?

New tears replenished the salty stream that had dried on Sarah's face. She'd loved Armand Richards since they were children, and had never known any other man in the world but him.

Her footsteps took her through the house, each room making her walk more quickly as she saw sumptuous wealth—but not her husband. She hurried up the winding staircase toward the upper levels of the mansion, listening intently for the sounds of her husband in the throes of passion, but heard nothing. Every well-appointed room was vacant. The seer had been wrong. Armand was not here. But it was clear that her husband had been here at one time. Perhaps he and his man-friend were out on the town, or secluded in another love nest? Sarah's mind took a sinister turn; she squeezed her eyes shut as she saw them naked together. Bile rose within her throat as images of her husband with this seductive man lacerated her spirit. No. This had to be fixed! This was the only way.

The opportunity their absence provided was perfect. She would do what she had to do—go into the wine cellar, the base of the house, and cast the spell. Sarah covered her heart and said a prayer for her child, and asked for forgiveness. She knew her prescription was wrong as she tiptoed down the long hallway, found the stairs, and descended to the first floor. The long walk gave her time to explain with contrition that she had to *do* something, could not just sit and wait for this to be *made* right. All she asked was that Father God would understand and spare her baby girl—despite what it said in the Good Book about soothsayers and spell-casters . . . or taking matters into one's own hands. This was a special case, and He had to understand her desperation.

Her bare feet stung with the cuts and abrasions she sustained from walking, crazed, through the woods, over bramble, across driveway gravel for five miles in the dark. The bag of black magic weighed heavily in her hand as she shifted the bulk of it onto her hip, extracted a black candle and a small box of stick matches, lit the candle, then clumsily stowed away the matches, and resumed her slow descent down into the damp cavern of the first level of the mansion.

Slick stone walls reflected the light from the sputtering flame,

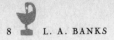

and the coolness of the room belied the humidity that made her summer robe and gown cling to her skin. Perspiration due to her shattered nerves seeped from her pores, sending a rivulet of adrenaline-filled sweat between her breasts and down her back. Undaunted, she began making the circle in the dirt, using the butcher knife to carve the strange star shape that the old woman had drawn for her on a crumpled piece of paper. Sarah's lips moved with purpose as she opened the Mason jar and splashed blood from the gutted rooster upon each point of the star. And as she set each black candle in place, and closed her eyes, constantly murmuring, the floor beneath her began to move.

Immediately plumes of thick, yellowish smoke rose, choking her in a sulfuric, blackening haze. The rack of wine bottles on the wall began to explode, sending shards of glass to cover her. Splinters from flying wood and glass cut into her skin like shrapnel. A scream choked by spit, terror, and smoke was torn from her throat as she ran and huddled in a corner against the wall.

He could not believe his good fortune. Fallon Nuit contained his amusement as his strategy took root. Providence of this magnitude couldn't have been conjured by the highest sorcerers of old. A fluke. A variable. A tiny rip in the fabric of supernatural law, all caused by a frightened, but foolish, woman. Jealousy had ironically released the green-eyed monster within her—along with another, more dangerous entity that the poor human creature obviously hadn't anticipated . . . nor had the Vampire Council. Pity. A gross oversight. They couldn't keep him incarcerated for a violation of their staunch, outdated High Council rules, as they had planned. There were things that even vampires frowned upon. Then again, there was this variable called luck.

"You have inadvertently been summoned to my lair," Nuit

crooned in a seductive tone toward the demon that arose with him from the billowing cloud of smoke.

"I was called, yes. That gives me the right—"

"No," Nuit replied with a lethal warning between his teeth. "You have no *rights,* but you do have the misfortune to be a demon trapped in a master vampire's lair."

Two formidable adversaries stared at each other for a moment. The snakelike creature appeared stunned, then outraged. However, when it offered no rebuttal, Nuit pressed on, his hunger for the fresh taste of blood, stoked by the scent of the frail female human trying to hide herself in the corner of his wine cellar, notwithstanding.

"Cohabitation without cooperation is not an option." Nuit studied his manicured nails and sighed. "Do remember that I am of the more evolved order of the dark realms, and now freed, I could make existence for you here torturous. But I am a man of reason."

The demon looked at him, and then glanced at the cowering woman on the floor. "We could come to terms. Fair exchange is no robbery."

Fallon Nuit threw his head back and laughed. "Indeed!"

Being unconquerable lies within yourself;
being conquerable lies within the enemy.

—Sun-tzu, *The Art of War*

CHAPTER ONE

DAMALI RICHARDS could still feel the electricity of the crowd and the adrenaline rush of her spoken-word performance pulsing through her veins as she entered the backstage dressing room. The club was jumping so hard it seemed like even the walls were sweating. The bass thumping from the extensive speaker system was like an insistent heartbeat that she could feel vibrating through the floor and smoke-thickened air until it entered her body through the soles of her feet. Dirty aqua-colored paint peeled at the corners of the cramped space, as though it was trying to escape the throbbing scene.

She glanced around at the ugly, stained brown sofa, and the sparse collection of wooden and metal chairs, immediately opting to stand rather than flop on any of the seating choices. How many performers' body funk had been permanently tattooed on that sorry excuse for a couch, she wondered? Even the one mirror in the room was covered with a white, filmy layer of grime. Yuck. And people thought this was the glamorous life? She, Marlene, and a five-man squad crammed into a dump. Pullease.

Sweat, icy yet burning, made her clothes stick to her skin. Her heavily beaded, Nzinga queen warrior headdress had suddenly become an intolerable weight on her damp scalp. Damali roughly removed it, tossing it onto a chair, and she held her shoulder-length locks up off her neck to give her overheated body a much-needed waft of air. The semiprecious stone and lion's teeth adornments, affixed to her locks with silver and copper wire, gently clinked as she moved her hair. She grimaced at the sound that was now too close to her skull. All five feet seven inches of her felt on fire. Being an artist was great, but this was no way to live.

"Lot of activity on radar tonight," Marlene said in a near whisper, as though talking to herself. "Most times we get a visit from one or two vampires. I'm sensing many."

"Yeah," Damali croaked. Her vocal chords still ached from the intense performance, so she kept her response short. Besides, what else was there to say to her manager, who was like a surrogate mother to their group?

Damali and Marlene shared a glance. They both knew what had to be done. Things were heating up. Before, one vamp might follow them, at most two. But ever since they'd turned the tables and went on the offensive a couple of times, seeking out the action instead of waiting for it to come to them, nothing had been the same. The rare random ambushes were now becoming a regular phenomenon. Valuable junior team members had been lost because if it. Irritation coiled within Damali. She'd told Marlene this shit would go down like that once they started hunting. Shoulda let sleeping dogs lie.

Marlene shot her a look that said *don't start.* Screw Marlene and her pious yang. Not tonight. Sure, she loved Mar like a mom and all, but wasn't feeling sister-girl right now. Yeah, they only went after vampires that were acting up. But that wasn't the point.

"You didn't hear me, did you?"

Damali cut Marlene a hard glance, then looked away. "No. What did you say?"

Marlene waited until the two women's eyes met again. "I didn't *say* anything. I thought it, and you didn't hear me in your head. But I'm able to read you loud and clear. That concerns me."

Total annoyance wrapped itself around Damali and she gave Marlene another glare to make her back off. She felt invaded. "I'm just tired, that's all. The past is the past. It's done now, anyway. Drop it."

"You need to tell us when you're having sensory blackouts. They're becoming more frequent, aren't they? You could have sent that to me without a word."

The other members of the team gave Damali a quick look of concern, but were wise enough not to get in the middle of the brewing dispute. More than likely they'd let the bullshit pass, because she and Marlene were always at it. Whatever.

Instead of answering Marlene, Damali forced her attention toward the Native American flutes, cowbells, and chimes that rested against large conga drums in the corner of the room. Her gaze scanned the sharp, titanium-based, silver-plated anchors that held the drumhead skins in place. She refused to answer Marlene's question. She didn't feel like dealing with that crap right now. There was something making the hair stand up on the back of her neck.

Tonight, the drum anchors were going in her belt, even if that music gear was Jose's, a.k.a. Wizard. He was da bomb in concert, but he didn't know how to use the disguised weapons as well as she did out in the streets. Summoning inner strength, Damali blocked Marlene's intrusion into her thoughts. She'd give Marlene a mental blank to consider while taking her time to figure out how to better arm herself.

The crew was so quiet it was eerie. Nobody said a word, and all were simply packing gear. That was not her team's normal behavior after a gig. The walls of the tiny room felt like they were closing in on her, swallowing her crew whole. Damali studied her weapons options.

Maybe a few silver-plated chimes would be a safe bet, too? Jose could do his thing on crossbow, his favorite weapon anyway. A sister could back somethin' up off her with the dagger-edges off the drum anchors and chimes, if it got crazy out there—same deal with the cymbals. Even though she reminded herself that when a cymbal disc was thrown dead-aim the edge was sharp enough to slice paper without hearing it rip, that fact didn't make her feel better tonight. Why not?

Her gaze instantly went to the Fender—Jake Rider's electric guitar, and to Shabazz's bass, and then to Marlene's electric violin. Marlene's line of vision followed Damali's for a moment before Marlene began assisting the others with equipment breakdown.

As Marlene moved to work with Shabazz, renewed tension wound its way up Damali's spine. Yeah, they'd better restring the instruments and put in the steel cables across the reinforced metal bridges. Tonight felt like a crossbow-necessary night, and the string instruments were easier to roll with. She might even get Wizard to hook up the light poles through the phony strap loops to lock and load additional crossbows. But Marlene needed to give up the walking stick as her only protection. Sistah better recognize, and deal with her violin like it had been designed—put the steel-based bow across the bridge and be ready to rock.

It felt like they'd need the light cannons out there, too, although at the moment, she couldn't exactly say why. Nah . . . this was no way to live.

She walked over to the drums and ignored the look Marlene cast in her direction. The dense scent of frankincense, sage, and myrrh had trailed into the room behind her from the stage. Damali licked her parched lips, tasting salt on them, and tried to inhale the protective fragrance, but felt herself almost retch.

Usually the aroma calmed her, its elements anointing her stage space—a required opening before a purple haze of dry-ice smoke was released as she'd enter a performance and claim it. The ring of holy water which had been poured around her in libation to bring forth the ancestors to channel-speak through her, and to encircle her while she spat out the truth of injustice, did not infuse her marrow with unshakable confidence tonight. Heavy bass still throbbed in her skull, now cranking the growing headache to a new decibel level with the ongoing club music that quaked the walls. Being a vampire huntress was no way to live.

"You all right?"

Marlene's question hung in the air as the other crew members paused in their tasks for a moment, considered her, and glanced at each other as though waiting for the green light to continue their equipment breakdown.

Damali just nodded. The crew resumed motion, but kept glancing at her from the corners of their eyes. She wanted to get back to the compound, where they stowed *off the hook* weapons. The equipment they took on the road was disguised enough to get through new airport security screenings, which meant it wasn't the real heavy artillery. And, yeah, it would be enough to stop a few predators. But if her senses were right, they were in for sho 'nuff action tonight.

The problem was, she couldn't half see. Her normal sight was fine, but inside her head, everything was blurry. Her third-eye was down. Had been that way for a couple of weeks, like static on a television. Intermittent static. Sometimes her mental radar was crystal clear, but at other times, like tonight, it was all snow. She hated this bull.

"We need to hurry up," Damali said out of the blue. Her crew stared at her. One by one they nodded, but nobody said a word. Damn, it was hot in there.

For some reason, the air-conditioned confines didn't cool her off either. Her skin-tight, thigh-slit leather pants felt like they were suffocating her, while the ropes of semiprecious amulets and stones set in thick silver around her wrists, and especially about her neck, began feeling like a humid noose. She began stripping them off, ignoring Marlene's expression of disapproval. The necklaces were practically strangling her. She'd have to chance having her throat exposed, just so she could breathe.

Unable to bear the weight of it, Damali cast off her wide silver belt, and the clatter of it against a nearby coffee table almost made her cringe from the piercing sound of metal connecting with the wood. The ankh earrings of amber and silver and onyx had to come off—they were all too heavy, no matter what Marlene said about the protective talismans that hung as guards to her jugular. Everything felt like it was holding on to her, grasping at her. She couldn't breathe!

"You're sure you're all right?" Marlene had stopped working over an equipment bag to hold her in a steady gaze.

"I'm cool, y'all. For real, for real," Damali finally muttered. There was no need to bring her foul vibe to the group. It wasn't their fault. Why alarm them if this was only a case of raw nerves? She studied the drum anchors one last time and then walked away from them. "Guess I'm just tired from giving it a hundred and fifty percent tonight."

The others in the room simply stared at her, their silence filling in the gaps with quiet apprehension. Yeah, they all felt it, she could tell. Oh, well, shit happens. They knew that, too. None of them wanted to do this destiny thing, especially her. They were trapped as guardians, just like she was trapped as a vampire huntress. There was only one choice that they'd all learned the hard way—band together or die, or worse.

"Let's just keep moving, people. Anybody seen my Tims?"

Marlene extracted the flat-heeled, amber-colored suede boots Damali had requested from a corner in the room and tossed them to her. Damali caught each shoe and bent to put them on. Slowly, her crew resumed their packing.

The sleek high-heeled boots she'd worn during the performance had become like anvils on her legs. This was not a high-heel, be fly and cute kinda night. This was a possible kick ass after a show deal. Despite the sheerness of the color-splashed, tie-dyed duster and embroidered midriff brassiere she performed in, they too felt like they were cutting off her blood flow, and made her want to scream. Her breasts, which she had always believed to be too small, now felt oddly pendulous, heavy, too constricted by her costume. The fragile silver waist-chain she donned seemed to push bile up from her gullet and into her throat. If she weren't almost twenty-one years old, and in top athletic form, she would have sworn that she was having a mild heart attack.

Damali peered in the mirror, appraising her once-bronze complexion that now seemed pallid—but was eerily relieved to see that at least she still had a reflection. What the hell was wrong with her?

"Somebody throw me a T-shirt."

Shabazz complied, and flung a shirt with the band's logo on it in her direction.

"Thanks." Damali gave her crew her back and stripped off the offending sheer top of her stage costume. The guys averted their eyes, as was normal, and as soon as she pulled on the cotton, she sighed. "That's much better. Now I'm good."

"You put a lot of energy into the show," Marlene said after a long pause while the group resumed breakdown. But she spoke in a calm voice, one almost too calm.

"Got a reputation to maintain, Mar." Damali made eye contact with Marlene and held her with a brief stare. *Read the double meaning in that, sis. Don't front on me—not with my crew standing around. Address it later.*

Marlene nodded but said nothing.

Cool. Damali relaxed a bit.

Oh, yeah. Everybody was on edge and needed to chill. She now wondered what Marlene, their seer-guardian, had sensed. When Marlene had visions, she got real cool—scary calm. Damali tossed her knowledge of Marlene's capabilities around inside her head and watched her mentor's body language. Only having a portion of one's skills to rely on was a bitch.

Maybe she should have just told Mar that she was going blind again tonight. But she hated the concept. What, and have the guys go back to treating her like a young buck? A newbie? Hell, no. This was *her* crew, and whatever was going wrong with her was temporary. All she had to do was look at Marlene hard to know it was gonna be on when they left, no doubt. Didn't need second sight to pick that up.

Jose glanced from crew member to crew member, his nerves also seeming raw. The fact that no one else had said a word had to be jacking with him. Their percussion man's dark eyes shifted nervously between Damali and Marlene Stone. "Yeah, you brought it to 'em, D," he confirmed after a hesitant glance up from his task of packing away equipment.

Small talk, a sure sign of nerves. She hated small talk. "Thanks, Wizard."

"You owned New Energy tonight. The club will never be the same—Warriors of Light Productions and you, lady, should get some good ink from this one in the press tomorrow."

Tomorrow? Assuming they made it through the night. Damali glanced at Jose and then toward Marlene. That crazy Mexican Indian always started babbling when he was hyped. She loved him just the same, but if their ace tracker was trippin'—then *damn*. Marlene blanched. Obviously Marlene got that message, too.

"Sho 'nuff, we brought it, Wizard," Damali said in a short pant, giving Jose a fist pound, trying to make him feel better as she did so. It was obvious that her mental wall against Marlene wasn't even working. But she also couldn't seem to completely catch her breath. Forget that, Wizard always talked a lot and his voice got louder when nervous. Tonight was no different. It made her head hurt.

She glanced at Marlene again. The colors of her manager's royal purple Afrocentric robe and glittering gold-patterned embroidery that matched her lamé pants were now too bright, and Damali briefly shut her eyes to that regal countenance. Jose's sleeveless black T-shirt and jet-black jeans stabbed into the center of the color array that danced beneath her lids. Silver from his large cross turned into a pinpoint of light just as she'd glanced away, and now she could feel herself taking in breaths in short sips.

"Get her some water," Marlene ordered, dispatching Jose from his semi-stooped position over a light kit bag.

Damali accepted a new bottle of spring water from him; she broke the seal of it with her eyes still closed and took a deep, cleansing swig. A metallic taste covered her tongue. The taste of nearby death made her appraise her crew with a wary eye. They couldn't afford to lose another soul in their group. By now she could definitely tell that they'd sensed the danger, too.

Everyone was too quiet, too laid-back, too methodical in the way they'd quickly dispensed with courtesies with the club management, fended off groupies, and then immediately began to break down the equipment to pack up to leave the club without a word. There wasn't the normal backstage revelry; there wasn't any discussion about getting something to eat, or general conversation even. Just a strange nothingness stood between them as they worked like robots at their tasks.

"I'ma go help Rider get the rest of the gear," Jose finally said in a low tone, leaving Damali's side. "Won't be too long."

"You cool?" Marlene asked again, giving her artist a level glance as she gathered up Damali's cast-off costume pieces and thrust them into her mud-cloth satchel. Marlene then looked at Shabazz, who didn't utter a word.

Damali only nodded in Marlene's direction. She noted that J.L., their lighting/keyboard man, also hadn't said two words since they'd entered the room. What was that about?

"Damali's always cool," Shabazz murmured.

Damali stared at him for a moment. Okay, Shabazz was always chill as the group's Aikido instructor/choreographer/bassist. Brother smooth, the director of ice. Martial arts warrior of few words, unless it was much rhetorical philosophy. However, Shabazz had murmured without looking up from helping Joe Leung disassemble and pack sections of the lighting grips and the digital keyboards that masked the vital computer tracking systems they needed. J.L. hadn't looked at Shabazz either, and those two were always in sync and made eye contact. No. Something deep was up.

She studied her crew hard. Marlene, their manager and the guardian seer on violin, normally bristled at the slightest trace of movement and saw everything coming with eagle eyes. What was wrong with Mar tonight? Plus, Marlene wasn't givin' up the tapes. She just kept trying to act like everything was cool, but it wasn't. Shabazz and J.L., also pair sensors—they could actually *feel* things coming, and could detect a location by simply touching something evil left behind—were tense, on guard, but weren't talking.

Jose and crazy Jake Rider, their guitarist and sharpshooter, shared the capacity to pull the taste and the scent of danger out of the air. They were the noses—and they hadn't been right all night. Then there was Big Mike, their soundman/music director, who could hear what nobody else could, and could also blow the mothers up, literally. An unmatched explosives expert from the era of 'Nam, tonight he was jumpy. That wasn't Big Mike's style. Brother was always laid-back, and the voice of reason in the group.

Together they possessed all five senses, plus the sixth of clairvoyance through Marlene, and yet she was supposed to be the omni-voyant one—possessing all six natural wonders as a vampire huntress, so they'd said. Yeah, right. She hadn't seen any of that grandeur materialize lately. For a while, she was *all that*. But as of a couple of weeks ago, she felt her gifts, as Marlene referred to them, sliding away from her fast. First her sight, and then some of her physical endurance. Her nose wasn't worth shit as a tracker these days. Taste and sound were off-kilter, too. Then, without warning, each attribute would come back stronger than it had been before. Like power fluctuations during a brownout. Go figure.

All she knew right now was that she was good at kicking ass when she had to—the streets had taught her that, although she'd give props to Shabazz for the Aikido refinement. But if the crew was buggin' this hard, then it was large, whatever *it* was. That was real.

"Where's Dan?" Damali finally asked. "I don't think it's a good idea to leave him behind this time. He's not a guardian, and if there's trouble out there tonight, he'll be at extreme risk."

"Weinstein is settling with the club owners, and going ahead of us to book a venue in New Orleans before we meet up with him in L.A. Probably the safest bet for his life is to stay away from all of this. The less he knows about this, the better," Marlene replied gently. "Daniel's a good man, but he's no guardian, and he definitely isn't a hunter. He has no skill, other than being a fantastic business manager. He should've stayed on the administrative side of things. I told him I had the other aspects of managing the band, but everybody wants to do the glitz and glamour thing."

"Yeah," Damali agreed. "Problem is, he came to an evening performance. Usually he just works the phones by day, ya know? It's getting too hot for him to be out with us, at any time, especially at night."

"I know," Marlene murmured, her gaze going toward the door. "He insisted this time. Wanted to personally experience the phenomenon of *Damali* so he could better promote her in contract negotiations, he said. I argued with him about it, and thought it was settled, and then he shows up tonight anyway, unannounced. Not good. Too dangerous."

"Every-damned-body wants to be in the mix," Shabazz said with a disgusted sigh. "The limelight. If they only knew."

"When we get back to L.A., I'm going to have to sever him for his own good. Let's just get our innocent home safely. We clean up whatever's out there tonight, and then page the limo to pick Dan up in the front, first, before the limo comes to pick up the team. I'll have to go back to doing the promoting as well as the books, I suppose. But in the meanwhile, I just have to think about what to tell Dan. I'll give him a nice exit package, though. It's at the point where we can't even expose a limo driver to this." Marlene chuckled sadly and addressed Shabazz. "Looks like you'll be driving our limo again, too, after tonight."

"No problem." Shabazz shrugged. "It's better that way. Just like old times."

J.L. gave a slow nod of agreement in response to Shabazz. "Yeah, man, but what's taking Rider and Jose so long to break down the set? It's time to bounce. We need those mics—stat."

"They ain't breakin' it all the way down," Mike reported in his deep Southern drawl.

"No, not tonight," Rider concurred as he reentered the small space followed by Jose.

Damali didn't comment. Mike Robert's dark face held a non-descript, poker-player blank expression that Damali was used to reading by now. Being an audio-sensor, she wondered if he'd heard anything in the charged atmosphere. That possibility was not lost on her. It was all in the way Big Mike kept stopping and tilting his head like a hunting dog straining to hear some-thing, and then going back to his task. His vibe didn't improve her nerves. Nor did Rider's or Jose's actions help cool her out when they came in the room, breathed deeply, stopped for a beat, and then began moving quickly to convert some of the gear.

Again Damali's gaze scanned the room, returning to Marlene Stone's eyes. Her manager hadn't changed her expression; it con-tained the same barely concealed tension that it had ever since they'd arrived at the club. Marlene tightened the beaded strap that held back her waist-length, silver-gray locks, and then picked up her walking stick, casting a second one in Damali's direction.

Catching the carved ebony quickly, Damali felt a renewed wave of adrenaline course through her. She needed her long blade, Madame Isis, but this would have to do. Marlene had promised she could have it when she turned twenty-one, but she didn't see why Marlene had put up such a fuss about her taking it a few days early. Marlene was getting on her nerves.

Damali walked over to the drums and put three titanium anchors in her waistband, and a razor-sharp chime in both back pockets of her leather pants. "No time to change outta stage gear, huh?"

"You know the drill," Marlene said in a firm voice. "Shabazz, you're lead point. You're out front to feel the vibe as we move. I'm right behind you, next to Damali—to keep an eye on any sudden movement."

Again, she and Marlene shared a stare. This one felt like a standoff. What the hell was Marlene doing giving her and her crew the move-out logistics?

"I decide when we roll." Damali glanced around the room at her team and allowed her line of vision to settle on Marlene. "Everybody clear?"

Marlene only nodded and spoke in a tense, quiet voice. "If you're up to it, fine."

"Yeah. I'm up to it, so long as you're clear."

"Very."

"All right. Normal formation, then. Everybody ready?"

Shabazz opened his one-button, black leather suit jacket and smoothed his washboard abs beneath the turquoise silk shirt, flashing a ceramic Glock nine stashed in his waistband, and then toyed with the small gold star and crescent dangling about his neck. His jaw was set hard. "I'm always ready."

Marlene cut a vicious glance at Shabazz. They all knew what that look was for. They had all agreed—no incidents that could further raise suspicion with authorities. It was hard enough trying to get out of Dodge after an attack without getting hung up in a search, or have it come out in the media that one of them was carrying a concealed weapon.

Damali smiled. She knew that both Shabazz and Rider were carrying. Neither had ever been comfortable with the crossbows. Well, a man had to do what a man had to do. She could appreciate that. Next time she'd smuggle her sword along, too, just like Shabazz had claimed his nine.

"Ceramic," Shabazz explained. "Breaks down and rode stowaway in Big Mike's FX case along with what appears to be stage smoke bombs, et cetera. Felt I needed Sleeping Beauty this time. As long as everything stays beautiful, she'll stay sleeping. Anyway, they can't detect the ceramic pieces in the airport X-ray equipment—it's all good. Special-effects gear was a solid cover . . . Chill."

Rider and Shabazz exchanged a fist pound, while Mike chuckled low in his throat. Jose and J.L. gave a nod of agreement. Mutiny against Marlene's rules was in full effect.

"We'll take this up back at the compound," Marlene muttered. "Anybody else got any contraband that can get us nailed by the police—if we make it to daylight?"

If? Aw, shit . . . Marlene didn't do "if." Homegirl was always sure—positive. *If* was not a good thing.

Everyone shook their heads and Marlene let out a long breath, closed her eyes, and then shook her head, too. "We move out." As soon as the words escaped her lips, she opened her eyes and briefly glanced at Damali. "On Damali's order."

All of them were silent as they waited for Damali to give the word. However, a sense of dread coiled in the pit of her stomach as she witnessed the oldest members of the Warriors of Light Productions team take a familiar stance. It was on her to lead the potential battle, but it was also on her to make sure she didn't lose any of her people. Tension threaded through the room with a palpable static charge as the group watched her for the move-out signal.

The traces of gray in Shabazz's dark locks, and at the temples of Rider's brownish-blond spike cut, made her wonder how long these warriors could keep up their protective vigil. Marlene was a fifty-year-old enigma, driven by something Damali realized she'd probably never fully understand. Sure, Jose and J.L. only had her by ten years, and were a decade or more younger than the core team members, but how long would it be before they either got nicked, or wanted a real life and defected from the group—just like the other guardians who'd tried to give this up, and then wound up worse than dead? She loved these crazy people. They were family, like brothers and a mom. Fuckin' A. Not one of them was expendable.

She looked at Jose's handsome amber-hued face, and J.L.'s lithe, Jackie Chan–type athletically honed body. Damali shook her head as she wondered how men as fine as Shabazz and Big Mike had never found permanent solace in someone's arms. This was no way to live. The money, the fame; none of it could be totally, freely, normally enjoyed. Sooner or later, they, too, might be lost, one way or the other. It was on her as the Neteru to see that that didn't happen. But what could she do, really, to indefinitely protect them all as they guarded her? Damned catch-22, as Rider always said.

As though sensing her unspoken question, Rider swaggered over to a chair and turned it around, propping his cowboy boot in the center of it, and then leaned on his knee as he spoke. "We're ready to rock when you are. Everybody here is grown. We know the deal. Fresh-packed the rhino bullets this morning with hallowed earth," he announced with a wide grin. "Put crosses on the blunt end to leave a brand on whatever's left."

"Got something for 'em in the rear," Mike said in a blasé manner, unfurling his six-foot-seven-inch frame from the task of packing small vials in his vest on the coffee table. The slow, easy action belied the power and speed that he could unleash from his huge, muscular structure. "Got enough of these holy-water grenades to make it look like a C-4 hit 'em. Picked up a lot of activity on my soundboards during the show, thanks to the computer rig J.L. hooked up. Comes in blips like radar. Cold body readings. It's more than one of 'em tonight. Problem is, though . . . can't tell you how many—just many."

"Me and Jose are ready," J.L. announced, receiving a nod of confirmation from Jose.

"All right, Mike. Then, no sense in having Wizard and J.L. put those stage lamp kits away, completely." Damali let her breath out hard. "Leave the instruments, though. We've gotta travel light, and we can't carry it all while armed. The club will send in a couple of bouncers or security guys to load up the limo and equipment van in the front. But we do need two bows, and ultraviolet Fresnel lamps out back. Keep the UV lamps near. So, gentlemen, you're on flank, with crossbows ready. One of you wear the battery-vest to light it up on cue."

"That's why I didn't fully pack everything away," Jose replied, locking together the last bolts to transform the stands from their lighting gear into weapons. Tossing a converted bow to J.L., Wizard caught a return volley of wooden ammunition and began loading it.

"You're pretty nice on the lights, man," Joe Leung said with a sly grin. "Like the new design."

"Let's wrap this discussion up," Marlene said. "Like Damali told you guys. Shabazz walks point with Rider at his back; both sharpshooters go first. J.L. and I flank Damali with a crossbow and my stake, and then Big Mike and Jose are bringing up the rear—with our lights, crossbows, and explosives. Look alive, stay alive. There's only seven of us left."

"Yeah, and we strut out there in a giant human cross formation, like that'll help."

"Save it, Rider," Marlene warned. "Not now. Nobody's in the mood for the sarcastic commentary."

"Truth," Mike agreed, making Rider scowl.

"We ain't got time for the jokes, man." Shabazz checked his gun without looking at Rider.

"Let's just everybody chill," Jose said in a weary tone.

J.L. nodded. "Word."

Again, silence settled on the group, albeit a strained type of quiet. Still one primary question nagged Damali as she studied Marlene. Together they had all the elements that could bring down a small army of vampires. What could have spooked Marlene to the point where she was double- and triple-checking basic stage exit protocol? Something was definitely not right.

"Hold up," Damali said, her hand on Marlene's shoulder. Even her mentor's toned form was wound way too tightly for explanation. "What's out there tonight that hasn't been out there before, Marlene?"

"I don't know," Marlene murmured. "That's the problem."

"Talk to me," Shabazz said, moving behind Marlene and getting her to face him. "I'm walking point, Mar. Have for you for years. Would die for you, baby—but want to know that I *will die,* you feel me? I'm first out the door, so I have a need for clarity."

Damali watched the strain lace its way through Marlene's expression and draw her mouth to a tight line as she struggled to answer Shabazz. He reached out and pushed one of Marlene's silver-gray locks over her shoulder. Damali could only stare at the two as their eyes held a private conversation, something un-fathomable between them that obviously went back a long way, and probably had more to do with an unspoken personal commitment than what was happening tonight.

"I don't know," Marlene finally whispered.

"Your old friend, Raven?" Mike asked, his question sounding like an apology when he asked it.

Marlene shook her head. "No. She hasn't come to me like that in a while. When she does, the vision leaves emotional pain, grief. But it's not this level of intensity. The problem is . . . I can't see anything tonight."

The revelation made the group go still. *Marlene couldn't see?*

"Mar, that's too freakin' deep," Damali whispered after a moment. She had to process what Marlene had said. Earlier, Marlene was reading her like a book. Now Marlene was blind? Just as they were about to go out the door? Oh shit . . .

"Yo, Mar, I'm blind, too, okay? Like, I can sense things aren't right, but can't put my finger on it. You knew that earlier, so what's up now?"

Her guys passed concerned glances between them. The admission was uncomfortable, and Damali had cast her gaze toward the back door as she'd spoken. Saying it out loud was like giving the flaw energy, and that produced a feeling of impotence like she'd never experienced. The cat was out of the bag, and it unnerved her.

"I don't know why I can't see right now, Damali." Marlene walked away from Shabazz and faced the wall.

"But how can you be blind when you were inside my head just a few minutes ago?" At this point, Damali was pacing and using her hands as she talked.

"I was all right until we were about to leave. It's like I've suddenly got no internal radar. Normally I can call stuff on a dime, like you can, Damali." Marlene turned around and her gaze swept the group. "Even Big Mike says he *thinks* there's multiple predators out there, but can't be sure. Big Mike is always sure."

"That's how I've been all day," Damali said, agitated. "You feel me? Plus, the whole crew is jumpy, like their specialty is off or something. I don't like this bullshit at all. I'm not having it."

"Damali, relax," Shabazz ordered. He went to Marlene's side, his hand briefly touching and leaving Marlene's cheek. "You, too, Mar. Be still. Relax. Concentrate. If both seers are blind, then what's outside is too big to jack with. This is out of Marlene's league. It's on you, Damali. We get a word, first, then we move out. Breathe, baby. Then speak on it."

Damali let her breath out slowly and closed her eyes, taking in a very deep inhale. She focused on her diaphragm, forcing it to regulate to a relaxed rhythm, and then she tried to imagine the blood flowing through her veins one cell at a time. The base of her spine became warm and fleeting images flashed in colors across her inner lids. Her fingertips tingled, as did the little Sankofa tattoo over her base chakra. She felt each vertebra in her back connect and fuse by the cord threaded through it, and then she opened her eyes, nauseated.

"Strong. Higher numbers than we've seen before," Damali said, dry heaving. "I think we're going to see some people we know. That's what's going to mess with our heads. That's probably what's making me sick."

Damali worked the knots out of her neck as she began to pace again. She shrugged her locks off her shoulders in annoyance, and then leaned against the wall. "I can't explain it. But, it's not clear. Everything is messin' with me—nothing smells right, nothing feels right, and my tongue tastes like it was dipped in metal and even spring water tastes like crap. All during the performance the sound seemed off-key, sharp, in my head, like nails down a blackboard, and my skin . . . everything I touch feels like it's clinging to me. I want to just get out of here. Now."

"Oh, fuck *me*!" Jake Rider raked his fingers through his hair, wiped his hand over his face, and then pulled his Glock from his waistband, checking the magazine one more time for good measure. "First it was Di'Giovani—and Gio was *so close* to making it to full guardian status. Then Kid Cruz—we lost his ass almost as soon as we started working with the punk, God rest his talented soul . . . when we can finally drive a stake through his heart. Then, fuckin' Dee Dee Henson—that bullshit was criminal. The poor girl was only nineteen. The way they died didn't make any sense."

The mention of Dee Dee made everyone in the group freeze then glance at each other. They all looked at Jose, and then down at the floor. Yeah, it was criminal. Rider was right. A damned sin what happened to their band sister and their newbie brothers. A damned shame.

Rider suddenly kicked the chair, toppling it with a loud clatter of metal that reverberated off the walls and through Damali's skeleton, and walked back and forth as he appeared to get fired up again just thinking about it all.

"Imhotep's island ass is probably down in Jamaica some-freakin'-where turning his whole family into a tribe of moth-erfucking vampires. Then, Hans Koehler, last week, just before that kid was about to blow up on the music scene as a part of our band? And not a body in the morgue—feds and local authorities all over our ass, and we've probably gotta psycho blast up an alley on Third and Market Street in Philly's historic district tonight? Kiss my natural ass, I tell you! Just kiss my ass! I'm ready to go back to L.A., folks—and all of us are working double duty on everything—there were supposed to be twelve of us, not seven. Shit!"

"Chill," Shabazz ordered.

"Chill? I'm forty-five and getting too old for this bullshit, y'all. This is no way to live. We need to find the main lair, soon, before we all go fuckin' nuts. Let's do this."

"Chill," Shabazz ordered again, his tone lethal. His expression was no-nonsense, and he didn't blink as he looked at Rider. "That's just the kind of hysteria that will get you iced. I don't want to have to roll up on you one day, just because you panicked and got nicked. I'd hate to have to do any of you, but . . ."

"For real, for real." J.L. laughed nervously. "I'd rather take on the Asian mob, or the freakin' Russian dealers. I can handle a drive-by," he added, tucking in his khaki T-shirt, hoisting up his fatigues, rolling his neck, and then checking the laces of his army boots before he straightened himself again. "Been there, seen it, done that growing up in Laos. I mean, we don't even know what we're dealing with out there tonight." He shook his head. "I've got a bad vibe. I've never seen Damali or Marlene look like this after a gig. Your run-of-the-mill demon, one or two vamps, are one thing, but this vibe is freaky. Don't wanna have to do nobody I know, you know what I mean?" He looked at Wizard, and then looked away.

"True dat," Jose added with a melancholy tone. "They call me Wizard because I can design some def shit, but I ain't no magician. Dis ain't da barrios either, man. Ain't the Columbians or da Dominicans tonight, boss. I jus' . . . I jus' hope Dee Dee's not out there."

Damali and Marlene glanced at each other. Everybody knew the Dee Dee situation was going to be the hardest one to cope with. When Rider had mentioned her name, everybody had paused. How did one put a stake in a teammate's lover and then have things go back to normal? Wasn't possible. Jose would be messed up for a long time if his dead girlfriend was out there. Before she'd gotten nicked, Dee Dee had been like family to all of them. Poor Jose didn't even have a chance to ID her body at the morgue, because like the rest of their dead crew, the bodies had vanished from the slabs before they could get there.

Damali's glance ricocheted around the group. Yeah, they all knew it.

"I gotcha back on that one, Wizard," Big Mike reassured him after a moment, pounding Jose's fist in the process. "Cool?"

"Yeah. I'm cool, man." Jose checked the settings on his cross-bow as he answered, but did not look up. "You do her, though, if she's out there. Okay?"

Mike nodded, his massive walnut-colored hand splaying across Jose's lean, sinewy shoulder. "The sooner we do this, the sooner we do this, little bro."

"And the sooner we can get on a plane, and can sleep for five hours before we land in the morning at LAX," Shabazz reminded the group. "Focus. We need a full day and the time the sunlight provides to check the compound out, and make sure we still have a secure base. They've got regular people like us siding with the vamps for power and money who can get past the vampire traps. Remember that. We don't even rehash or strategize on the flight, because you never know who's listening. So let's just do this and be out."

"Might be nothing," Jose offered. "We've been strapped up before, all ready to rock 'n' roll, and only one or two of 'em was out there—or none, and we just had the heebie-jeebies."

"That's the best way to get yourself nicked, or worse," Damali warned. She carefully chose her words and spoke with full authority, trying to be sure that her team was clear about the danger this time out. One by one, she looked each crew member in the eyes. "Don't let your guard down—not at night. Not tonight."

"I got Raven," Shabazz said quietly, watching Marlene, "if she's out there. Nobody should have to do a person they've loved. You don't have to carry that burden, baby. I'll carry that load, if it comes to it."

Marlene nodded, but the emotional wear from his reassurance almost made her face appear to age as the group waited for her response. "Thanks."

Damali let a tender gaze rest with Marlene's. It was clear that for all of Marlene's hard edge, the woman was breaking inside. Made sense, now, why Mar had been riding her so hard all day. She must have telepathically picked up Raven nearby, and it had to hurt Marlene so badly that their auxiliary seer was slowly going blind. Marlene's voice had been just above a whisper when she'd spoken to Shabazz. Damn.

"You good?" Marlene asked Damali after a moment, shifting gears and obviously submerging her own pain.

"Yeah, I'm good," Damali responded on a long exhale, while pushing herself away from the place on the wall where she'd been temporarily leaning. "I'm always good." She had to say something to get the group's confidence back. But the question remained, if Marlene was blanking because of Raven's possible presence, then who was out there that was making *her* blank? Seeing Dee Dee would definitely hurt, but wouldn't rock her to the core like that. It had to be more than that.

"Then, let's pray," Marlene began, joining hands with Damali and Shabazz until each member of the team was linked in a circle. "May the power of the Most High, the Giver of True Light protect us, and send a battalion of warrior angels to flank us and cover us . . . let no weapon formed against us prosper. Let our circle remain unbroken. *Ashé.*"

A dull chorus of "Amens" followed, and one by one hands slipped away from hands, and palms gripped gear and weapons in the place of human flesh. Damali looked into the eyes of each of her mentors, guides, trainers, crew, who had become her beloved family—like older brothers, people that she'd never had connections to by blood but who were now linked to her soul in spirit . . . just like Marlene had become the mother she never had.

Whatever was waiting for them, whatever hunted them, had a darkness more vast than she'd ever sensed before, and if any of the team of seven fell on this full-moon eve, she wondered whether that would be the final stake driven through her own heart. Damali glanced around at each member of her team and gave them the nod. There was only one way to find out what was in the streets.

"Let's do this."

CHAPTER TWO

DAMALI LISTENED beyond the steady drone of the air-conditioner compressors that wafted down the vacant alley. The low hum resonated through her as she tried to get her bearings. Humidity hung about the guardian-huntress team like a thick cloak. It was hard to breathe in air so dense. The summer heat combined with the dampness felt like a shroud. She glanced at her squad and the way everyone's shirts had begun to stick to them just that fast. Nervous perspiration was also a probable cause. Extra adrenaline was a good thing. Her ears strained to detect anything abnormal while her team's footsteps echoed against the gray, rounded cobblestone as they walked in formation.

This was an alley probably filled with ghosts, she told herself, her gaze sweeping the terrain. Original architecture, old buildings, hidden openings. She hated shit like this. New buildings were clean, better, easier to spot a sudden movement against. The bricks probably hadn't been replaced since the sixteen hundreds, and the Society Hill alley was still as narrow as it had been during Ben Franklin's era. Joint even emptied out to the old slave-auction square. No wonder everybody had the creeps. Stupid developers had cranes up a few blocks away digging in slave burial grounds, too. Who knew what else they'd dug up? All she knew was they'd better chill, before they unearthed some real deep shit. Maybe that was all she and the team had sensed. A massive, disturbed gravesite.

From the corner of her eye, she glimpsed a rat scurry behind a Dumpster. Others on her team had seen it, too. Yeah, they were on guard. Cool. Everybody had clutched their weapons tighter, and the muscles in their arms had tensed. That was good. Nobody was sleepin' on the job. Might save their lives if they noticed something as small as that.

But there should have been more noise coming from the club and the streets beyond the alley; more sound. Damali tilted her head. Something was wrong. It didn't take three seconds to process the answer. Just as she thought. No security. Not even the cops were out there. But that didn't account for the eerie absence of sound. The human vampire helpers had obviously been there to create a diversion, and had gotten any witnesses out of the alley—but that still didn't answer the sound question. When she heard Big Mike's footfalls stop behind her, Damali glanced over her shoulder at him and listened harder.

"It's too quiet," Big Mike remarked as the team cautiously paused in the alley before advancing.

Shabazz just nodded, flexing his right hand and rolling his shoulder. "No cops. No back-door security. Nobody out here going for a smoke—you know when it's dead like this, trouble's brewing. I don't like the vibe out here. I'm feeling the hair stand up on the back of my neck."

"I don't like it, either," Jose agreed, breathing deeply and closing ranks tighter while they all surveyed the dark, narrow back street. "I'm tracking a scent. Coming from that direction," he added with a nod.

"Sulfur." Rider sniffed the air and quickly hocked and spit

on the ground in disgust. "I hate the taste of that shit. I'm just glad it's not raining."

"Time for the Twenty-third," Marlene muttered, her line of vision glancing to Dumpsters, darkened doorways, and then up to the fire escapes that hung above them like huge, blackened skeletal remains.

Damali nodded and started walking again, her team resuming their original formation. *"Yea, though I walk through the valley of the shadow of death, I will fear no evil . . ."*

One by one the members of the team picked up strands of the psalm, advancing slowly as their voices became one low harmonic chant. Dense night surrounded them, the transparency of the air around almost becoming a thicker texture that made it feel like they were trudging through wet sand.

Shabazz abruptly stopped, forcing the group to come to a halt behind him. "Wait," he whispered. "You feel it?"

"Like walking through the swamp," J.L. said. "But you can't see anything."

"It's too quiet—you can't even hear the club music inside, or traffic," Big Mike murmured. "We're in a zone."

Damali turned in a slow, three-hundred-and-sixty-degree circle. All eyes were on her as she spread her arms out, her walking stick in one hand, and splaying her fingers on her free hand to feel the nothingness. They were in some kind of silenced area or cocoon. It was too freaky, and way too dangerous. Something invisible could snuff them out without a sound being heard by anyone but them. "They've got us in some sort of sound bubble. Vamps don't normally roll like that. They come upon you silently, but they can't block exterior sound."

"Damali might be on to something. This is different," Marlene murmured.

"Too much like a setup," Shabazz agreed.

Mike rubbed his jaw and glanced at Jose and J.L. "You ain't said a mumblin' word, bro."

"Now, you all are reaching," Rider said with a nervous laugh, fingering his gun.

"Oh, it's there," Damali reassured Rider, growing defensive and testy by his arrogance. "Something's out there."

She didn't care what anybody said, the density had changed around them. Everything around them felt weighted and as though it was pulling them down. It was creepy, like a gate to the dark realm had opened. Marlene had told her about the phenomenon, but none of them except Marlene had ever claimed to experience it.

"Mar, you're the expert on this one. What's your take?"

Marlene let her breath out slowly and used her stick to point to the fire escapes, thin sidewalks beyond the cobblestones, and then motioned out toward the wider asphalt street beyond the alley. "Notice how the colors around everything are off, aren't what they should be—gray isn't gray, black isn't black? Seen this before. Only once. Wasn't good."

"Demons?"

"Possibly."

"But I thought we all sensed vamps tonight?"

"We did. That's what I can't figure out."

Damali looked at Marlene for a moment. Hold up. Her mind lunged at the facts. The two entities don't travel together, demons and vamps. Plus, demons were fixed to locations . . . like a house or a building or within a host body they'd possessed, unlike vampires that could freely move about as long as there was no sunlight.

Big Mike opened his vest and took out two vials attached together on a long leather cord. Raising his arm above the heads of his teammates, he began swinging them in a hard circular motion until the two objects at the end of the tether became a blur. "Then let's light this joint up."

Hurling the vials fifty feet before the group, they exploded against the cement with two small pops of broken glass. Holy water trickled from the shattered containers, and then suddenly ignited the asphalt. The flames quickly spread, moving swiftly back toward the group, covering the cobblestoned ground around them as though a river of gasoline had been lit at their feet with a match.

"Jesus H. Christ!" Rider's line of vision followed the edge of the flame.

"It's like we're standing in the middle of Hell!" J.L. hollered.

"Down!" Damali yelled, as the flame suddenly stopped twenty-five yards out from where it began and disappeared into the street vents, which gave way to a screeching, fluttering cloud of movement. "Bats!"

Hundreds of the flying vermin circled their heads with beady, glowing red eyes and huge, menacing fangs, diving at the team in a high-pitched aerial attack.

"It's too fucking many of them to shoot! They're moving too fast," Rider shouted.

Damali and Marlene swung wildly at the offending creatures, and kept the swirling mass from descending on the group using their walking sticks, while J.L. and Jose spun in erratic circles, trying to get a clear shot at the multiple enemies smaller than the stakes their crossbows held.

"Save your ammo. Don't fire. It's probably only one giving the illusion of many," Shabazz said, cool control lacing his order. "Wizard, J.L., lights on. Damali, Marlene, cover 'em. UV lights up—and back that bullshit up. Now!"

Jose and J.L. worked feverishly to free the halogens and Fresnels in their duffle bags, hooking them immediately into the battery packs slung over their shoulders, and then sent beams into the fluttering black mass.

Immediately the cloud dispersed, then reconstituted itself into one form, and then separated into multiple forms just beyond the flame, yards away. The eyes of the beasts glowed red within their slits. Huge fangs protruded from the creatures' deformed mouths, stretching gray, death-pallor skin over their overpacked jaw lines. Their limbs seemed elongated, unnatural, and yellowing, hooked claws turned their hands into razor-sharp weapons. And the sounds they made . . . then their jaws unhinged. *What the hell* . . . These were not normal vampires!

"Crossbows up," Damali ordered as the group's focus trained on the shadow that was still shape-shifting before them. "We need to take all six of them out pronto, people."

A series of low hisses emanated from the forms in front of them. With lightning reflexes, Damali spun toward a sound on her left. J.L.'s body had also turned immediately to address the hiss at his side, which made him instinctively fire at the sound. Jose fought off an attack from a creature that leapt over him using the blunt end of his crossbow, but his UV light crashed to the ground in the struggle.

"J.L., reload, now! Get some light on our men and cover 'em!" Damali ordered, her attention snapped back toward the remaining beasts. But for a few seconds, she watched the creature that had been hit.

Pinned to the brick wall at their left, the hideous creature struggled against the stake in its center. Dying, it began transforming back to what it looked like upon death. That's when she saw it. In only an instant before it disintegrated into dust, leaving the awful stench of sulfur behind it, she saw it. The throat had been ripped out. That was not the normal vamp bite. It was not the typical dual puncture wound at the jugular. The thing looked like whatever had attacked it, and had converted it to this type of creature, had half eaten it in the bloodsucking process. Vampires had a much smoother signature than that. So, what the fuck were they up against?

J.L. had quickly reloaded and closed ranks tighter. Jose was in position, but his new light didn't have the beasts in range. A screeching chorus erupted from the slithering forms before them, which kept multiplying, splintering, exponentially growing as though they were cells of evil splitting under the microscopic focus of the slayer-guardian team. In a quick tally, Damali counted thirteen in all.

"I hate to inform you, Shabazz, but it ain't one trying to fake itself as many, brother," Rider quipped as he took aim. "As far as theory goes, we're screwed!"

Mike lobbed the first wave of the offensive, using the vials as Shabazz and Rider opened up and began firing rounds of hallowed earth. Jose and J.L. kept the walls to their left and right clear, hitting targets that crept up the bricks with their joints turned backward, scaling the mortar like grotesque, fast-moving spiders, and occasionally picking off a predator that had made its way to an overhanging fire escape.

"Dead aim, bro," Jose shouted as a creature dropped behind J.L. "Watch your back!"

J.L. couldn't turn fast enough, but Damali was on it, her long ebony stick spearing the creature, sparing J.L.'s life, causing her to use the wall as leverage to flip out of harm's way to attend Marlene's side as she battled two demons on her own.

The two women, in tandem, went back to back, forcing the creatures into Jake's firing range. Shabazz reloaded, flanking Jake, but the magazine jammed. The two creatures were on him in an instant, and he used a trash can to fend them off, kick-boxing the entities back until his arm could reach a stake still mounted in the bricks. Deftly breaking it off, he speared one, avoided a swipe by the second one, catching the stick Damali hurled at him, and plugging the creature as he went down on one knee. But the creature that had escaped being staked had caught Shabazz in the back of the head with a sharp kick just as he got up.

"We've got a man down!" Without weapon in hand, Damali hauled to Shabazz's side. "Freestyle combat, motherfucker!" she hollered, avoiding a swipe, and using a hard kick to repel a creature. "Keep firing, Rider! Cover us, Shabazz is wide open!"

Rider's dead aim incinerated the creature Damali had kicked. J.L.'s crossbow released a stake that connected with another in the base of its spine. Jose fried the side of another monster's face, a beam of light blinding it just long enough for Marlene to retrieve a stake off the ground and finish the job. Big Mike dropped a load of holy water explosive near Shabazz and Damali so that Marlene could help him while Damali continued to fight.

"You see how they move?" Damali yelled, breathing hard, her glance darting from predator to predator. "You all peepin' how much of Rider's ammo we need to put one of them down?"

Marlene tossed Damali her stick, and joined the unarmed Shabazz at his side. With two canes at her disposal, Damali spun, catching one advancing beast with a broadside slam against its jaw, and staking the other that had leapt at her without needing to turn around. Her vision was back. She could sense them coming at her. The heat of battle snapped her focus into keen awareness. Adrenaline pumped through her system. Her ears rang.

As the first creature she'd hit ran at her again, Damali fly-kicked it, her boot landing against its stomach and making it lose enough balance for her to spear it. She kept vigil to protect the fallen Shabazz and Marlene, who was helping him, circling her downed teammates, brandishing the walking sticks. Three more creatures came at her, and she ducked as Jose's crossbow released a stake that whirred past her and caught the beast in the center of its forehead. Smoke rose from the flaming target, nearly choking her and making her want to vomit. Big Mike had brought one of them down with a trash can, so she could finish the job with a stake. He then released more holy water vials, sending a bombardment of liquid that torched two creatures that were trying to get near Shabazz and Marlene.

Putrid smoke was everywhere, making the team's eyes burn and sending foul, scorched air down their throats and into their lungs. Rider dry heaved, and covered his face as he kept firing. The dazed Shabazz was on his feet now. Marlene had an arm under his elbow as they both stood side-by-side, ready to join the fight again.

"You scratched?" Marlene coughed, her line of vision constantly sweeping the area as she spoke.

"No. The cut is from the fall," Shabazz muttered, wiping blood away from his eyebrow.

"Big Mike, douse it with holy water, ASAP. I love you, too, Shabazz. But let's not play with any open wounds." Marlene glanced at Shabazz with concern, then her focus instantly returned to the retreating hissing forms that their group now outnumbered.

"Sonofabitch!" Rider hollered, still pumped with adrenaline and turning around in a wild circle as his gun failed, too. "It had to be at least fifteen of them out there. I had to hit 'em with four or five hallowed-earth bullets to put one of those bastards down. It was never like this, gang. Freaking dirt jamming my magazine, and shit. Look at this shit!"

"It was thirteen of them to be exact," Damali muttered, kicking at a pile of ash. "Never seen this many, or like this."

"Anybody else cut?" Marlene repeated, carefully appraising her team. "Status, before we start moving and get ambushed. Reload what we have left."

"Opened my knee up when I went down for a second," J.L. muttered, looking at the gash in his fatigues.

"Douse it, and close up the wound, fast. The blood'll draw 'em back like sharks," Damali ordered, bending over with her hands on her knees as she took in huge gulps of air. Then she stood up and walked slowly toward her teammate who was hanging back from the protective circle of the group. "Wizard . . . Jose. Jose!"

Jose didn't answer. His line of vision was trained to a dark corner of the alley behind them. His battery pack had dimmed and his lamp was on the ground. Damali saw him swallow hard and slowly bring his crossbow up to his chest.

"Let him do it," Marlene murmured, stopping Damali's advance.

"No. I told him I got his back," Big Mike interjected, stepping in front of Marlene and Damali. "No man should have to put his own woman down."

"She's in there, man," Jose choked out on a strangled swallow. "She's calling me."

Two red, glowing eyes appeared in the corner of the dark alley.

"Give me your weapon, Wizard," Big Mike ordered.

A hiss came from the corner where Jose stared.

"There must be something Marlene can do—some spells, something, man. Take her to a priest, an exorcist . . ."

"We been through this, little brother. Now give me your weapon. There's nothing we can do for Dee Dee now. Did she nick you?"

"No . . . but all she wants me to do is hold her before she dies, she wants to be at peace. Just once."

The group nodded, which seemed to be the assurance Jose required. He slowly handed Big Mike the weapon.

"You'll give me a chance to say good-bye, right?" he asked, stepping toward the shadows.

"Steady, Mike," Shabazz said low in his throat. "Over our brother's shoulder. Let him draw her to where you can see her."

"Be prepared to take Jose, too," Marlene murmured to J.L., "if Big Mike misses. Dee Dee will be on him in two seconds."

Jose hesitated, and looked back at his teammates. "She's afraid, that's all, and so alone. Can't you hear what she's saying?"

"Yeah, I can hear her," Big Mike replied quietly. "She ain't saying what you think, though."

The two eyes in the corner of the alley disappeared for a moment, and then reappeared in the same spot as though the creature had slowly blinked. A form stealthily came forward. The group held in a collective gasp. The alley was silent, save for the hum of the air conditioners. What was once their beloved Dee Dee flicked a long, pronged black tongue out upon a hiss. Talons had replaced her once-neat French manicure. Her grayish-green skin was peeling away from the skeleton of her face, and her glowing eyes sat in black, dark sockets. Her nose was merely two holes. This abomination of their friend had a sly smile on its face, a taunting grin that flashed huge, saliva-slicked fangs. Damali wanted to hurl.

The team glanced at each other, all sensing that the beast was inside Jose's head, cracking his skull with its call. Damali's heart hurt from watching her teammate writhe in emotional agony. But the situation was too delicate. Nobody made a move, lest they catch the living lover, Jose, their teammate, in the crossfire.

It was clear that he'd make a lunge to try to spare her the stake. This had to go down smooth to save their brother.

Jose stepped forward slowly. "Dee Dee, baby. Nobody is going to hurt you. We're going to help you. You're still one of us."

Like hell . . . Damali glanced at Marlene and the fellas and shook her head. Even though it was eating her up inside to watch Jose battle this thing, there was no other way. She almost couldn't watch him calling to the woman he loved like one would call to a beloved house pet that had been hit by a car and had hidden under a parked vehicle to die alone in fear. It was pitiful.

There was only one focus, however. Get Dee Dee in range. As soon as Dee Dee's clawed hand reached out, and a glimmer of her fang-distorted face showed past the next set of Dumpster shadows, Damali gave the order. "Fire!"

The stake released, sending a whooshing sound past the group, nearly grazing Jose's shoulder, but connecting with a screaming target that instantly combusted where it once stood. Rider was still trying to fire rounds from his jammed gun when Jose dropped to his knees and covered his face with his hands. Damali watched his shoulders shake as Big Mike tried to help Jose up, only to have him shrug away.

"He'll be all right in the morning," Marlene said in a distant tone.

"Dirt—shit! You can't even find good hallowed earth these days!" Rider yelled, spitting again and attempting to reload his jammed gun. "He ain't gonna never be all right."

"Were any of us?" Shabazz added solemnly, collecting Jose under his arm so he'd stand, and then shaking Big Mike's hand. "Your brother just saved your life—even though right now you just wanna curl up and die. Was hard for him to take that weight so you wouldn't have to. Recognize, and let this go."

Jose nodded, wiped his face, and pounded Big Mike's fist.

"Told you I gotcha back," Mike reminded Jose, throwing an arm over his shoulder.

But the fact that Big Mike warily appraised Jose's skin from head to toe first, was not lost on the group.

"He's clean," Big Mike finally muttered, offering Jose a fast male embrace, then handing him back his weapon.

"I can't get her voice out of my head," Jose whispered.

"And you won't," Shabazz said in a harsh tone, collecting their gear and still surveying the perimeter beyond the group. "That's why you can't afford to fall in love, let somebody get under your skin like that—their voice will be in your head until the main vamp is dead. You'll be in hell, and want to take your own life every night when one of them assumes her voice to fuck with you . . . or tries to climb into your bed to make you forget she's dead. That's why I wanted Wizard to kill her—so he'd remember that when the succubus comes for him. His hell is brand-spanking-new. Ask me how I know."

"Leave him be," Marlene warned. "One step of awareness at a time."

"Maybe you haven't noticed, Mar, but we seem to be running out of time."

Marlene and Shabazz held each other's gaze in a deadlock before Shabazz turned away and looked up at the sky.

"We need to move out," Damali said quietly, sensing the environment, and then she looked up at the sky. "But I don't think it's safe yet." She glanced at her group and they nodded their agreement. The team was wired, still breathing hard, and pumped from the battle. "I know we all wanna get out of here, but we need to be strategic, and not just run headlong into another setup."

"She's on-point," Shabazz said, nodding in agreement. "Our slayer is coming into her own."

Marlene glanced at Shabazz and looked away.

What was *that* about? Damali assessed her team with caution. "We should hold up for a moment, and make sure we're clear. I can hear sound coming back, but it's not all the way back, yet. Soon as it does, and traffic can be clearly heard, we move." Again, her gaze went to the heavens.

Mike nodded. "She's on about the sound."

"When we get back to the compound, we need to have a meeting." Damali glanced around at her battle-weary team. "Anybody notice the death-wounds these things sustained to turn 'em?"

Damali's question was met with silence.

"Did anyone get a good look at their throats before they flamed?" she asked, repeating the question more slowly. She let her breath out hard when her team just shook their heads. "Well, it wasn't the normal two-hole vamp bite that turned these things into whatever they are, that's for sure." She wiped her hands off on her backside and picked up a walking stick.

"Yeah. Baby girl is coming into her own," Shabazz muttered as the team collected their ammo.

Marlene glared a Shabazz. "That's enough!"

"Talk to me, Marlene," Damali ordered. "What's up with the vibe?"

"How's everybody's ammo?" Shabazz's question was an open diversion, a tension release valve, more so than an actual need to know.

Damali looked at him and Marlene hard and let it go. Later.

"Low, and fucked up," Rider retorted, still angered by his jammed magazine. "Well, this has been fun."

"Crossbows are on E," J.L. said, his expression worried.

"Almost out of grenades," Mike added, throwing Marlene her

walking stick after retrieving it from a pile of smoldering, putrid ash on the ground.

"Sound's back. We're clear to move out," Big Mike announced.

"Let's roll," Shabazz said, throwing Damali a stake he'd picked up. "Time to call the limo."

Marlene and Shabazz glared at each other, but didn't say another word as they walked. All Marlene did was grab her cell phone out of her satchel and punch in a code and hang up. But it was the way the seer had flung the cell phone into her bag that Damali noted.

"Shabazz is right," Damali chimed in, taking the lead between her sparring mentors. "This alley is hot territory now that we have sound back in it. We've kicked up a lot of dust, made a lot of noise, and the cops are sure to be here soon. Let's gather weapons, the limo will be here in a second, and we can get Dan, then jet. We can do damage-to-equipment accounting in the limo, and repack everything so it passes muster at the airport."

"We didn't get all of them," Rider reminded the group as they neared the alley's exit. "Look alive."

"Page the limo again, somebody," Marlene said, her voice monotone. "Then, Big Mike, you sweep it before we get in— use the remaining grenades for that. Just splash a load of holy water in there, as per usual. If something's in the limo that shouldn't be, we'll know as soon as it catches fire."

Mike nodded. "Right, boss lady. We're real low on my holy water that burns 'em up like fossil fuel, though. From there, it'll be hand-to-hand." Big Mike took out his cellular, punched in the code, and sighed.

"J.L., can you spare a stake for everybody from your grip?"

The group turned their attention to J.L. at Damali's comment.

"I've got two," J.L. said, tossing one to Shabazz. "Jose, what-chu got?"

"One," he said, laughing sadly, and then handed it to Damali. "Use it to do me if you have to."

Damali shook her head, and handed it back to Jose. "You're clean, and didn't get nicked by a vamp. Just because she was jacking with your head, doesn't mean you'll turn. It'll just hurt your soul . . . So, keep the stake. I don't need it. Protect yourself while we walk. Peace?"

"Oh, I get it," Rider said. "Just dog the white boy in the group. Just leave him assed out with a fucked-up clip that won't fire, nothing in his hand—"

"I gotcha back." Damali chuckled, walking up beside Jake and elbowing him. She patted her waistband that contained the drum anchors and handed him one of the chimes from her back pocket. "Never even got to use them."

"Now I feel better." Rider outstretched his arms and then slapped the center of his chest. "Chimes and drum anchors bring a man up close and personal—I prefer long-distance relationships with the vamps. Dig?"

"You cool," Big Mike said with a grin, tossing Rider a vial. "Feel better, now?"

"Much improved, good brother," Rider replied with a nervous laugh as he caught the vial and kissed it.

"I hope you saved a bullet for Dan, just in case," Marlene said quietly.

The group stopped walking for a moment.

"Yeah," Shabazz muttered and checked his jammed weapon, firing once to be sure it would again. "Been thinking about that—he was away from sight, you know."

"This shit can get to anybody," Rider said, now growing somber. "There but for the grace of God go any of us at any time."

"That's what makes this all so ludicrous." J.L. ran his hands through his sweat-slicked black hair. His dark brown, almond-shaped eyes held an intensity that made Marlene acknowledge his unspoken comment.

"I know," Marlene whispered, placing a hand on his shoulder, and forcing him to keep walking with the group. "We're in too deep to get out, but we're all still human. One day this will all be over."

"Don't promise the man a check that will bounce, Mar." Shabazz looked at Marlene hard.

"When we find the main lair, it'll be over, right?" Damali's question hung between them as the limo approached. A hundred questions also ran through her mind. What kind of lair were they searching for? These creatures were different than regular run-of-the-mill vampires, but their weapons still worked against them as though they were normal vamps, albeit it seemed to take twice as much of the auxiliary-type weapons to put one of them down. Stakes had been effective, but the hallowed earth and even the holy water had been slower to take effect. Too weird.

The group backed up when the driver opened the door and a smiling Dan leapt out.

"What in Hell's name was taking you guys so long to page us?"

Dan's upbeat persona made the tension ease its way from Damali's shoulders. She said a silent prayer as Big Mike approached him. Please God, no more tonight.

"Hey, what's with the water thing?" Dan laughed and batted at Mike's ministrations. "The show's over, I don't need to be anointed by the spirits," he added, chuckling.

Mike ignored him and turned to the driver. "Step away from the vehicle."

"Why?" Seeming indignant, the driver opened up his coat to allow what he obviously thought was going to be a frisk, only to swear under his breath as Mike flicked water at him. "Crazy bastards. Damn."

"All clear," Mike called out, after having administered the test to the inside of the vehicle, also spraying the trunk and under the chassis. He helped Damali in first, saw to it that J.L, Jose, and Shabazz were also inside safely, and then got in himself, while Rider took Marlene's elbow.

"This ain't no way to live," Rider murmured to Marlene, whose gaze still scanned the horizon.

Marlene only nodded, but Rider's firm hold made her pause. He dropped his voice and spoke quickly as the group assembled themselves within the vehicle and their attention was on Dan, who was chatting away, keeping them distracted.

"What was that soundproof thing about? Was like what happened down South, right? You've seen this before, or am I wrong?"

"Yes. It was just what I was afraid of—and we'll talk about it later."

The two older warriors climbed into the vehicle and shut the door behind them.

"Anybody hungry?" Dan said in a cheery voice as their limo pulled off. "Chinese, ribs?"

The mention of food made Damali cover her mouth and fight to swallow down the immediate nausea the suggestion brought.

"What?"

All eyes had turned to Dan, and he just shrugged, totally confused.

"Piles of dust, broken glass, empty rhino shell cases with crosses on them, dirt splattered everywhere—freakin' wooden spikes all around . . . and *the stink*. What do you make of it?"

"I don't know, Malloy," Detective Berkfield muttered, stooping down to study an empty shell case. "It looks like somebody was back here firing enough ammo to start World War Three, but as per usual, nobody heard anything, everybody was supposedly partying inside the club, and down here there's no residences with neighbors close enough to have seen anything from a window. Godammit, these music-and-drug sons of bitches are involved somehow, and I'm going to pin their rich, slippery asses soon—or die trying. Plus where's our backdoor squad cars, anyway?"

Detective Malloy shrugged, lit a cigarette, and inhaled slowly, allowing the smoke to escape from his bulbous, pale nose. "Same place as they always seem to be when this crap goes down—diverted. Doesn't it seem strange to you that they always show up just after everything goes down?"

"Don't start with the conspiracy theory, Malloy. I can't deal with that, too, right now. All we need is an Internal Affairs investigation going parallel with this bull."

Malloy leaned his angular form against the wall, considering the red ember as he took another steady drag. "Eventually, we might have to stake out their shows with our boys, and put one of our cars in the alleys, and one to two of our own men inside. Tonight, everything was jake in-house, but we definitely missed the action out here. Sooner or later the action behind the scenes will out. It's just a matter of time. Problem is, if these kids keep dropping like flies, and then the bodies keep disappearing from the morgues, we're gonna be on the media and department hot seat."

His short stocky partner stared back at him with a scowl.

"That's a lot of resources," Berkfield said with a grunt, standing up slowly and brushing off his wrinkled navy suit. "We've already got our team spread thin from that drug bastard, Rivera, in L.A., to a squad watching Warriors of Light Production there, to a stakeout near Fallon Nuit's supposed base of operations in Beverly Hills for Blood Music, as well as monitoring one of his holdings in New Orleans. We might have to cut some of that back, especially the New Orleans detail. That place is probably a vacation home, and there's been no activity near it for months. Now we're supposed to expand the mission to run around the country following all the hip-hop concerts—when a lot of our boys are still on terrorist detail?"

Berkfield let his breath out hard and shook his head, grime and sweat plastering wisps of brown hair to his shiny, balding scalp. "I'm getting too old for this bullshit, Paul. Honest to God. I need to get a life."

CHAPTER THREE

CARLOS RIVERA looked out over the chrome balcony of his North Hollywood club. Saturday night was prime time for Club Vengeance, and again, the place was loaded. Techno, hip-hop, salsa, it didn't matter. The people came. The artists came. They all waited in line outside, hoping to get in. It was the place to see and be seen, just like he'd told his boyz it would be. The crowd brought product. Once again, it was time to expand.

Making his usual rounds through his establishment, a sense of vitality pulsed in him with the beat of the music. There was nothing like the feel of money, except power.

"Yo, Carlos," a regular patron shouted as he passed.

Oh, yeah, he was king.

He nodded and signaled to the bartender to give the man a drink, even though he couldn't remember the man's name. Smiles from gorgeous, scantily clad women graced his path. He smiled back, but kept walking while trying to decide which one of the harem he'd have tonight. His bouncers gave him a deferring nod as they kept their posts. This was a helluva long way from East L.A. . . . a long way from souped-up Chevy's, gang-banging in the streets for turf, drive-bys, and listening to his mother and grandmother's wails as his sister died like a dog in a crack house. He'd told them all that he'd get everyone of his own out of that madness, or die trying. Oh, yes, it was great to be the king.

"What's the count?" Carlos leaned in toward his head bouncer as he assessed the size of the throng.

"Twelve hundred bodies and rising," his employee muttered with a sly grin.

"And product sales?"

"Through the roof."

Carlos exchanged a fist pound, nodded, and then threaded his way back through the crowd. Where was Alejandro?

If his little bro and his cousin could just grasp the understanding and commitment it took to run a business—a series of businesses. Pure disgust picked up his tempo as he briefly spoke to patrons, and headed back toward his office. Street product turned into Laundromats, corner stores, and then converted into apartment buildings. The nineties had been good to him. Real estate bought a man leverage, just like firepower did.

Leverage meant expansion. Other lines, multimedia in X-rated videos, Web sites, phone sex lines, everything had a dirty basis in this country, and then the masters converted it into clean, cold cash. One day, he, too, would be a master of the game—he could taste it, like fate. A small taste of power was never enough. It was better than any drug he plied.

Carlos kept his line of vision steady. Yeah. Soon. One day. After his other holdings had produced, then came the club, and increased shipment levels of product, new products like Ecstasy, and designer packages. More money meant more guns at his disposal, more mercenary soldiers. That meant more territory—which had to be run vigilantly, efficiently, or you'd lose your damned control, then your life. What about this didn't Alejandro and his compadres get? A man had to have skillz. Had to strategically build an empire.

He dismissed the sudden melancholy, peering at his glistening platinum Rolex watch, and then glimpsing himself in one of the mirrors as he passed. Carlos Rivera liked what he saw—a young man, in top form from working out, wearing alligator shoes and belt, a custom-tailored, gunmetal gray Nino Cerruti suit, maroon bandit collar, silk shirt, manicured hands—not marred from picking fruit or performing other manual labor—and a smooth barber cut. He ran his palm over his jaw line. Fine, oh yes, he was indeed the man.

He glimpsed himself again and kissed the heavy silver cross that he always wore in place of the puny gold one he'd ditched as he'd gained more wealth. His family was too superstitious. So what if the first one had been blessed when he was christened? So he'd even traded up on his cross, a piece of jewelry, which was the only concession to the women in his family. Just like he'd upgraded his car and women and everything else around him. Carlos alighted the floating staircase to his sanctuary. He was blessed.

Entering the more quiet confines, he went to his private bar, selected Remy, and poured himself a drink. He took a sip and studied the rim of the crystal glass, watching the light form a prism against it. His mother never owned anything beyond Dollar Store plastic.

His mother and grandmother were so naïve, refusing to accept the gifts from this new life that he could offer them—only because they believed in fairy tales . . . good men didn't do bad things. Good men, like his father and uncles, were poor, immigrant bastards who died young under the weight of a factory, or in the sun picking fruit for men who also stole to own those factories and those farms.

Blood Music had snubbed him, though. He'd have to have someone from his organization pay them a visit. It was pure bullshit that they wouldn't send their artists to his club to perform, just because some nobody had bought it over a month ago not far from his establishment. What the hell? People died in the alley every day where he'd come from. He'd certainly lost enough men in gun battles, nudging out a respected space between the Russians and Asians. Even the Italians now gave him some props. The Dominicans and the Jamaicans had been a problem, but they'd come to terms. It was all good. Negotiation was always possible, and there were always weaknesses in any operation that would allow an alliance to be formed.

He let his breath out hard. Nobody snubbed him. Maybe he would just go to Blood's competitor, Warriors of Light Productions, and have them in . . . but there were people there he didn't want to deal with. The shit was complicated.

A vibration at his waist drew his hand to his cell, but the 911 on it along with Alejandro's code made him circle his wide glass-and-chrome desk, set down his drink, and add his gun to his wardrobe.

"Talk to me," he said slowly, answering his brother's page.

"You gotta come down here, man. It's fucking chaos!"

"Come where, bro? You ain't making sense."

"The station, the morgue. They got Julio, Miguel, and Juan is in the hospital—he don't look like he's gonna make it, though, man. Can't let their family do the body ID, not when you see what's left."

"See what's left? What the fuck, man? Who did this! Where did it go down?"

"I don't know who did 'em. But you know it's got to be bad, I'm telling you, if I agreed to come down to do the ID. I went to pick up Julio, Miguel, and Juan from their positions at the clubs we got alliances with on Santa Monica, they were all meeting up at the last one on the list tonight, the transactions up to then were smooth, but when I got there, it was off da hook. Cops everywhere, body bags . . . You should have seen our boyz—they're fucked up bad."

Carlos paused, silence strangling the digital line between the brothers. His mind raced through his organization's long list of adversaries and business deals pending, trying to quickly assess who in the mix could be sending a message, about what deal, about what part of his territory? His cousin and two best friends?

"Where were they shot?"

Again there was a long pause before Alejandro spoke.

"That's the thing. They weren't shot."

"Stabbed? What the fuck, talk to me!"

"Naw, bro . . . more like half eaten."

"Glad you could finally come in here on your own recognizance, Rivera," Detective McKinsey muttered with a disdainful grin. "My partners, Malloy and Berkfield, will be so sorry they missed your visit."

"Cut the bullshit, man. My family is in there on trays." Carlos bristled as he waited for the slow process of gaining entry, the muscle in his jaw pulsing as his mind worked the puzzle of who would be bold enough to come for his inner circle like this.

"Yeah," McKinsey said with disgust, "we can have us a little conversation, later. I take it your enterprises will keep you in L.A. for a while, especially when you see what's left of your posse."

"I was there, man, when they came with the ambulances,"

Alejandro murmured to his brother, still stricken. "I don't need to see it again. I'll wait for you out here."

Carlos didn't respond to the comments from either of the so-called men standing before him. How many times had he seen one of his own on a tray, in a casket, on a sidewalk, whatever—it came with doing the kind of business he did. Pussies. In a war, there were casualties. Collateral damage, they called it on the news. In a war, there was a body count. In a war, there were soldiers, and some of them got shot. And in a war, there was territory gained and lost based upon who had the strongest men.

They left Alejandro where he stood and proceeded to the cold rooms. Carlos almost knew his way there by heart, just like he knew prison entry-and-exit procedures, and he waited while McKinsey got them through yet another layer of the system's security.

"Thought you should see this, Rivera, especially since a young artist died the same way not too far from your club, and not too long ago. Thought you might want to finally have a conversation about that, given the heat is now turned up and coming in your direction? If you bastards are duking it out in the streets for some new turf, we know that goes on all the time—but you all really have to lighten up on your style of doing hits. This bullshit causes media attention, now that drive-bys are old hat."

Carlos continued to ignore the fat asshole beside him; the man's cheap polyester suit made him want to vomit.

"Just open the door," Carlos ordered in a low sneer. "If you guys can't handle it, I might know some people who know some people that can."

The two exchanged a glance of pure hatred as McKinsey pushed open the door.

"See if your people who know some people can handle *that*," the detective muttered, hailing the coroner on duty as they approached a table.

Frozen where he stood, all Carlos could do was stare at the gruesome remains of his cousin and best friend. Nauseating bile rose to burn his esophagus and coated his tongue.

"Chilling, ain't it?" McKinsey said with triumph. "Even for you, huh?"

"What the fuck . . ." Carlos's voice had become a gravelly whisper, trailing off in horror as he made the sign of the cross over his chest.

"Throats ripped out, some instrument sliced down the center of the first victim's chest, halving it, cutting through the esophagus, aorta, and the hearts are—for lack of a better observation, eaten away. Frontal attack, though," the coroner said in a monotone voice. "The one over there has his left arm hanging by a thread of ligament and cartilage. The lacerations look like he tried to block his throat, but the victim's arm was apparently snatched away by a significant force before his throat and chest cavity were opened up. We found, of all things, something that looked like a huge animal claw lodged in it. We're running analysis now to determine if this was the weapon used, or if this was dropped on the body afterward as a little leave behind marker for this ritualistic killing."

"Weapons fired everything in the clips," McKinsey added, his smile one of vindication. "Oh, your boys were strapped and went down with a struggle—full metal jacket type of shit in that alley. We found enough rounds back there to light up half of L.A., but of course, nobody heard or saw a thing—except Juan DeJesus. Alas, his tongue and the lower half of his jaw are missing, like somebody kissed him and decided to take a bite out of his face. He's in a coma, lost enough blood to flat-line him within the next twenty-four hours. So, suffice to say, we don't have a witness who can *speak* to the assailant's whereabouts—or give a description."

"I've seen enough," Carlos whispered, exhaling quickly, and only allowing a tiny sip of putrid air back into his lungs.

"Bet you have," McKinsey muttered, following Carlos's hasty exit from the dead room.

Carlos felt his body go hot and cold at the same time. Perspiration had formed beads on his brow; he could sense the moisture before he swiped at it. The detective leaned against the wall as Carlos bent and sucked in air with one hand bracing himself against the elevator door.

"Madre de Dios," Carlos whispered, again crossing himself. "When I find out who did this . . ."

"Want to talk to us first? Like maybe tell us a little something about your drug operation; in exchange, we might be able to give you a little amnesty—and bring down whoever's shaking up L.A.? Fair exchange is no robbery, Carlos."

"I don't know what you're talking about," he said more calmly as the elevator opened and he regained his composure. "I run a clean business. Whoever—"

"More like whatever," McKinsey corrected. "Pit bull rings—you all in that illegal betting business these days? Maybe somebody let your boyz get eaten and took odds on how long they'd last in the ring? Or, are you all doing exotic animal bouts—moved up from dogfights to lions, tigers, and bears, oh my? Something for the wealthy crowd to entertain them beyond mere drugs? What is it, Carlos?"

"I'm going to the hospital, unless I'm a suspect and you're holding me?"

"No, we're not holding you." McKinsey sneered. "We'll let you back out on the street as lion bait. One way or another we'll find out the connection between your club—all of its dirty little secrets—and who's also offing Blood Music and Warriors of Light Productions artists."

Carlos let the comment pass, never flinching as McKinsey mentioned Warriors of Light. He let his line of vision settle on his distraught brother as the elevator doors opened. Damali Richards had been passed over somehow, too. She was like him, a survivor from the old neighborhood . . . and the only one inside the music scene whom he could trust—that is, if he could get to simply talk to her again.

"You already have my attorney's name on file—if you want to bring me in for real questions," Carlos spat out, pacing quickly out of the too-close confines of the elevator. "And tell Malloy and Berkfield they can suck my dick."

He hated hospitals. More than the smell, he abhorred the rocking, the wailing, and the sense of no control people had over their fates as they waited for a sign of good news. Men in white coats, white men, who thought they were better than him and played God, were always in control in places like this, keeping the bereft at their mercy.

"His mama is there with the family," Alejandro murmured, nodding in the direction of the DeJesus clan.

As soon as Juan's mother saw them, she began a new bout of loud sobs, and it took her daughter, younger son, and an older female friend from the neighborhood to keep her in her chair as she screamed invectives toward Carlos in her native tongue.

Juanita, her daughter, approached the two men, once her mother's wails had been subdued and had given way to piteous moans.

"He's in intensive care," Juanita whimpered, going into Carlos's arms when he opened them for her. She hid her face in the lapels of Carlos's suit and wept as he rubbed her back. "Promise me that you will find out who did this to him."

Saliva in his mouth had suddenly grown thick and salty, and Carlos bent to kiss the top of her head, stroking it, and then looking up to the ceiling, fighting the buildup of moisture in his eyes. Her mother's moans, her flurry of Spanish prayers, the cry of a woman against his chest . . . how many times, Father God, would he have to hear the wail of women as death took its sweet territory within his?

"Look at me," he ordered in a gentle voice, lifting her chin with one finger. "I promise you, with my word as my bond, that whoever did this will know no peace as I hunt them down like a dog in the street. Juan was . . . is my best hombre. Like a brother. Your family is my family. *Mi casa es su casa, comprendre?*"

With trembling fingers the young woman traced his cheek, her large, brown eyes now red from tears, her face distorted by pain and streaks of white crusty tear lines. "My mama won't allow you into intensive care, upon her orders. The cops came and asked us questions about who we knew that could do this, who my brother ran with . . . I told them I didn't know. But, if you know . . ."

"I swear to you on my father's grave, Juanita, neither Alejandro or I know who did this, but we'll find out."

"Get away from my daughter! Get away, get away!" the older woman shrieked, coming out of her wailing haze, temporarily lucid enough to see her only remaining grown child pressed against what she considered evil incarnate.

"I have to go to her," Juanita whispered, opening his hand and placing a small gold cross within it. "My grandmother swears this is the only thing that kept him from being totally eaten like the others." Slipping out of his hold, she turned back once. "It was under his shirt . . . he's had it ever since he was an infant. He was christened in it. It was dipped in holy water with him as a baby. May it guide you and protect you. Find them."

He stood with his brother on the outer edge of the surreal scene, transfixed. Alejandro stood by him silently; a huddle of women and a little boy, who had suddenly become the man of the house, rocked in the waiting-room chairs. His best friend was dying, his other tight friend dead, his cousin gutted—his job now was to go to his aunt, his mother, make the rounds, pay for all funerals—even the imminent one, Juan's. Men had to be assembled, a team to search and destroy, his boundaries had to be reinforced—tomorrow the news would hit the media, and wannabes would try to push up against his weakened borders. Old vendettas would resurface, and he'd have to show the old timers that this had not interrupted his operations, or his security forces.

He glanced at his old lover from his youth as he turned away. Juanita's innocence washed through his soul, making him remember Damali, forcing him to wonder what a life with someone like her would have been like. Reality knifed at the illusion. He shook it off as he and his brother crossed the linoleum floor and bolted for fresh air. They probably would have had a boy, like Juan's little brother, one that he couldn't protect or provide for, one waiting for his turn to seek his own fortune; a daughter who would have few choices; a woman who would one day become old and fat and grieving as that son perished in the streets or went to jail, and that daughter became a baby's momma; and he'd work like a mule to drink himself to death for pennies— but not before beating the beauty from his woman, or being laughed at as an old bum by the young, up-and-coming lords of the jungle.

CHAPTER FOUR

~·•◦•·~

IT WAS still dark when their flight touched down in LAX. The three-hour West Coast time differential had not been on their side. Despite Dan's incessant chatter, they were able to get him to catch an airport van at curbside and go home, while Big Mike and Shabazz waited for the rest of the luggage. Damali and Marlene had to practically body slam Dan into a shuttle to get him to leave.

But now that her team was all assembled, walking two abreast through the concrete parking lot, Damali missed Dan's cheerful banter. Big Mike had been able to dissuade a few weary groupies from barraging her with autograph requests, and she wondered what it would be like if they were megastars like the ones on the Blood Music label. How would they hunt vampires, then? How would they come and go at will under fairly anonymous circumstances as a smaller club act? But that level of fame was the least of their worries. She'd deal with that if and when it ever came up.

The Dee Dee thing would take a long time to heal, and she glanced at Jose every now and then to be sure he was all right. Then again, how was he supposed to be all right? The man looked positively shell-shocked, and the rest of the team was walking in silence like on a funeral march. In a sense, they were.

Big Mike released a grunt as he lifted and set the FX boxes on top of the four-by-four rack and secured them.

"Me, Marlene, Shabazz, and Jose can take the Hummer," Damali murmured, her attention off in the distance. "Mike, J.L., and Rider take the Jeep."

"Need to stop and get more ammo before we roll up on the compound at night," Mike said in a tired voice. "It ain't daylight yet."

"Sho' you right," Shabazz muttered.

That was the extent of what anyone had to say as they all climbed into the vehicles, turned on the ignitions, signaled each other, and pulled off. It was so quiet within the Hum-V, Damali swore you could hear a pin drop. She didn't even reach for the radio to tune in to her favorite station. Thumpin' music seemed inappropriate, given the circumstances. She just let the events repeat and run like an endless loop videotape inside her mind as Mike flashed her with his headlights to get her to pull over next to the cathedral.

Shabazz rolled down his window, and pointed his nine in Mike's direction to cover him as he went up the wide, cement steps, and rang the bell using the code that would get a response. A few minutes passed, and the church door cracked open. A briefcase was handed to Mike, and a hand extended. The edge of a black robe cautiously peeped out of the huge red door, and a trembling hand made the sign of the cross on Mike's forehead. Then the door shut hard.

Mike raised the case toward the waiting vehicles, and got back in the Jeep and pulled off. Damali followed him. Marlene's hand went to the two-way radio and tuned in to the other vehicle's frequency band.

"Everything okay, Mike?"

"Yeah, Mar. More holy water, hallowed earth . . . I got enough to sweep the compound, and some to spare."

"Good." Marlene sat back in her seat and stared out the window.

Jose had never even taken his eyes off the distance. He just didn't seem to care. Shabazz had pulled his gun back in the window, and patted Jose's shoulder, but Jose didn't acknowledge the touch. Damali just drove.

Highway turned into narrow, one-lane roads as their two-car caravan snaked its way up the misty, North Hollywood mountainside. Commercial districts had given way to residential communities until the houses became mansions separated by vast expanses of land. The full moon cast a bluish tinge on the rows of tall pines and redwoods and made the dense foliage take eerie shapes as they approached the place they called home.

Damali stared at their fortress that was set on a high vista surrounded by time-activated ultraviolet lights. All shrubs and trees had been removed from the landscape, except a few tall palms on the outskirts of the property—for safety purposes. Steel gates were still closed down over the bulletproof-glass windows and skylights. The clean edges of the modern concrete design didn't appear to have been disturbed. Tonight it bothered her that the brightly lit building looked more like a prison than a place to live.

"Seems clear," Damali said into the radio receiver as she pulled the Hum-V to a stop behind the Jeep in the driveway.

"Yup. But only one way to be sure," Mike answered from the other vehicle.

"Jose, why don't you sit this one out?" Damali looked at him when he didn't respond, and glanced at Marlene and Shabazz.

Shabazz gave her a nod, and he, J.L., Big Mike, and Rider all exited their vehicles on cue.

J.L spoke into his transmitter as he walked ahead of the four-man sweep team. "All sensors are still operable. The normal alarms haven't been tampered with. I'm going to open the garage. Mar, you drive the Jeep in, and I'll flood the interior with UV. We could have picked up an unwanted passenger."

Shabazz leveled his gun toward Marlene to cover her as she jumped out of the Hum-V, ran over to the second vehicle, and engaged the ignition within the Jeep. Intense lamps lit up within the garage over the other parked sedans. Both trucks rolled forward slowly. The ground team had already gone in and was ready to fire at any intruder. Damali sighed. Normal people didn't have to go through this mess just to come home from a business trip. She watched the garage doors slowly seal them away to safety, and as the team went room by room, she couldn't help feeling a twinge of resentment.

"We need to have a meeting before any of us goes back to sleep," she said in a weary tone. "I know everybody is beat up, tired, and through—but we've gotta deal with this now."

A series of disgruntled mutters followed her as she led the way to the war room. People dropped their bruised bodies on the seat closest to them, fanning out to claim director's chairs, metal stools, the sofa, and an armchair. The crew looked like hell. But they also seemed relieved. J.L.'s systems and monitors were operating at normal levels. Damali walked over to the expansive metal table in the middle of the area that was littered with equipment and weapons and hoisted herself up to sit on it.

The war room was mostly metal and concrete; maybe they should have all just met in the study or game room or even the kitchen, just to get away from the madness. They had all worked so hard at making every other room and the studios in the compound feel warm, lived in, like a real home—but the weapons area was where the illusion ended. No amount of art, plants, cool furniture, or serene colors could disguise that.

She knew all of them were maxed out, stressed beyond the edge, and for a moment Damali wondered whether or not a more comfortable atmosphere might make the conversation feel less invasive. She was also worried about how Jose would handle the details that needed to be discussed. Then she immediately banished the thought. They had to deal with this head-on.

"Damn," Rider said, dropping his weapons on a nearby table with a clatter and flopping on the sofa. "I need a drink and a good card game."

"First light, you're on." J.L. eased into a director's chair with a groan. "Feel like I got my ass kicked."

"Me, you, our old friend Jack Daniels, and anybody else who doesn't have second sight can play poker with us, and I challenge you to shots." Rider leaned his head back against the wall and closed his eyes. "Times like these, whiskey is a man's best friend."

"As soon as it gets light outside, I'm finding me some barbecue ribs, potato salad, greens, and a cold beer," Mike said, sitting heavily in an armchair. "Then, I'm calling up this fine sister who—"

"How can you think of food at a time like this?" Marlene just shook her head. "Or anything else? You guys don't need to pollute your bodies, either. Everyone needs to focus, and keep their systems clean—"

"Been telling you that pork will kill you, brother," Shabazz warned, taking off his gun and examining the clip. "And be careful about the sister you decide to spend some time with."

Big Mike laughed his deep, rolling-thunder chuckle. "Takes my mind offa thangs, Mar. Shabazz, you know I can't eat that vegetarian bird food y'all keep pushing. 'Sides, a brother needs a little TLC, if you get my drift."

"But you need to lose the pork, Mike." Shabazz shot Big Mike a disapproving glance.

"A man who hunts vampires for a living is not trying to tell Big Mike to worry about pork killing him, or did I hear wrong?" Rider slapped his forehead and let his arms fall to the back of the sofa. "Put me out of my misery."

"It's bad for your health," Shabazz countered.

"I need some real food . . . might even have me a taste for some Creole."

Rider opened his eyes and gave Big Mike a scowl. "Do not even talk to me about anything that has to do with Louisiana. That topic is off-limits."

Damali chuckled and before she could open her mouth to ask the question about the dreaded city, Marlene had held up her hand.

"Girl, you don't even want to know."

"But I hear you, Mike. We all need a break after what just went down tonight." Shabazz shook his head. "Me, I'm going to find my jazz spot." He glanced at Jose. "Man, some cool-out music might help. We can hang, if you want? We can go find us a brew, maybe?"

Damali watched the interaction, quietly assessing how each team member was talking about everything but what needed to be discussed. "I might go shoot some pool, then find Rider and J.L. and whip their butts at some cards—as long as the joint you hit has my extra-hot barbecue chips."

"You can shoot pool, but you can't play cards with us, darlin'. You and Marlene have been permanently banned from all games of chance, even Scrabble—because you ladies cheat with your gift."

"We do not!" Damali laughed and hopped off the table to stand in Rider's face.

"We're just good," Marlene chuckled. "But I'll leave you guys to your games. I have some research to do."

Just as quickly as it had erupted, the mirth slid away from the group.

"Marlene is right," Damali said with a sigh. "There's a new entity out there that we've never dealt with before. So, I suggest you all get some more rest and play hard when the light comes up, because we're gonna have to work hard come nightfall."

All team members nodded agreement, except Jose, who just continued to stare at the steel-covered windows.

"Work hard, play hard, and carry some serious heat," Shabazz muttered.

"Correct." Damali cast her attention toward Marlene. The subject was on the floor, and it was time. "These things die like vampires, and suck blood. But they hiss, not a normal characteristic of vampires. They leave a horrible signature bite—"

"They ain't smooth at all," Shabazz added. "Normal vamps talk a lot of shit. You don't even see the bite coming till it's too late—but from what Damali described, they totally jack up their prey."

"Can't be demon, though, can it?" J.L's gaze went from teammate to teammate as he spoke. "Each one of the people we lost had been attacked in a different location—just like Blood Music's people, according to the newspapers. Demons are usually linked to a place—a house, an abandoned facility, or inside a host body."

"Right, J.L. And the host body doesn't incinerate on impact. The demon flees, and it will torch, but the human body just dies a normal death." Damali waited, her focus on Marlene.

"Marlene, tell her," Shabazz urged. "Tell her about the house in New Orleans."

Everyone watched the team matriarch slowly stand and walk

over to the sealed window. Marlene leaned against the steel beam and spoke in a low tone. "There was a mansion down there that had what we all assumed, for years, was a demon sighting. Same thing happened—the absence of sound, and one hell of a fight to put the thing down. It slithered into nothingness, and we thought it had been destroyed. The host body was unfortunately killed."

"How long ago?" Damali's arms were folded over her chest. For some strange reason the information was making her breathe hard, and again, her second sight was wavering. "And why didn't I hear about this before?"

"It happened a little more than twenty years ago," Marlene murmured, and then her gaze slid away from Damali's. "I thought it had to do with my own coming of age as a guardian, with no bearing on what's been going on here. Every one of us has their own private tale about how they were summoned to this destiny, I'm no different."

Nervous glances shot between her crew members, and then each of them looked away. She didn't like it. "Fine. But what did that thing from twenty years ago look like? How did it manifest?"

Marlene took in a deep, cleansing breath and exhaled slowly. "We thought it was an Amanthra demon—ugly things that look like a cross between a snake, a huge spider, and a panther, hence the scaly facial appearance and fluid movements and power. The hiss is like a snake's, but it also has big cat properties, like a panther, and growls low in a rumble. Jaws unhinge to attack—the snake part. Its fangs and bite are deeper than a regular vampire's. Retractable claws, moves fast—the panther aspect. Joints able to turn backward and give it scurry motion like a spider's. Eats flesh. Hideous creatures."

"Now where did some shit like that come from?" Rider was wide-eyed, his expression incredulous.

"Demons have to be released, or conjured up, brother." Big Mike rubbed his jaw and stared at Rider. "You and I both know that."

"Right. New Orleans." Rider sighed. "Need some black magic to bring them to the surface. Vamps can just do their thing and don't have to be called. Guess that's why they're at the top of the food chain—or the bottom of it, as the case may be."

"Vampires are incredible creatures, if you really think about it."

This time the entire team just stared at J.L. for a moment, stunned.

"What?!"

"Hear me out, Rider," J.L. argued. "Think about it. What makes a vampire so deadly is they have the ability to blend in with humans. They can transform into bats, wolves, mist, smoke, leave no real odor trail, can invade dreams, and feed without detection. Leave the body drained with only two puncture wounds—but most of the time they cover up the kill and make it look like an accident to keep authorities at bay. As an entity, they are extremely effective."

"Smooth, like I said," Shabazz muttered. "Most times they're cool, don't cause a lot of static. They stay on the down low to keep the public unaware."

"Sexy, too," Big Mike said in a distant voice. "Can make you wanna slap your momma."

"I told you, we were not going to get into that discussion," Rider said with a scowl. "Almost got yourself bitten that time."

"Yeah . . . I did, didn't I?" Mike chuckled. "Guess I been cooped up too long."

"People, can we stay focused?" Damali walked in a tight circle. "What brought this Amanthra thing up from Hell?"

"This demon is one that has province over revenge."

"All right, Mar, but that's another difference. Vampires aren't just bent on revenge. They're about power and feeding."

All eyes were on Marlene as she spoke.

"There's a South American legend, and another similar one from ancient Kemet . . . the three creatures' aspects of the demon are found in those respective regions. Hence why it has to be released using incantations from those cultures."

When the group looked like their understanding had glazed over, Marlene pressed on. "Big snakes like anacondas and cobras, and jaguars—a cousin to panthers—are found in South America, and the Kemetians were always partial to the big cats. Spiders, I can only assume, had the South American influence. No matter. Someone conjured up that particular revenge demon, or made it, or whatever, in some dark-arts ritual long ago. We thought we'd dealt with it years ago, and now it appears to be back. That's what I need to research. So, while you guys are drinking and carousing, I will be in the occult bookstore and scanning the shelves at the Botanica to get answers."

"But the eyes," Damali persisted. "These things had vamp eyes, and from all the police accounts and the stuff in the papers, they said the bodies were drained of blood. That's vamp action. Plus, a wooden stake wouldn't do a revenge demon. Would it? That's a vampire weakness."

"I know," Marlene murmured. "That's what concerns me. It's almost like a hybrid."

"You have *got* to be kidding me!" Rider leaned against the back of the sofa and closed his eyes. "Now I *know* I need a drink."

"Think I'll skip the ribs and the fine sister and join you, brother," Big Mike said.

"Jazz ain't calling me like Rider's bottle of Jack Daniels, right through here," Shabazz agreed.

"How about if I just make a package-store run and we open up old Jack right here in the compound, dudes?" J.L. glanced at his monitors. "If Mar is breaking out the dusty black books, I'll need a shot. Hell, I'll even stop off and pick up some chips for Damali, too."

For a moment, no one said a word. Damali began pacing, as the group remained silent. Revenge?

"Oh, God . . ." she finally muttered. "We have to figure out how these things multiply, how to kill them at the source—did you see the jaws on those things? And they're strong as shit!"

"Yeah," Rider agreed. "Not to mention the smell. Vamp breath smells like walking death—but not sulfur. That's a demon thing. That's what was throwing our noses off track. We couldn't figure it out. Normal vamps are too cool to stink until the moment fangs are out and they're two inches from your jugular, which I might add, is when it's too late for you to worry about their hygiene or post-morning breath. But it's not a sulfur stench."

"Stop it!" Jose was off his metal stool and headed for the door. "I need a day before I can dissect this shit. Dee Dee is dead, people, and you're talking about her like she was an animal!"

Mike moved aside as Jose pushed past him. Quiet settled on the group. No one stopped Jose as he stormed down the hall and slammed his bedroom door behind him.

Damali turned toward the window as she heard the steel gates engage and begin to lift. Weak golden light began to filter into the room around them. Blessed sunlight. It was dawn. She wrapped her arms about herself and closed her eyes. "Everybody take a shower, crash . . . go out, and get your heads right. This was a tough one."

Rose-orange dawn filtered through Damali's private bathroom window, framing the lush indoor ferns and glinting off the rock garden surrounding them. Morning. The only time when she felt safe to undress, be vulnerable, and be unarmed long enough to wash the heat of battle off her. Thank God the compound sweep showed no invasion here. She didn't have it in her to go one more round. There was just too much to think about, so she let it go for now.

Damali allowed the steam to claim her as she stepped up the slate bricks and then down into the tub of the Jacuzzi, facing the shower spray and closing the etched-glass doors behind her. She plunged her face into the pummeling water, covering her eyes with her palms, breathing deeply and willing away a sob. What the heck was wrong with her? Ready to cry? Over what! The Dee Dee thing was over, and she had to shake it.

The beauty of the room that had been designed as a haven for her within the compound now made her feel like a kept exhibit at the zoo. All of it was a magnificent, gilded cage.

Trying to steady herself, she turned and allowed the hot water to beat away the tension from her shoulders, neck, and back. She had to think of the positive—just like Marlene had taught her. Had to stop trippin', as her crew would say. Yes, it looked like Eden in her bathroom. Yes, they had ensured there was plenty of light everywhere, albeit through four inches of impenetrable glass. Yes, she was blessed to have people around her to protect her, and to have money, even fame. But God in Heaven, this was no way to live.

Her breath came in short bursts mixed with anger and despair, and she leaned her head back to allow the water to rinse through her locks. She remembered her martial arts training. Breathe deep. Relax. Find your center without struggle. She could almost hear Shabazz's voice in her mind as the knots in her shoulders began to unwind.

But that was easy enough for the team to say, when they could each go out alone. All of the guys got to go out by day to undisclosed locations, and return relaxed . . . kicking secret smiles between themselves. Joking with each other in guy code that anyone could read. She grabbed the soap and began lathering her hands as well as the sponge she'd picked up. After Raven was history, Marlene had Shabazz. Nobody was stupid. Some days they'd be gone for hours, and come back all glimpses and sighs. And she was locked in a gilded cage—most times with a zookeeper on her hip if she did venture out of it.

Damali took her time, soaping away all the anger as she made huge circles with the natural sponge on her skin, enjoying the texture of it as it slid against her. Where would she go anyway, even if she did sneak off alone? There was no one to make her secretly smile. There wasn't a soul she knew that she could risk putting in danger, just by association. Her thoughts immediately went to Jose, and it made her shoulders drop as she let out her breath fast in pity for him.

Tears came from a source within that she couldn't explain even to herself as they ran down the bridge of her nose and dropped into the swirling abyss of the drain. They were so happy, he and Dee Dee. They had a right, didn't they—to live and love and be as one? Now look at this shit. One of her guardian brothers was all screwed up and dying inside. She flung the sponge at the shower wall and it left globs of soap against the bright Moroccan tiles. The sound of the splat made her close her eyes, and she grabbed the shampoo, blindly feeling her way to open the bottle, squeeze a large blob into her palm, set it down again, and apply the lather to her locks.

Blues and yellows from the colors of the tiles hovered as an image inside her lids and then disappeared. Yeah . . . where would she go anyway? She was living with the equivalent of five brothers who could kill with their bare hands, and Marlene who was no slouch as a perpetual guardian den mother, either. Damali chuckled sadly and let her breath out more slowly. Her twenty-first birthday was in a few days, and this ragtag family would celebrate it. That was cool. It was a blessing, she supposed . . . to even have people around her who cared. At one time she didn't.

But there would be no quiet table in the corner of a restaurant, there would be no roses coming from anyone she could call special. And there would be no evening out, *ever.* No nights like she was beginning to fantasize about. The only person she knew that wasn't afraid of her brother-squad was history—Carlos was old news.

That his name even popped into her mind made her begin to roughly rinse the soap from her hair. She was not going there *ever* again. Damali kept her eyes shut tight, allowing the pulsing water to beat sense into her brain. That was five years ago. She was fifteen. She hadn't met the Guardians. Was living life on the edge and in the streets, then. Had narrowly missed sleeping with the man too many times.

Picking up the conditioner more slowly, she opened the bottle, studying the light lemon-colored fluid and the fragrance of it as she poured it into her palm. Once she'd set down the bottle, she played with the slick texture between her hands, and shut her eyes again as she bent over, throwing her locks before her, adding conditioner to her nape and working it out to the ends of her locks with care. What if?

She turned and faced the spray, noticing that it was beginning to cool. But the change in temperature as it gradually went from piping hot to lukewarm felt good on her body and clean scalp.

At one time, they were from the same world. She could remember him taking her by his people's house to get a grub on. Regular, nice folks.

He'd been the one to tell her to run away, and had had her back when her drunken foster father tried her one, and only one, time. Even she didn't know that by the time of puberty she'd become as strong as a grown man. How would she have known, especially when her body still looked like a regular kid's? But she'd kicked that old, perverted bastard's ass—then had to jet the scene. Carlos had been there, waiting for her . . . arms opened wide. And he'd teased her about being a church girl in hip-hop gear. Had made fun of her for not giving it up during his many attempts to break her in . . . but was also very cool about it, in a strange, respectful sorta way.

The thought made her laugh. Before he'd blown up in the drug world, she remembered thinking how he might have been the one. Had she not been so scared after that foster care attack, maybe she would have given in—but Carlos had messed up. Rumors of a shootout had been enough to make her back off.

A shiver ran through her and she quickly doused her hair under the water, half chuckling at herself for being so stupid. Fate had conspired to keep his boys ever present, or to always have his pager go off with a 911, just when things could have gone too far. She'd made it to fifteen without incident—a long time in her world. But she'd seen too many of her girls from 'round the old way get pregnant, die, or be hurt, or all of the above. That had kept her cool. Made her wary. She wasn't going out like that.

Yeah, a cold shower was probably in order. Anytime she was back to putting Carlos's face on a fantasy lover. Thank God Marlene had found her. Thank God she'd never slept with anybody, or gotten pregnant. She'd seen so much in other people's houses that there was a definite link in her mind between men and disaster. Who needed a man? What was all the fuss about sex, anyway? Probably just like another drug. Thank God she always argued street politics with Carlos and didn't go down that slippery path of dealing and jail with him. But, what if? Nah.

He wasn't the one; when she would finally make that decision it would be a righteous brother—and she hadn't run up on anybody yet that was worth the risk of satisfying that one curiosity she had. Marlene said be patient. Marlene was wise. Marlene had helped her get herself together and launch her career. Marlene would know . . . Yeah, but, Marlene was old, too. On the other hand, though, Marlene was gettin' some.

Why she was even thinking about this was beyond her. They'd just been through a high-stress situation; Jose was all messed up, and now there was some new entity to contend with. Maybe she was like Big Mike: just wanted the basics to relieve stress. Good food, good loving, and go to sleep. Mike was a trip.

Damali felt the temperature shift in the water again, but it had oddly warmed up. Probably one of the fellas got out. Cool. That meant she had a little more of the tank to herself. Today she didn't feel like being *as one,* a team, or sharing. She'd just stand here until the water got cold enough to chase her out of it on its own.

Besides, at the moment, it felt just as good as someone massaging her shoulders. Carlos used to do that for her. Now nobody did. . . .

Damali lolled her neck, the rhythmic pummel against her skin making it tingle. Thick rivers ran down her naked form and just the flow across her breasts, past her abdomen, down her legs sent a tremor through her. He'd been the one to listen to her rap, said he'd make enough money one day to showcase her in his own club. Somebody to dream with . . . but that was before she fully understood that she could never go there, not the way he made his money. Ever. Knowledge was power, he'd always say; the guardians said that, too. But at the moment it was a bitch.

She let her breath out hard. Damn, those were some good old days, though, when everybody was scramblin', but could be free, and laugh despite all the tragedies the streets offered. Same diff. Hanging out at rave parties, free styling on open mics, dancing until sweat poured off them and they could practically wring out their clothes. Eating barbeque chips with a soda pop in her hand, dropping the bandana for souped-up cars drag racing at night . . . the night. Her man's red Chevy bouncing, engine gleaming set up high and mounted in a cut out of the hood— Carlos wasn't scared of shit. She missed the freedom of it all. That's what she missed about him, he wasn't scared of shit.

"You will not go there," she whispered into the rain of the shower, using the words to help stave off the memory of his touch.

Yet the temporal awareness pulled her deeper into the pulsing spray, making her close her eyes once more. The sound of the water became a blanket against any other noise in the compound. They had come so close. They had been talking, had become all deep and philosophical, down by the beach, right about dusk, his boys weren't around, and his pager was off.

His finger had traced her jaw on that one particular day. She remembered. Yeah . . . and it had trailed across her collarbone, the edge of his finger nudging away her light blouse, finding a point on her breast that had made the tips of both sting. The memory washed over her like the water from the shower, warming her. If people hadn't walked by; if his boys hadn't found him. If his sister hadn't OD'ed later. She'd wanted him so badly that night, if he'd only known.

Unable to stop the torrid memory that beat on her hard, just like the spray, she allowed it to seep into her pores and take over her thoughts. How could she get it out of her head, when it was the closest she'd ever come to being conquered—different worlds notwithstanding? He'd been the only one to touch her like that, or make her feel anything like that. Especially when he'd brushed her mouth, and had followed the invisible trail of his finger, replacing the path with kisses at points along the way. Then a sudden heat had covered one of the stinging pebbles, a tongue, then the gentle graze of teeth, pulling at it with warmth that soaked through her sheer top, made her lean into the lips that suckled her as the sensation soaked her panties.

Without permission her palms cupped her breasts, creating tiny waterfalls at the edges of her hands. A slight shudder forced a quiet moan. It happened so fast, so out of the blue, so crazy. She squeezed her thighs together, feeling her own inner river spill over the thickened lips between her legs. This was nuts, she told herself, as her palm slid down her wet belly toward the heat-slicked source. For weeks she'd been in this perpetual agony. She swallowed away another moan, letting it come from inside her throat when her finger touched a part of her that now craved something she'd never had.

Trembling, the returned coolness of the water didn't bother her. What if . . . Then she felt it, an awareness of being filled from behind, a shaft of heat traveling up her center, quaking her uninitiated womb.

The sensation was so real that she found her hands flat against the tiles, the texture almost boring into her palms as her head dropped back and her hips writhed to a rhythm that even the unexplored could comprehend. Phantom pleasure dipped her spine into a deep sway; she couldn't get enough air. Her back felt like it was being anointed by kisses, a bite at her shoulder. Her head tilted of its own accord, exposing her neck in offering, the sensation of a deep, passionate bite sent indescribable delirium through her whole system. Her lips parted to give way to ragged inhales and exhales that transformed into a staccato pant. Just once . . . Please . . .

A burn like fire ringed the engorged delta that she now opened her thighs to allow full entry to . . . from behind, something invisible but that felt so real . . . pleasure so unthinkable that it literally buckled her knees and made her cry out.

Carlos's face blurred and new intense eyes, intoxicating, drank her in. The tight rim of her valley ached so much that it began to spasm as she moved her body to draw friction from the shower wall, her vertebrae separating as she flipped over and her back hit the tile and the water beat against her face, her collarbone, her breasts, her stomach. Shards of ice-hot need tore away shame, transforming it to liquid anguish that ran down her legs. Her quick gasp reverberated back as an echo, and she could feel it cast prisms of energy through her bloodstream. The burn was all-consuming, and she wasn't even touching herself. Her hands were splayed against the wall, her nails beginning to dig at the tile as her mind grappled with the explosive sensations. If this was what it felt like . . . Oh my God . . .

Years of wonder, frustration that had made sleeping at times torture . . . Had turned her pillow into a lover until she gasped alone in the quiet. Movements often so frantic that she feared her bed would be heard by the others. Hot tears streamed from the corners of her eyes, mixing with the spray that pelted her. A sudden weight felt like it was crushing her, making her skin ignite as it slid against her, again causing her to turn her head for the sensation at her neck, exposing her jugular, wanting to feel that force against her throat. She didn't care. Profound, erotic heat swept through her. Then it was gone.

Breathing hard, she glanced around the empty room. The shower, now freezing, made her immediately shut it off and wrap her arms about herself and shiver. Then she rocked, her eyes closed, one hand over her mouth. Unable to stop shaking as aftershock tremors slid between her legs, gently petting the molten surfaces as though a good-bye kiss, and evaporating like the stream, she wept.

For a long while she sat on the edge of her bed, staring out at nothing. This thing that had happened was so private, so humiliating, but so gloriously paralyzing that she couldn't even tell Marlene. What could she say? How did one explain something like this, especially to someone who was practically your mom? What—so the team could whiteboard it and draw a weapons diagram for the shower? She was only glad that Marlene's second sight had been spotty lately, and she could put up a wall against her when these feelings manifested. But she still strained to sense whether this private invasion had been detected. Damali became very, very still. No. Whew. She let out a sigh of relief.

She couldn't fathom fixing her mouth to describe a sudden onset of severe horniness, that's all it was. She glanced at her pillow with disdain, total inner shame making her face feel hotter. Once in a while had become too regular. That's all it was. The mood just descended on her followed by a mind-blowing fantasy about an old lover who was now practically an enemy. Oh shit.

She rocked. Because she wanted more of what that had felt like, regardless of what prompted it. The awareness was sobering, even if her body didn't want to comply.

Not Carlos Rivera, ever. She rocked. But her body was still trembling and on fire. She rocked. Because she now had an idea of what it felt like. If he walked in the room right now, it would be over. No. She rocked. The incident in the shower had left her thirsty for more, hadn't released her. It just made it hurt worse. She rocked, trying to breathe steady through a new wave of want that licked a coating of memory between her legs. She groaned, closed her eyes, and stopped rocking . . . knowing that one day, no matter what Marlene said, she wouldn't be able to say no.

Then she became very still. It felt so good that she had offered her throat?

Oh shit . . .

Damali covered her face with her hands, leaning over until the back of them rested against her thighs. She breathed slowly. The plush terry cloth towel felt too heavy on her wet hair, and she snatched it off and tossed it, not caring where it fell. She had to get out of here, get some air. Go for a drive. Clear her head. See some people from the old neighborhood who still lived normal lives. Buy some chips and soda pop, and chocolate. Go Roller-blading on the pier at the beach. Eat tacos. Laugh to keep from crying, or running screaming into the fucking night!

Spying her black jeans and a peach tank top she'd laid out, she stood. She was outta here.

It was late afternoon when she returned. Damali glanced around at her ragtag team. Rider was leaning to the side, as was J.L., and both appeared to be trying to hold themselves upright in their chairs. Big Mike was sprawled out on the sofa with his eyes closed, snoring, and his burly hand over his stomach. Shabazz was nodding in the armchair, and Marlene looked pissed off enough to spit nails. Guess everybody had a good time. She sure did. Kicked some butt at pool, had her a taco, chips, and even a brew.

"How is he?" Damali nodded and signaled with her head toward Jose's room within the compound when she fully entered the weapons area.

"Messed up," Rider muttered sullenly. "How the hell do you think he is?"

"All right. That's enough." Marlene walked over to the sofa, kicked Mike's foot to rouse him, and glanced at the metal bench that stretched twelve feet long. "Big Mike, go in there with him and make sure Jose keeps the shades open. Give our man plenty of sunlight."

Mike yawned, stretched, nodded, then got up and left the room. Marlene sat on a stool and looked at Shabazz and Damali for a moment and then cast her gaze around the team before sending it out the large double-reinforced, bulletproof window toward the hills. "Why don't you all get some real rest? The red-eye flights are tough, Rider and J.L. are dead drunk, and we don't know what nightfall will bring."

"I'm going out again for a few hours—alone."

Damali ignored the glances of concern that ricocheted around the room. She needed space. Period. Five years of this was like Alcatraz.

"We'll discuss that in a moment, but first we need to deal with Jose's situation."

Damali stretched and moved toward the beige leather sofa by the wall that Big Mike had abandoned and flopped down on it, while Shabazz got up and took a high metal stool facing Marlene. Rider let his breath out in a long, weary exhale as he turned a ladder-back chair around the wrong way and sat with a thud. J.L. just glanced up from his laptop computer and stared.

She needed to know Jose was all right, but she also needed to break camp again. The streets were calling her. A little bit of sunlight just hadn't been enough.

Damali tried to keep her fingers from drumming on the side of the sofa with impatience. What the hell was wrong with her? Jose was her boy! Damali looked at Marlene, willing her with her mind to speak, but hurry up.

"Poor bastard was talking to her in his sleep, just like he was the whole ride on the plane," Rider said after a moment, shaking his head. "If he didn't get nicked, I can't figure it out."

"You see the paper?" J.L. folded up the newspaper and tossed it toward Shabazz like a Frisbee.

"Yeah," Shabazz muttered, catching it with one hand and passing it to Marlene to inspect without looking at it.

"Dee Dee was pregnant," Damali whispered, swallowing hard, her gaze trailing to Marlene's and then out the window. She didn't even respond to the newspaper that had been tossed around. She wanted to clear her conscience about Dee Dee, first. She hated secrets, and had hoped Jose and Dee Dee would have told their own tale. The team shouldn't have had to learn about their baby this way.

"Our sister asked me not to mention it when she found out." Damali sighed hard in frustration and sadness. "They were so happy, and didn't want to blow their high if the group had a negative reaction. Wanted something private of their own to keep between them for a little while. That's part of why Jose couldn't do her last night." She swallowed again and shut her eyes briefly. "The other part is because he loved her."

"Aw, shit . . ." Rider stood and began pacing. "Then you know what we're dealing with, right?"

Marlene just nodded as Shabazz wiped his palms over his face and let out a loud breath.

"We gotta find the lair, soon. Jose's energy is dying . . . Dee Dee had a part of him inside her when we toasted her." Rider stopped and studied the group. "How long does that give us, Mar? Weeks, days, months, before our man just buys it as his energy drains away? Plus, Dee Dee didn't look like a normal vamp—so what are we dealing with, in terms of time, to either send the main demon back where it belongs with a ritual, or kill a master vampire? This is crazy!"

"I don't know." Marlene tossed the newspaper to Damali without even opening it. "We're down a guardian—and we need to address that, first. You know that."

"Maybe you haven't been counting, Mar," Rider shot back, "but we ain't exactly in a position to win friends and influence others to join this crap. Not after what was in the papers."

"What about Dan?" Shabazz's question made the group go still.

"Dan is an innocent," Damali whispered. "I don't want to see another one go out like the others did. They died before they even got a quarter through basic training—they hadn't even gotten to the compound, and we thought just keeping them on the edges of the activity would make them safe. No, Shabazz. Bad plan. We need somebody who can hang."

When the group nodded, Damali relaxed a bit and sat back. All of this was beyond insane. Both activity and the attacks had mounted. Why, even if it was a demon, was it targeting artists?

She wouldn't even allow herself to imagine what had taken place in her shower.

Damali opened the paper and looked at the headline news. She nearly gasped. Her gaze momentarily stopped to assess Carlos's eyes, and then she read on. An immediate chill swept through her and she struggled not to cover her mouth with her hand. The team didn't need to see how much she was still concerned about him. That wasn't their business. But this was horrible. His best friends, and cousin. . . . Damn, she knew all of them. Her gaze went back to his eyes, and she touched his photo and immediately closed the paper. When she looked up, everyone was staring at her.

Marlene's gaze again went around the group and she allowed her line of vision to linger on each face for a moment before she went on. But she held Damali in her sight a little longer than she'd peered at the others, and then eventually sighed. "Because a few of our own have been compromised, J.L. will need to come up with some new gear."

J.L. nodded. "I'm on it . . . I just hope Jose can assist—"

"That's just it," Rider argued. "If his mind is locked with the bloodline of suckers that bit him, then he is a walking breach. And, truth be told, we aren't even sure it is a vamp that got Dee Dee . . . we don't know what that demon Marlene was talking about can do!"

"He hasn't been bitten!" Damali corrected. Her voice had escalated unintentionally and her skin was crawling. She needed to get into the sunlight, outside, and get real air.

Again the group fell silent, and slowly one by one they nodded.

"Look," J.L. added after a moment, "we have made this place as tight as we can. We've got UV floods surrounding the compound to light it up like a stadium at night. Freaking planes mistake it for LAX, already. Every window is bulletproof glass for the strength.

"We've got infrared motion detectors lacing all entrances, windows, even the vents. Steel grates shut this place down like a tin can at dusk, with reinforced steel doors and frames mounted into a foot-thick of cinder block, with ultraviolet lights in every room that can go on with a panic button—plus with sprinkler system trips in all the halls, in case one gets in here and we have to dose the joint with holy water . . . and we've got motion detectors and computer visuals to not just track human intruders, but we've rigged the capacity to pick up forms that don't show up on infrared—but just give off cold. It picks up a form that's lower than environmental temp and shows a blip. However, as we know, people . . ."

"We can't stay in here twenty-four/seven." Damali let her breath out and stood. "I'm ready to do this thing, ya know. Like, when's the last time I could just hang out down the way *at night,* and kick it with the kids at the rec center—which is what we're supposed to be trying to do? Helping people. Giving back. I miss—*people.*" She spun on Marlene and looked at her mentor hard.

"Mar, for real. When's the last time Big Mike could go do his thing with the kids in the church basements, or Shabazz could go do his thing helping ex-offenders transition? Hell, when's the last time Rider's been able to go play some poker, or J.L. could go hang out in the spy shops to make some new yang, without anybody worrying about what time they had to get back here? Huh? Now he's gotta come up with some new gear and tracking systems all by himself. We won't even talk about this bullshit that just happened to Jose. All he wanted to do was sit outside and sketch and be with his woman and play his music, and our poor brother's been so messed up since they turned Dee Dee that he doesn't even draw anymore! Hell, I can't concentrate—can't deal with the spoken word thing right through here—and that's our bread and butter!"

Shabazz gave Marlene a look, and she stilled it. The silent communication between them grated Damali so badly she wrapped her arms around herself to keep from choking them. "The guys should be able to get tore the hell up, play poker . . . Mike should be able to spend the night with some sister and eat till fried chicken comes out of his ears, Shabazz should be able to go to a real jazz club at night, Jose should be able to fall in love, and I should be able to go party my ass off at a club of *my choice*—especially when I turn twenty-one. Demon or vamp, I'ma get lit. Tore up. I'ma dance, act crazy, and have a blast . . . might even get laid, okaaay."

Her team looked stunned, and Rider seemed to instantly sober up.

"Thank you for trying to get us all a weekend pass, Sergeant." Rider laughed tensely as Damali circled the weapons table. "But somehow I don't think the general is going for it. I can pass up Vegas."

They all kept giving each other fishy glances, but for a moment, none of them spoke. Whateva. She was too serious. Fuck this living in prison with little outings to make it seem like they had real lives.

"This destiny is a hard sacrifice," Shabazz finally murmured, his eyes holding Marlene's gaze as he spoke. "None of us have been able to totally do what we used to do. And as a seer, dropping your guard under the influence of alcohol or get-high won't be pretty. Think you've seen some scary shit before . . ."

"I know, I know, that's why I don't go there," Damali snapped. "But all the other rules are draining the life out of the team. And I, for one, am not going to live the rest of my life in a jail cell—techno pop as it is!" Her hands had found her hips and she glared at Shabazz, and then at Marlene. "Don't we have some damned barbeque chips, or some soda in this joint?"

They all stared at her.

"Oh, pullease, spare me with 'the body is your temple' speech. If I'm gonna die, then whateva. At least I can have some fun before I buy it. I'm going out."

"That's not advisable," Marlene warned, her voice low and tense. "It's late."

Damali turned her attention to J.L, ignoring Marlene. "Hook a sister up with some crazy-mad-shit to take out on the street. I am sick of this living scared, but acting like everything is cool. The damned vampires have us hiding, even in daylight now. Was a time when one or two chased us—then we flipped the script and went after a few of them. Now, apparently, it's on. L.A. is hot—crawling—and we don't have to look for them, they're finding us on the road now. And we've got demons? Sheeeiit." Damali glanced at the clock and pointed toward it. "You call this late, Marlene? Little kids go out in the street later than this!"

Shabazz stood and retrieved the cast-off newspaper, and opened it. "Club Vengeance is smoking," he murmured. "A body dropped there a little while ago, and now it appears that an old friend of yours just lost two compadres, with one in the hospital about to turn, too."

Rider cocked his head to the side as Damali slowed her exit. "Thinking what I'm thinking?"

"Thinking that maybe Marlene might want to get us booked at Vengeance?"

Rider nodded at Shabazz. Damali kept her alarm in check. That was the last place she wanted to do a gig, for more than one reason.

Big Mike's fast entry to the room drew everyone's attention, and his eyes studied the floor as he walked. "Gotta get him to a hospital."

Marlene was on her feet. "What's wrong?"

"He's gray, Marlene," Mike murmured. "Looks like a drug addict going through the DTs. He's incoherent, breathing is irregular . . ." Mike paused and cast his gaze toward the sun beyond the window and then closed his eyes. "If he dies here, they'll sweep the place. Little brother ain't gonna make it through the night if we don't get him some type of medical attention."

"That's just it," Marlene whispered. "They can run tests, put an IV drip in his arm to rehydrate him . . . but in the end, what's killing him isn't in the medical books. Not theirs anyway."

"Mike is right, though," Damali said quietly. "We have to at least get him help while we look for this thing. Nobody in here is a doctor. We do soldier stuff, can do some healing, can pray, but this might be beyond the laying on of hands."

"I agree with Damali," J.L. commented, his voice a soft murmur. "Can't just wait this one out."

"Might buy him a few days, or more, while we do our thing, and it will keep the authorities from going for a search warrant to come in here, maybe . . . but how are we going to secure him in the hospital? At night?"

Rider's question made the group simply stare at Big Mike.

"They already have one in there that's about to turn," Shabazz reminded the group. "If DeJesus dies today, then in three days he'll wake up."

"So, what do we do, just watch Jose die in here?" Damali began pacing again. Her mind shredded the options and she leaned her forehead against the wall in frustration. "Maybe that's our lead, and we should follow it when it wakes up and turns.

Let's take Jose over to the hospital while we still have some light. Just three of us—me, Mike, and Rider. We can post one man—Mike—by Jose until they run whatever battery they can on him there. Rider and me can see if we can find Carlos's boy and lay low until dusk. They always mark one about to turn, so something will come for DeJesus, and maybe me and Rider can track it."

"Why do I always get involved in the—"

"Because you're a nose, Rider," Damali argued. "Jose is down. That leaves you." She blew out her breath hard. They were all getting on her nerves. "Two of you guys, J.L. and Shabazz, stay here and work on weapons and keep it tight here. Marlene, you work the phones and get us booked with Club Vengeance—and leave a message for Carlos that I want to have a word with him, one on one. He might talk to me."

She pushed herself away from the wall and let her breath out fast again in disgust. "Don't even say it. I know. Me and Rivera go way back. Chill."

CHAPTER FIVE

"THE DOCTORS said he was extremely dehydrated, like his fluid levels had been siphoned out of him. Plus, he had too many white blood cells in his system, same as if our boy was fighting off a virus." Big Mike sat down heavily in the hospital waiting-room chair, leaning his huge forearms on his thighs, his head dropped and his massive hands clasped.

"He *is* fighting a virus," Rider sighed, leaning his head against the wall while in his seat and rubbing his palms over his face. "How long's he got?"

"Damn, Rider," Damali whispered. She stood and walked in a short back-and-forth pace before her team members. "Don't go there. Okay? If we have to bring him to the hospital every few days to get him dosed up, then that's what we do. But don't ever talk about one of our own in the past tense."

Rider cast his line of vision to the bank of elevators and offered no further comment.

"They're gonna put him on IV fluids and heavy doses of antibiotics for a few days, then, if he responds, he can come home." Big Mike glanced up at Damali. "When he responds. My bad."

"A few days," Rider said, his tone far-off and quiet. "That

kid is like a little brother to me. Guess I'm just trying to brace myself . . . seen the inevitable too many times not to go there. I hate surprises."

"Okay," Damali murmured, her voice more gentle as she went to Rider to place a hand on his shoulder. "I hear you. I'm sorry. This situation is messing with all of us. It's too close to our core."

Rider nodded and covered her hand with his and closed his eyes.

"Did you find out anything about DeJesus?"

Damali's question made Rider look at her.

"He bought it, first light at dawn this morning, before we got here."

"Takes three days, usually, for one of them to fully turn." Big Mike stood, making Rider stand with him. "That means we have a few days before he climbs off a morgue slab."

Damali and Rider nodded a quiet acknowledgment of what had been learned the hard way. It was going down just like she'd thought.

"Then he's gonna try to go find Poppa—or Momma. Whatever bit him."

"Rider's right." Damali leaned against the wall. "All we can do is hope that Jose comes around before this one starts going back over old ground." She let her breath out hard. "They always track back to where they'd last been before turning."

"Just like bloodhounds, trying to pick up the scent to find their maker—to find and identify their pack, their own particular vampire family line," Rider said in a weary tone.

"Yeah," Mike whispered. "Then that group marks off it's own territory. But that's what's been so weird about the recent activity. At first, it seemed random . . . like no order to it. Just a vamp here or there that would pop up, find us, and then we'd dust it.

Or, we'd find a small nest and get to them first. Now, there's a pattern, almost—"

"That's because it's concentrating, like nests are forming alliances or something . . ." Damali said thoughtfully. "And the dangerous part is, we don't know why. They might all be vamps, but vamps are very clear on feeding grounds, and whose turf is whose, right? Like the drug dealers."

"Okay," Rider said. "What's the plan—or dare I ask?"

"Big Mike, you stay with Jose, like we talked about. I'm not going to lose him . . . or you, Mike. So stay sharp. Promise." She waited until Mike nodded and he pounded her fist. "Rider. You do the morgue detail with me later."

She laughed when Rider started shaking his head.

"I know, I know, Rider. Not your favorite place to be—but we need to keep a tail on DeJesus. That's why we took the four-by-four and the Hummer. We'll take the Jeep, and leave the Hum for Mike. Cool?"

"Aw'right. Shit."

Damali smiled. "Rider, hang here and try to chill. I'll come back and get you, and then we'll do the Coroner's Office together—but you keep tabs on the hospital morgue, see if they moved DeJesus downtown yet for an autopsy. Turn on the monitor and your transmitter if you leave here for any reason, so J.L. and the team can stay with you. We don't want to lose you either, Jake Rider. You're a perpetual pain in the ass, but we still love you."

"Now I have to be LoJacked like a car? Aw, man, gimme a break." Rider let out a resigned sigh and ran his fingers through his hair.

"And where are you going, lil' sis?"

Mike's question made Rider stop complaining, as both guardians looked at her hard with concern.

"You know where I'm going," she said.

"Be back at Rider's side, or mine, before dark," Mike said, his tone telling her that he'd brook no argument. "We're not trying to lose you, either."

Damali shrugged off the security frisk as the bodyguard completed it. Bastard didn't need to feel her up, just check for a weapon. She didn't have a gun, so what the hell?

"You can follow me," he told her, smiling too much for her liking.

She let the irritation pass and steadied her line of vision to focus on Carlos's office door, looking beyond the guard's too-tight black T-shirt, which strained against the muscular bulk that made up his stocky frame. When she entered the room and saw Carlos, his silent appraisal both grated her and worked on a section of her emotions that she'd turned off. She didn't even want to name the conflicting sensations in her head right now. This was business.

He rose briefly, sitting after she had. "Long time no see," he said in a quiet voice. "It's cool," he told the bodyguard who had ushered Damali in. "Practically family."

Damali watched the man leave them with a nod, and returned her attention to Carlos. He looked healthy. Color was good. It was still daytime. All good signs. She glimpsed the reflective surfaces in the room. He gave off an image. But the question was, could he have become one of the vampire helpers—human traitors that sold off his friends and family for power? He'd risen awfully fast.

She studied the lines of tension in his face; he still wore his silver cross. And, Lord help her, the man was still fine . . . had the body of life, showing every rock-solid definition in it through his turquoise silk shirt . . . the color looked good on his bronzed skin. Leather pants. She would try her best not to remember those black leather pants.

"You look good, too," Carlos said after a moment of surveying her again with a knowing smile. "Life seems to be treating you well."

"This isn't a social call, Carlos." She kept her voice even like her gaze. Arrogant bastard. He got on her nerves.

"I knew it wouldn't be," he replied, leaning forward on his desk, but still seeming relaxed enough to be amused. "Your people called and wanted to book a gig here. I figured that with Blood Music blowing up large, and doing this worldwide simultaneous concert, maybe you'd finally changed your mind about never performing in the hottest club network in L.A.?"

"Yeah. Saw the news about the international concert in the papers, and every entertainment show has been blasting it." She stared at him as his smile broadened.

"I told your manager that it was cool for you to perform here." Carlos took his time choosing his words, his gaze holding Damali's. "What I didn't tell her was that, since the sons-of-bitches have snubbed my clubs repeatedly, I would love to see somebody else pull some of their profit—maybe move on their territory one day. Then I heard from you—the only one who could do it. Welcome."

Damali shook her head. "That's not why I'm here, either." She watched him carefully ease back and assess her. "I'm here because of what happened to your boys."

Something in his expression shifted. A deep sadness registered in the depths of his eyes—pain, remorse, guilt—it flickered past her so fast that she almost didn't see it. Then he lowered his gaze, smoothed the front of his silk shirt, and looked up. Pure, chilling fury reflected back at her now from his handsome face. Any sign of vulnerability was gone.

"I appreciate that you came to pay your respects, and wanted to book an event here as a peace offering between you and me. Thank you. You've always been cool people, D. Always had my back, even though we've had our philosophical differences."

She watched as he stood and walked to his bar. She wouldn't correct him, however. If he thought she was here as a mourner, so be it. If he thought the gig was her way of paying homage to his crew—so be it. And yet, she wrestled with that knowledge.

"Do you want a drink? I need one to talk about this shit."

"No. I'm good."

"Yes . . . you always were," he murmured, pouring a drink for himself, studying the glass with a chuckle, and then returning to his chair behind his desk. "Still holistic, my barrios church girl. Amazing."

"Carlos, what happened?" Her voice was a murmur as she tried to shake off the effect of his intense appraisal.

"You've read the newspapers." He smiled.

"I wanted to hear it from you."

He took a sip of his drink and let the liquid roll over his tongue. "I know about as much as they know. But I'm glad that you finally came to me . . . without my having to call you . . . at least not in the traditional way."

She cocked her head to the side.

He chuckled and took another sip of his drink. "Let's say you've been on my mind lately . . . been calling you from here." Carlos tapped his temple. "Perhaps, since all this went down. Who knows?"

She remained very, very still as her fingertips began to tingle, all senses keened and readied with adrenaline.

He briefly closed his eyes with another sip of the dark liquor and breathed in deeply, then smiled sadly as he swallowed. "What are you wearing?"

Almost rendered mute by the question and the expression on his face, she raised an eyebrow.

"The perfume? The scent. Name it for me."

"What?"

"Just name it, so I can remember it."

"Okay, look," she said, standing quickly and walking to a far end of the room. "This is way off track. I wanted to ask you—"

"My bad," he cut in, his smile widening, then tapering off as she leveled a warning glare at him. "I've lost a lot of *hombres*. My inner family. Juan this morning. . . . Then you walked through my door unannounced. . . . And I wanted to just forget about everything but you for a while."

"I'm not a drug, Carlos. Never was, and never will be." It was odd, but she'd meant to use a harsher tone when she told him off. She had to find something else in the room to stare at besides him.

"Then I guess you still don't know your own power . . . one that can leave a man strung out. It's dangerous not to know one's own power." His voice was quiet, and his expression tender before he looked away.

"Did you get high this morning or something? You're talking crazy, and we're way off the subject of why I'm here." Her comment was sarcastic, but just didn't have the desired effect upon him. It was supposed to piss him off, get him to stick to the subject, and not make him look at her like that . . . not with the expression that allowed her to see his soul beneath the hard façade.

"You know I never touch my own product. That's how I stay in control and wealthy." His tone was calm, but there was a slow, intense smolder of offended dignity within his eyes.

She could feel her breaths coming in quick bursts of fury. His cool demeanor was messing with her head, and he was so blind! "You are not in control of what's going down here, Carlos. You need to get with that."

"Sit down," he ordered, now standing himself. "What do you know that I should know?"

All sexual tension vanished. Again, like a shape-shifter, his expression had instantly changed; giving way to the hardness of spirit that had driven her from him in the first place. He rounded his high-backed leather chair, abandoned his glass on his desk, and walked toward her so quickly that she reflexively went into a fight stance.

"What is wrong with you?" He seemed absolutely appalled that she was prepared to defend herself from a strike as though he'd hit her. Taken aback, he moved away.

She blinked and relaxed.

"You think I would hit you? Why?" Hurt and stunned anger filled his eyes. "Have I *ever* hurt you?"

He circled her and she matched his motion as they both walked counterclockwise to each other.

"If you know something, D, then tell me. Who did my boys? I know you'd come to warn me if you knew . . . heard something on the streets, right? But you're so jumpy that now you're making me wonder. Don't fuck with me, baby. You know me well enough to know better than that—it would break my heart to have to . . . well. Lemme just say, don't go there. Talk."

"You're threatening me, now, huh, Carlos?" She'd stopped walking. "Did I just hear you right?"

He looked away toward the glass wall that overlooked his

club. "I didn't mean it like that. We're all on edge."

"Your boys," she said, nearly speaking through her teeth, "chose a lifestyle—your lifestyle—that constantly puts them in danger. It puts other people in danger, and it weakens our community from the inside out."

Carlos chuckled and his shoulders relaxed. He walked further away from her and collected his drink, and then sat down heavily in his plush leather chair. He let out a breath and took a sip.

"Oh, baby . . ." He shook his head and laughed harder, the tone becoming sadder. "You came all the way down here to preach at me? God bless you, you haven't changed a bit. I miss our arguments about my business." He took another sip from his glass and chased the ice in it with his finger. "I really do."

His melancholy rooted her to the middle of the floor. It was an inexplicable dance, hers and his. He opened up very tender places in the center of her chest, and could just as quickly send a steel cage of protection crashing down around it.

"Listen," she whispered. "I am sorry about your family. No one should have died that way."

He looked up at her and simply nodded, but when he swallowed hard, suddenly it was difficult for her to speak. She found herself drawn to sit back down in the chair in front of him, leaning forward on her forearms with her hands folded. His hand covered hers and they both closed their eyes for a moment, allowing a long ago-memory presence before they both sat back.

"I did come to warn you," she murmured, holding his gaze.

"Talk to me," he told her in a quiet tone, no threat in his voice.

"I'm glad you're still able to wear a cross."

"I use to wear the little gold one that was a gift from my grandfather, given by my grandmother . . . you know I used to never take it off. This one replaced it. That's all."

Damali nodded. "Promise me you won't stop wearing one, though. And, if you ever see anything . . . unusual that frightens you—"

He laughed, cutting off her words and opening his desk drawer. Carlos shook his head as he reached in it and produced a huge, custom-designed silver automatic magnum. Setting it down carefully between them, he then slid it toward Damali with a grin.

"I don't do fear. But I do vengeance very, very well. Named my club for the skill."

"That won't work, Carlos. You can't shoot what you can't see. You have to use a higher—"

"Still trying to save my soul, baby . . . and make me give all this up. What's in the center of this desk is what keeps the balance of power, not this," he chuckled, holding his cross out from his chest. "This is jewelry." He pointed to the gun, and returned it to the drawer. "That is power. And we all make choices . . . the subject of our running debate. Maybe one day we'll see eye to eye?"

She inhaled slowly and let it out even slower, the tightness around her heart became so heavy that she needed to stand, needed fresh air. She turned away and walked over to the wide glass and cast her gaze down to watch the club readying for the evening onslaught. "You took one path, I took another a long time ago. I just wish you could see. Every day that you stay in this, the less chance you have to get out, and the more in danger you are, just like everyone around you—dark draws to dark . . . and it's already eating your boys, alive."

Her back was to him when she heard him stand and come toward her. She didn't flinch when the heat of his palms touched her shoulders as he massaged them. Nor did she pull away when he placed a gentle kiss against her neck. To her surprise her head tilted to yield to his mouth. She watched his reflection in the two-way mirrored glass and then shut her eyes. Just this morning . . . if only. God help her.

"I'm already in too deep, and you know that, Damali. It would take a miracle . . . it's a way of life once you choose this road, and there's no turning back—until you die." He inhaled deeply, sending a hidden tremor through her.

"Then, you go to Hell. It's so simple. Why fight it? Hell now, or Hell later. There's only a few choices for a man in my position," he murmured.

He'd breathed his statement behind his kiss, and she could still feel his breath as it swept the moist marker of where his lips had been.

"Not always," she whispered. "Sometimes miracles happen, if you believe."

He rubbed her arms and then stepped away. The loss of his heat sent a shiver through her and she unfolded her arms to wrap them around herself.

"Maybe you're right," he said. "You are here . . . you cared enough to come to ask about my family, and even still try to chastise me about my lifestyle. After all these years, I guess some prayers do get answered."

As she stood watching him lean against the edge of his desk, his words knifed into her. Guilt spread and fused with old memories, becoming a palpable pain that made her palm find the center of her own chest. She had to make him understand her true purpose, and yet never give away her team. But, from way, way back, she also owed him enough information to keep him from an attack. If he perished from his lifestyle, that would be hard, but she could live with it. That had been his path, his choice. Yet, she couldn't have him stalked by something beyond his comprehension.

"There's something not human going after your family—and I'm not sure why, Carlos. And regular ammo doesn't work."

His gaze was tender when he considered her words and his smile wasn't haughty, just weary. "I know," he said. "Whoever did this wasn't human. Even in turf wars, there are rules."

"No," she corrected, still trying to get through to him. "I mean, it's not from this world. It's a demon."

He chuckled sadly and shook his head. "Now you sound like the grandmothers. Damali, go home. Baby, I got this. When you come to perform, I promise you I'll have men at every door, and won't let anything happen to you. Thanks for agreeing to a gig here to bring back the crowds . . . and for the condolences. I'm cool."

It was useless. There was no way that his mind could absorb what she was trying to say. She let out a long breath, and gave up.

"Just keep your cross on."

He nodded and smiled at her.

"You be well."

"I will. Tell your mom and your family I asked for them."

"I will, baby. I'll walk you out."

As he neared her again, she stopped, and put her hand in the center of his chest. Her mind sealed it with a prayer. It didn't matter if he wore a cross, a Star of David, a star and crescent, a medicine wheel, a Yoruba amulet, a crystal, a Buddha, whatever . . . each member of her team was protected by these symbols of faith because they believed. They all came from various cultures, and brought their ideologies with them. He had to understand that the symbols were powerless without the faith behind it and an affinity toward the light.

"Oh, Carlos . . . you have to listen. This is worse than anything you could imagine."

"I'll be all right."

"I wish you were on our side." She looked away, not able to gaze into his eyes any longer, and not able to be this close to him.

"So do I, sometimes," he whispered with another deep inhale of her.

"If you do find yourself in a situation that you've never encountered before . . . and if your gun fails, do one thing for me at the very end."

"You know the only way I'll go down is fighting." He took her hand, found the middle of her palm and pressed a kiss into her hand, then folded the kiss away within it.

"Say a prayer to God if you find yourself going down. Make that the last thing you do, if it comes to that. Promise."

He nodded, and released her hand. "If is a mighty powerful word. I don't plan on going down. That much, I'll always promise."

"I know," she said softly, walking beside him. "None of us ever do."

She sat beside Rider saying nothing for a long time, just staring at the horizon as the sun set. Dusty mauves and muted blues formed a blanket covering the sky, which tried to hold its own with violent golds, pinks, and oranges, battling for the last of its light against evening. Night would not be kept at bay, no matter how hard the sun fought against it. Even the largest planet in the heavens had to follow what was natural law. Damali shook her head and sighed. How was she supposed to fight a pull that strong—indefinitely?

"Been a long time since the team did two-by-two detail. Just two from the team on a stakeout so a person could talk, really get to know the other guy whose back you're watching," Rider said in a quiet tone, his gaze fastened to the building across the street as he toyed with the jade cross at his neck.

"I know," Damali murmured, still looking at the sky. "Shame that we haven't had much breathing room ever since Marlene started us hunting. Liked it better when we left shit be. If something rolled up on us, then fine. If not, that was most cool. Today was the first time in a couple of months any of us went out alone."

"Yep. Was a time when I rode solo—got a bottle of whiskey, found a good poker game, selected a beautiful woman, and paid my tabs in the morning. Now, I'm rolling with the Magnificent Seven, or what used to be the equivalent of the Dirty Dozen, to God only knows where, or why. Nobody coulda told me this, then. Ain't life ironic?"

She nodded, checking the weapons in her belt and the Isis blade in her hand. Rider had made her smile despite her sullen mood. "Was a time when I had a bunch of girlfriends, and we all hung out and partied, and the biggest thing we were worried about was what to wear to the clubs—or if our fake IDs would get us in. Then again, some of us did have more than that to worry about. Don't get sentimental, Rider—it wasn't all good. Foster care was a bitch. So was being a runaway." She laughed and then swallowed hard as she looked at her sword.

"Ain't life ironic."

She didn't answer him and just allowed her fingers to trail the multiple blood grooves of the silver-plated triple blade, and eased it back into its ancient mahogany scabbard, holding it with both hands between her knees while she and Rider waited.

The ornate gold handle commanded her attention as she studied the goddess cast from Kemetian pyramid metals that slayed a serpent, wondering how many high priests had used it to defend themselves. Running from the authorities as a kid, fending off drunken adults, even running from a gang shootout was deep, but not as off the hook as this.

"You like her?" Rider asked. "She suits you."

"Thanks . . . yeah . . . she's beautiful."

"I remember being your age once," Rider said in an unusually gentle voice. "Had me a girlfriend and a Harley, was doing the all-American thing and rode all over creation, screwing, having fun—that was the seventies." When Damali chuckled, he laughed. "Honest to God's truth. I wasn't always a sharpshooter, just like Shabazz wasn't always an Aikido master. Wore my hair in a long ponytail, didn't worry about taking a bath, the weed was good—no bullshit in it like now—got in more bar fights than I care to remember, was locked up a time or two . . . the good old days."

"You're crazy, Rider, you know that, right?"

He laughed. "Yep, I am. That's why I lifted Madame Isis for you from Marlene's footlocker. That old bird got it from the Knights of Templar, and knowing those guys, it probably came from the Vatican. You weren't supposed to take it off the compound until after you turned twenty-one, lest it fall into the wrong hands. But, I figured, what the hell? A few days early won't hurt. You're as good as grown. Plus, I've seen you fight; it won't get taken from you, that's for sure." They both stared at each other. "All right, I admit it. I can pick a good lock. Don't ask."

She studied his face, the way the lines were starting to form in it from the wear and tear of life, and the way the edges of his eyes crinkled with mischief. He still wore cowboy boots and a seventies relic, fawn-colored suede jacket. All that was missing was the ten-gallon hat. "You're good people, Rider."

"Why thank you, darlin'. You ain't such bad people yourself."

He blew out a long breath. "And, although you're strong as shit, and have all these abilities, you're still young and human. Just so you know, we've all been working on Marlene for you."

Damali looked at him with a questioning gaze.

Rider nodded. "I don't need second sight to know that soon you're going to have to ride solo a while yourself. You can have the blade and the Far East contraptions. It would make me feel better if you had an equalizer, though, dig?"

She smiled.

"Like I told you, I do the all-American thing, a Harley and a gun. This white boy ain't trying to go out with a crossbow or guitar planted in his chest. Period. That's the one thing me and Shabazz agree on—like the fact that J.L. needs to tighten up the vamp detection rigs at the compound. I told Far East he was all that and two bags of chips, but J.L. has gotta recognize that things are heating up—all over. Can't be casual these days, ya know? Things are changing."

She nodded, but sensed that Rider was trying to work his way around to another deeper conversation. It was all in the way he was going on and on in what seemed like circles. "We've got a lil' somethin' for 'em. Don't worry. I hear you."

"Some shit is just natural law," he pressed on, "and Marlene is gonna have to deal with that." He turned around in his seat to face her. "Do you know what I'm saying to you?"

She glanced out the window and nodded. Her smile faded. She had to remember that Rider was a sharpshooter, and sometimes he was patient to hit his target dead-aim. But there was no escaping what he really meant. On the surface, the conversation could go one way, while they avoided speaking on the layer right under it. Very cool. It allowed both parties room to decide to go deeper, or not, and also save face.

"It's wearing you out, kiddo."

"I know," she whispered, half embarrassed, and half relieved, and yet totally unprepared to be having this conversation with Rider, of all people. Life was weird. Go figure.

"If you need to . . . uh . . . well . . . I say, get the Carlos thing out of your system. Or, if it's somebody else, hell, you're young. Just use a condom. There. I've said it. I've weighed in on it." Rider glanced at her and shot his gaze out the front windshield as he turned back around in his seat. The color had drained from his face as though saying those four words had been more embarrassing for him than for her.

"I'm not sure why Shabazz and Marlene are so dead set against you doing what's normal with anybody," he rattled on, talking a mile a minute to obviously cover his discomfort with the subject. "They keep looking up at the stars and pacing around like nervous parents." Rider paused and rubbed his hand over his jawline. "I don't claim to understand what they're so uptight about—but maybe you oughta just ask them outright, ya know? Stop beating around the bush and dropping coy hints. Shit, you ain't shy about anything else."

Rider had hit her right between the eyes with his own direct brand of truth, and for a moment, no words formed in her stunned brain. Then, out of nowhere, she laughed hard. "Why are you all up in my business tonight, Rider?"

For a while he just stared out the window and then closed his eyes. The shift in his mood worried her.

"Because I love you, sweetheart. You're the closest thing I have to a sister. You remind me so much of Tara, too."

"Tara?"

"Yeah," he whispered. "She was the one who used to ride on the back of my Harley."

She studied the way the muscle pulsed in Rider's jaw. Curiosity drew the question from her. "What happened to her?"

"I had to put a stake in her heart in Arizona." Rider looked at her with a sideways glance.

Damali opened her mouth and then closed it. What could she say? That was the last thing she'd expected him to tell her. Damn . . .

"I know. There are no words. And thanks for respecting my privacy . . . for not just bum-rushing my psyche to find out."

"I don't like it done to me, so I don't do that to any members of our team."

He nodded. "You need to tell Marlene that, too. She's too nosy."

"I will," Damali promised with a sad smile.

"Well, don't get all down in the mouth. The Tara thing is history. That's how I met Jose, and probably why I, more than anybody, know where he's at. Long story." Rider wiped his hands over his face. "I don't want to talk about it." He gripped the steering wheel and focused his attention on the morgue. "The last thing I'm gonna say about it is: life is short, unpredictable, and at times, fucked up. So have a blast while you can, kiddo. Taste it all before your number is up. Sermon is done, pass the plate, discussion over."

"Thanks, Rider." She touched his arm and then removed her hand. The pain that she registered in his system brought tears to her eyes, but she blinked them back to preserve both their dignities. She only hoped that she'd transmitted healing empathy when her palm had grazed him.

He nodded and looked away to the building again while she focused her attention on the precious gemstones in the blade's handle. She didn't know what else to say to Rider, and companionable silence seemed to be the safest haven now.

She peered at the seven stones that Marlene had said each

represented a color of the chakra alignment described in Eastern philosophy—the invisible energy fields that governed a part of the body and spirit, denoted by a specific hue running up the human spine, and so placed on the sword, made grip-ridges that were perfect for her hand. Three blades each etched with Adrinka symbols down the lengths formed a unified trinity that came to a fierce point. The stuff of legends, and now it was hers.

By design, its triangular shape had the ability to open a hole in a body that couldn't be closed. Made of Vatican and North American silver, and South American alloy cast with Dogon steel from the motherland, it had been fired in Samurai furnaces, parts of it passed around the world from female Neteru to Neteru until it was completely constructed. That's what she'd been told. Fascination claimed her as she studied the object that had been created era by era, religion by religion, each culture represented within it, so they said. An early birthday present, according to Marlene, ever since the planets aligned. What did that mean? But she was glad that Rider had swiped it and thought to bring it along. Madame Isis was something she knew could get the job done.

However, the fact that it had been "borrowed" from Marlene worried her. She tried to make herself feel better by using the word "liberated" to describe what Rider had done, and to define what she had accepted as a coconspirator. Damali laughed softly to herself. Marlene was gonna have a cow. In fact, where the heck did Marlene get a blade like this? There were so many questions, and so few answers . . . and who were the freakin' Knights of Templar?

"Maybe you shouldn't have taken this, even though I was complaining about wanting to try it out." She'd kept her gaze on the windshield when she'd spoken. Too many thoughts were battling for dominance in her head at once. "Marlene said it wasn't time yet."

"You know," Rider said, laughing, "if Marlene didn't want me to give it to you yet, she would have stopped me. Nothing gets by that old girl. She's smooth."

Damali smiled. "What did she say?"

"To be careful, like she always does—and to have a good time. Then she sighed and left the room."

Damali sat quietly again, thinking about Rider's comment for a moment.

"Did Shabazz say anything?"

"No, like the rest of us, he knew sooner or later it would be time."

She looked at Rider now. "What's this time thing? Ever since the planets lined up, the team has been talking in code—acting weird. I feel like there's this big secret and nobody's telling, and I don't like it."

"Did you ask Marlene?" Rider now looked out toward the horizon, his smile becoming gentler.

"I've asked Marlene, and all she says is that when I'm ready, I'll know."

"Just what a mom would say." Rider chuckled and leaned his head on the steering wheel. "It's not my place. And it's definitely not my forte. Ask Shabazz about the alignment."

Damali found herself laughing, amused as her teammate squirmed under her questioning. "Rider, c'mon. You are the bluntest person I know. Frogs leap out of your mouth daily— and your style is straight with no chaser, right between the eyes. Give it up."

He laughed, sat back, and shook his head. "Not on this whole slayer subject. Mar let you have the sword because you wanted it bad enough to sneak it. She left the room smiling. That's all I'ma say. Let it rest."

"All of us are acting weird, though," she whispered, the amusement gone from her tone as her thoughts drifted with her gaze. "It's like something within the team is changing. Getting stronger, or I don't know, but it's different . . . and it's changing the whole dynamic. Even the music is stronger; the crowds at the shows are getting bigger. Hell, I feel different, too, and I can't explain it. Everything is getting on my nerves."

"Okay," Rider finally said, making Damali look at him again. "What happened back at the club? I know we're all worried about Jose, and this graveyard shift ain't happening—but you seem beyond concentrating, or worried. Like, this Carlos thing."

"There's not much to say, Rider." She pulled her gaze from his and sent it out of the car window, sweeping the terrain for the slightest movement. "The sun's going down, you need to stay focused—like you said, we haven't done a two-by-two in a long time." The last thing she wanted to discuss was Carlos, or the primal pull that came with him.

"So, is Carlos a source, or what?"

"No. He doesn't know anything. He's bent on going after whoever did his posse. He's been attacked, but I don't believe he's a source. Whoever—"

"More like *whatever*."

"I tried to tell him that."

Her comment made Rider sit back, and it brought her attention away from the window momentarily. Her teammate's expression flickered between indignation, concern, and possibly a tinge of jealousy. It was amazing to watch.

"I didn't give us up. I told him to keep his cross on and pray if he went down. Period."

"Oh," Rider said, with a sigh of relief. "For a minute there

I thought the handsome bastard might have messed with your head."

She would not dignify the comment. Her gaze returned to the building. "This place is crawling with police. They're expecting a break-in at the morgue. They think it's some ritualistic message system of turf warfare between the gangs. Remember what the newspaper speculated, and the police comments said?" She stopped and waited for Rider's nod before continuing. "DeJesus won't turn for at least forty-eight more hours, given he died earlier this morning . . . and vamps don't wake up till the third nightfall."

"So, what are we doing here, then?"

"Frankly, I don't know. We should go back and get Big Mike—and stand watch over our own, with him."

Rider stared at her for a moment. "You haven't been making clear-cut decisions lately, have you noticed that?"

"Oh, bullshit. We're all jangled. There's a lot coming at us at once. So, my bad . . . I miscalculated the turn time—but nobody else caught it, either. But we do know that they always send one to mark their victim. So gimme a break, Rider."

"Aw'right, aw'right. Chill. Just an observation, Damali. You can loosen your grip on Madame Isis now."

"No, I can't," she whispered, her head nodding in the direction of the building.

Her arms immediately pebbled with gooseflesh as what felt like an electric current ran through her. Blurred images flashed through her head, making her temples throb. Her tongue became covered with a metallic taste, and her vision became keen enough to see the grains of sand within the concrete steps across the street. Damali blinked twice. She heard a bird rustle in the trees, and the cicadas sounded way too loud. What in the world . . . ?

For a moment Rider stared at her. "Talk to me."

"Can't you smell it, taste it?"

Rider leaned forward, closed his eyes, and breathed in. "Sulfur." He opened his eyes and looked at Damali hard. "You picked it up before I did, li'l sis."

"Yeah. I did," she murmured, the new awareness making her grip tighten on the handle of her blade.

"You're growing up on us," Rider finally said, his expression tender, his voice soft. "Soon, you won't need a chaperone."

A companionable silence enveloped them for a moment.

"What do you think of the sulfur, kiddo?"

"A newer one—the scent isn't strong enough to be the master of the line. Remember how Shabazz and Marlene described it? I personally never ran up on a head vamp, or a head demon, but they have. Said once you got it in the back of your throat, you wouldn't forget it. Whatever came here is probably checking on their newest member so they can report back. When the new vamp or demon thing wakes up, they'll take it back to their lair."

"A damned vampire escort service." Rider glared out the window. "Now what?"

"We follow the stench when it leaves this area, and hope it materializes into a solid form so we can see it. Right now it's moving through the air, staying masked in an invisible form so it can get inside the morgue past the cops, but I can smell it. Sooner or later, it has to materialize, because it's gotta feed tonight, then go back to a lair, somewhere."

"Sounds like a plan, li'l sis. Let's rock and roll."

CHAPTER SIX

STOREFRONTS PACKED tightly together squeezed as much commerce as they could out of the available space. Upper floors were made into tattoo dens, beauty parlors, massage parlors, secondary restaurants, and apartments roomed above fresh-fish and produce stands, eateries, and dingy but interesting shops. People milled about still bargain-hunting, couples strolled hand-in-hand, groups of young partygoers laughed loud and traveled in huddles, while tough teenagers and dirty-apron-wearing waiters hung in doorways or on the corners catching a smoke. It was chaos; it was bustling activity; it was life.

Spices from exotic Asian cuisine mingled with the heavy smells of old cooking oil from Chinese fast-food takeout joints. Splashes of colors, smells, writing in a language she didn't understand, foreign tongues, known words, drug dealers, gamblers, upstanding citizens, mothers with children, little kids, wealthy people, street urchins, a morass of humanity wedged itself into a few square blocks of mayhem. From somewhere roosters crowed. Garbage reeked. Traffic horns blared. Rap music fought for attention against world music and the whiny, high-pitched Chinese mandolins. Sound came from everywhere: cars, opened doors, restaurants, people's living quarters. Men argued over cards, a baby cried, lovers grunted as bedsprings squeaked, a junkie vomited in a rooming house, a dispute erupted over the price of fabric, cell phones beeped. All of it pummeled Damali's heightened senses. She was near nausea, but she pointed the way for Rider—who was cool enough to just drive.

"We're a long way from the hospital and Mulholland Drive up in Hollywood Hills, li'l sis," he finally complained when she signaled him to pull over. "Chinatown ain't no place to be jacking around in the alleys on a hunch."

"Save it, Rider. I know what I'm doing. Sit tight. Just keep a visual." Damali climbed out of the four-by-four before he could answer her, unsheathed her blade, and narrowed her gaze within the dark passageway she'd entered at a full dash.

In the distance, she could hear Rider contact the compound on the Jeep radio, but her nerve endings were on fire. Adrenaline and something else she couldn't describe made the blood flowing through her veins feel like lava. Her ears strained in the quiet so hard that she was sure they had lain back against her skull. Her grip tightened around Madame Isis.

The stench became thicker, concentrated, and it filled her nose and coated her tongue, making her spit. It was as though roaches were crawling over her skin. Her breaths came in short pants now. She didn't blink, as the darkness suddenly no longer became an issue. All her senses were heightened more than she'd ever known them to be. It was disorienting, yet thrilling at the same time. She could see layers of reality. A heat trail from a cat. A vicious stray dog saw her and quickly backed up, abandoning it's feeding in the garbage. Yeah, something else not human was with her out there, just as she'd thought. The dog was the tip-off. Animals always knew.

Heavy fumes of grease and garbage collided as steam from a kitchen vent filtered over a Dumpster. Dampness was all around her. The sound of a steady drip, drop, drip, drop came from the air-conditioner condensers. Their hum everpresent, she heard beyond that and listened to the small stream of water flowing down the alley's gutters in a noisy trickle. The garbage dripped a yellow, icky liquid that was the telltale sign of maggots. She shivered as she now heard the larva squirm. Her own footsteps echoed. Something skittered by. Fuck it. It was on.

She swung before she saw what it was. All she had to do was feel the hair on her arms shift and she knew where to strike. A pair of red-glowing eyes opened, then the form quickly filled in around them. The puff of lingering smoke transformed into a feminine shape of blackness in the dimly lit space. Yellow flood-lights glinted off massive fangs, and a hiss escaped the creature's face on a black, pronged tongue. Half hidden by the shadows, only a hint of vulgar, scaled cheek could be seen. Sulfur trailed the entity like cheap perfume.

Electrified, Damali moved with sudden force. Making a slice against the night as the thing before her vanished, she missed. Instantly off balance, she used the momentum to spin around and to keep the beast from attacking her from behind. The screech of rage the creature released filled the air, and her blade was still vibrating. Madame Isis was singing, creating a harmonic frequency that sent another surge of strength through her.

In the distance she heard the four-by-four door slam. Two more figures stepped from the Dumpster shadows. Males. She watched as their jaws unhinged and the dead-flesh scales on their faces split and bled green ooze to accommodate the massive fangs. She kept the female in her peripheral vision. It was smil-ing, watching the show. She'd deal with that skank in a minute. But she could feel it, sense that the two males were about to spring. It was as though their thoughts moved the air ever so slightly, like a subtle breeze. She was ready when they leapt.

Damali ducked, rose, and caught one in the chest, puncturing its lung with the direct point of her blade, and struck the other with a long slice across its throat. As the second creature fell back, grasping its neck, Damali doubled back and delivered another blow across its already wounded windpipe—but this time she landed the blow with more force. The female leaned its head back and released a bloodcurdling scream. A head rolled to Damali's feet and she kicked it away, and stood legs wide, Madame Isis held at a ninety-degree angle while the skull burned and turned to dust. Satisfaction claimed her as the first creature writhed in a slow incineration from the hole her sword had made.

Sudden movement—the female vampire sprang at her. Rider was about to be toast as he neared the battle-hot area by the Dumpsters. Damali somersaulted away from the lunging female to quickly stand in front of Rider, her sword leveled and her gaze darting to every surface, every puff of steam, and every skittering insect in the alley.

"I told you to stay in the car," she yelled at Rider.

"Screw that!" he said fast, holding his Glock above his shoulder with both hands. "The general gave other orders."

Three beasts came out of the shadows bearing fangs. When Rider took aim, Damali blocked his shot, using the wall as leverage to immediately mount an attack. She flipped toward them. When she landed, and spun, one was at her back, the other two were in front of her. Rider fired. The creatures before her hesitated for a second to hiss in Rider's direction. She could feel the one behind her become airborne. Rider was screaming for her to watch her back. An opportunity flashed. The advantage was opened as another round of Rider's ammo went off.

Damali's response was immediate. Isis was aimed to take out a heart—one jab, she plunged her sword with her full weight behind it. The crack of breastbone, then softness echoed against the brick walls. Creature slime ran down the trilogy of blood gutters on her blade. A direct hit—through a vampire heart. Madame Isis had been baptized. Flames burned where vampire blood polluted the weapon until it once again gleamed silver. The second vampire hesitated then rushed her. His abdomen was Damali's target. Isis found it. The creature wailed as silver entered his gizzard and came away with entrails. The disemboweled entity dropped to its knees clutching its stomach, trying to hold in its slowly igniting intestines. It all happened so fast, but to Damali it felt like slow motion. Seconds to react.

Moving with feline speed, Damali stepped aside, avoiding the swipe from behind as the third creature landed against the ground, making a lunge at the flaming dust. She summarily severed its head while it roasted with its brethren vamps. Breathing hard, Damali spun around in a circle. Then looked up as something identifiable as a female entity dropped down to the Dumpster.

"Bring it, bitch! You're the one I want anyway!"

"Damali, no! Leave that one, and get back in the Jeep! Get outta here before more of 'em show up!"

She couldn't help herself. Rider's hysterical pleas seemed to drive her forward. As long as there was a human in the alley, an innocent, she couldn't stop fighting. Something fragile within her had snapped. She wanted this female vampire like a junkie craved crack. Damali rounded the Dumpster, ascending to the top of it with one pull, leveraging her weight with the bottom of her boot against the side of the metal container. A claw made a swipe. She ducked, swung her sword, but missed. Rider was circling, trying to get a shot off, but Damali's boot found the beast's chest and connected, making both the creature and Damali fall backward.

Landing on the ground with a thud, and although temporarily

dazed, Damali immediately jumped up, angrier than she had been when she began. The creature hung from a precarious grip on the end of the fire escape. Rider fired a round, but missed as it swung upward and grabbed the next rungs. Damali was back on top of the Dumpster in a flash. The beast turned and smiled at her.

"You can't take my place," she hissed. "He's mine." Then it slithered through a vent and was gone.

"Damn!" Damali walked back and forth on the Dumpster top for a moment then jumped down, appraising Rider. "You nicked?"

"No," he said very carefully. "You?"

"Hell no. I wish one of them would even think about it."

His expression was very calm. Too calm. "I think they already have, li'l sis. What the hell was on your mind, going into an alley with no backup, and trying to do that many vamps alone? That's not procedure—ever."

"I don't need a lecture, Rider." Damali began walking, but didn't sheath her blade. "I need your ass to shut up and drive. And we ain't going back to the hospital until I find that bitch."

"Okay." His tone was laced with sarcasm as they reached the four-by-four. He held her arm as she opened the door. "Standard op—we always sweep a vehicle before we get in."

"Bullshit," she snapped, shrugging out of his hold. "If there's something in there, I got something for it." She hopped in, drawing a dagger from her waistband, thrusting Isis into the floor of the vehicle with vicious force.

"I'm sick of this shit! My people are dropping like flies, we're practically imprisoned in our own home! I want a life. So, either way, dead or alive, or otherwise, the bullshit ends tonight! We track that bitch, and drip holy water on her head, torture the truth out of her. I wanna know where the main lair is."

Rider climbed in behind her warily, and his gaze went to the sword stuck two inches into the steel floor of the Jeep. "I'm calling Marlene as we drive," he said, reaching for the radio, and flipping on the UV high beams that rimmed the Jeep's roof.

"You do that." Damali fumed as they backed out of the alley. *Punk.*

"Where are we going, and how are we supposed to find something that just slithered through a Chinese kitchen vent? Huh? Answer me that?"

"We track it—just like I brought you here. Or are you losing your skills, Rider?"

Her breaths were now coming in short bursts. Perspiration ran down the center of her back and beaded on her forehead and upper lip. The muscles in her arms and legs twitched. Her hair stuck to her scalp. Her heart was beating a hole in her chest. Images flashed in her mind, the bright colors making her close her eyes to the blur of passing traffic. She couldn't sit still. The feeling of maggots covered her skin. Each exhale was bringing a guttural sound up from her throat. She began to rock.

"West on Wilshire to La Brea," she ordered with her eyes still shut tight.

She could feel the vehicle turn and move, and although Rider had stepped on the gas, he was driving too slowly. "Now!"

"Mar, Shabazz, J.L., this is Rider. We have a situation."

"Speak to me," Shabazz replied in a tense command.

"Our Neteru is . . . well . . . going through some pretty fucked-up changes. Dig?"

"Where are you?" Marlene yelled. "Talk to me, Rider. What's going on?!"

"I've got a lock on them," J.L. said fast. "Wilshire, in Chinatown."

"Mar, she's rocking, and burning up." Rider glanced at

Damali, and then trained his eyes toward the street as he drove faster. "She jumped out of the Jeep before I could stop her, and ran down a blind alley with Isis drawn like a freakin' Samurai, and took out three of them by herself."

"Blood lust," Shabazz murmured. "Bring her in."

"Now," Marlene said, the panic clear in her voice.

"Fuck you, Marlene!" Damali came out of her daze, and put her hand on the wheel, making Rider swerve. "I'll cut his freakin' heart out if he doesn't follow this scent."

"Uh," Rider stammered. "Look, you heard the lady. I'm not arguing with her and Madame Isis. New plan, gang."

"Damali, listen, baby," Marlene crooned through the radio. "Come home. You don't understand what's happening to you."

Damali leaned her head back. Something inside her bubbled up, a strange heat that connected with sound and forced a battle cry through her lips. The primal yell echoed and bounced off the interior of the Jeep cab. Rider swerved to take the speed up to eighty as he rounded the corner onto Venice Boulevard on two wheels.

Rider glanced at his gun—Damali's eyes met his.

"Don't even think about it," she warned. "Draw it and you lose an arm."

"You hear that shit? You hear that shit, man?! What the fuck? Is she turning, what the fuck is happening?! Am I driving a vamp, or is our girl over the edge? Explain some shit to me! *Now!*" Rider's gaze shot between the radio, Damali, and the road.

"It's going down," Shabazz said in a controlled voice. "Phase one. Battle prep. Stay with her, Rider. J.L., get me audio to Big Mike."

"You do that," Rider said, watching Damali as she closed her eyes and began rocking again. "Yeah, you get that big, lurchy motherfucker on the horn and tell him I need backup, stat! We're getting ready to hit the Santa Monica Freeway—going west."

"Stay west," Damali said quickly. "Don't lose it."

"Li'l sis," Big Mike said softly. "It's time to come home."

She ignored Mike's entreaties as the images in her head tore at the gray matter in her skull. Blood was everywhere. A bedroom. A man. Mirrors. Police. Sulfur. A black cavern. Female eyes. A hiss. Waves. The beach. Then she saw Carlos and almost vomited. Thick, salty emulsion covered the inside of her mouth and her hand cupped over her lips while she choked the sensation back down.

"She's about to lose her cookies in this Jeep, guys. Our girl don't look good."

"Baby," Marlene said, calling to Damali. "Baby, talk to me. Tell me how you feel."

"Like shit," Damali replied, gulping hard, then taking in and letting out fast, shallow sips of air. "I'm burning up. Can't get the scent out of my nose. My skin—it's in my skin. The beach. It's down at the beach. Under the pier. But a house, or something. I can hear it hissing." Too nauseated to continue, she leaned her head back and panted, wiping at her forehead in anger. "I will cut that bitch's throat out! Five of our men, plus Jose—Dee Dee? I'll gut her."

"Rider. Did she pick up the scent before you did?" Shabazz's question had come quick, stabbing through the radio with its intensity.

"Yeah, now that you mention it." Rider peered over at Damali, then sent his gaze back to the highway signs on US-10.

"She's getting stronger."

"No shit."

"Rider. Chill. Put on a mobile transmitter so we can walk you through this."

Rider complied, watching Damali as she yelled again, writhing in her seat.

"Talk to me, y'all," Rider said. "I'm dealing with something here I've never seen happen. Understood?"

"You're in no imminent danger as long as you stay out of her way when she hunts," Shabazz told him. "Do *not* get between her and a kill. Stay alongside her, watch her back and yours, but do not try to bring her hunt down for her. Natural law is in full effect."

"You ain't gotta tell me twice, brother."

"Yo, Rider," Mike said. "Her hearing, her nose, tactical senses—everything is overloading right now. Don't touch her, because the reaction is swift. She's wired."

"I am looking at a young woman who stuck a sword into the floor of the Jeep—plunged two inches deep through steel like it was a butter knife and the fucking Jeep was Parkay—with a three-bladed dagger in the other hand, and you are counseling me not to touch her to hold her back? What are y'all? Nuts?"

"Rider, you need me to leave Jose and come out there for backup, brother?"

For a moment there was no answer over the radio from any of the guardians.

"No," Rider said slowly, still appraising Damali from the corner of his eye. "Can't leave Jose alone. I'm just worried, is all. She doesn't look good."

"Mike, man your post and stay with Jose," Shabazz said after a moment. "If he's better, bring him in tomorrow morning—*do not* travel at night. There's a lot of activity topside, right through here."

J.L. looked at his monitors, drawing nods from both Marlene and Shabazz. "It's not real good for any of you guys to be rolling at night," J.L. told them, strain lacing his voice. "The terrain is red-hot. Rider, if you can get Damali back in, and if Mike can stay put, we might be able to get everyone home in one piece."

"Got you," Mike said with a nod. He leveled his gaze at a nurse who came in to check on Jose. When she opened her mouth and looked at her watch to signal visiting hours were over, he stood. "*This* is my brother. I don't leave till he leaves—now handle your business. You want to be the one to call security on me?" He continued to stand as the nurse checked Jose's pulse and IV and then made a hasty retreat.

"How's Jose?" Marlene asked.

"Sleeping. Rehydrating. His color is back. He looks good."

"Uh, folks? We're coming up near the pier. You want to return to the immediate issue at hand?"

"Let her get her run out," Shabazz ordered. "When she crashes and burns in the morning, we'll all talk. For now, you have one job. Bring her back here safe—untouched. Put that wire in your ear and turn on your transmitter so we can stay in communication with you as this goes down."

Before Rider could bring the Jeep to a full stop, Damali was leaping out of the vehicle and had yanked the sword out behind her. She immediately began running, her legs eating up the distance with a lightness and a freedom she'd never experienced. The cement gave way to wood, which gave way to sand, and her locks lifted from her shoulders; breeze and salt air slapped her face as she ran. Every cell in her body felt beyond alive. The sword in one hand and a dagger in the other, there was no such thing as fear. An aura of faint blue light covered her outstretched sword arm. Sand hit her backside as she parted the grains of it with furious boot thuds—running, hunting, whatever was out there, she would chase it back to Hell.

"She's on the move," Rider puffed into the narrow electronic bar that bounced over his mouth as he ran, trying to keep pace.

He pushed his tiny earpiece in deeper to keep it from falling out, then released the safety on his gun.

"Stay with her!" Marlene's voice had gone from panic to a near-shriek.

"Easy for you to say. I'm forty-five. It's sand. She's twenty yards ahead of me, and stroking like Flo Jo, dammit. I can barely keep a visual." Drawing ragged breaths, Rider gave chase, and then stopped short of the edge of the pier as Damali's form disappeared.

"Houston," he murmured through deep huffs into his mouth-piece, "we've got a problem."

"Talk to me," Shabazz said in a whisper. "Where is she?"

"Under the pier, and it's waaaaay too quiet for my liking."

"She's in a den," Big Mike said. "How's your ammo, Rider?"

"Low as shit—to be in a zone."

"Rider, use the lights. Get back to the Jeep and hit the lights," J.L. told him.

"I can't leave her under the pier," Rider said, his breaths steadying as he went in deeper under the pier.

"Get out of there, Rider," Mike pleaded. "She'll be all right, man. You won't be."

Ignoring the team, Rider went still deeper, listening to the waves lap against the shore and the poles, his feet sinking in the wet sand as he walked. A whiff of sulfur made him turn. Slits of glowing red opened before him from behind a pole. Hisses—claws at his ankles began to pull him down. His gun dropped when something strong slammed into him, the weapon sum-marily eaten by a wave. He struggled as he felt himself grabbed from behind and his head forced down. The cross on his neck strangled him from the hold at his back; something clutched his shirt. He tried to fight against it but his punches connected with air. He managed to yell; he heard a chime and a whooshing noise, then a bloodcurdling screech as the sulfur smell thickened. His boots were in a vacuum seal that felt like cement.

He could hear the team calling to him, Marlene hollering prayers. His head was being forced to the side. Whatever had him from behind would not let go. Then he heard the chime again, followed by a whoosh. Two sets of eyes before him parted and scattered deeper into the darkness. The pull at his feet suddenly released and he dropped to wetness, covering his neck with both hands. The waves licked him. He shut his eyes, waiting for them to descend upon him like sharks and begin feeding. Prayers echoed from his mind and from his mouth. "Dear God, not like this!"

"Get up."

Traumatized, Rider kept his eyes shut to the voice in pitch black. "Fuck you! Just do it and get it done!"

"Rider, get up," a familiar voice said in an amused tone. "We need to get out of here."

Almost afraid to look up, he peered into the blue-black around him, his eyes adjusting slowly to the moonlight that filtered between the pier boards high above.

"Damali?"

"Let's move, dude. Unless you want to wait for them to regroup and come back?"

Rider grabbed her outstretched hand and pulled to right himself, noting how easily she'd helped him up. But he reserved comment until they had jogged back down the beach and locked the Jeep with them in it. He leaned his head on the steering wheel and let the tremors abate when his hands shook as he tried to put the key in the ignition.

"Sonofabitch! Don't do that again, okay? Enough to make a grown man piss himself. Shit!"

"Everybody: status!" Shabazz's voice bellowed through the radio.

"We're coming in," Damali said, her tone blasé. "We'll pick up Big Mike, unless he's okay till morning."

"Rider, the slayer's condition; your condition?"

Rider sat up slowly, wet sand and sea clinging to his body and clothes as he stared at Damali. Her expression was more peaceful, like the sudden onslaught of whatever had taken her over had passed. "One of 'em got me from behind," he said. Strain made his voice sound tight, as he thought about the horrible possibility of being nicked. "Check my back, D—I mighta got a scratch from a vamp. I think I'm hit." He peered over his shoulder, grabbing at his shirt, panic making him scrabble at the wet cloth. "Check me out, for real—I'm hit!"

There was silence on the radio—all anyone could hear was static.

"They never nicked him," Damali said in an amused tone. "That was me who grabbed him from behind and moved his head out of the way so I could throw my dagger without taking off his ear. Couldn't talk to him with a baby Isis between my teeth. Needed one hand to grab his slow ass and pull him out of harm's way." She slapped Rider on his shoulder and rubbed his spine as he pulled away with a sullen expression.

"They never broke the leather on his boots. I had his back. Madame Isis had mine. We're clean. Got two more—but two got away. One of them, the female, is headed for the beachfront properties . . . but police are up there. I wonder, maybe staking out one of Carlos's boys' residences?"

"Come back to the compound, now!" Marlene ordered. "Mike will travel by day if they release Jose sometime tomorrow."

"I'm cool," Mike said. "Go back to base."

"She's not even breathing hard," Rider snapped, exasperated. "And is now all smiles. This is bullshit."

"She got her run out," Shabazz said. "The blood lust has passed. Bring baby-girl home."

CHAPTER SEVEN

"YOU ARE grounded, Miss Thang!" Marlene walked in a circle as the rest of the team sat silently in the weapons room. "And, don't you *ever* curse at me, ever! What was that, 'Fuck you, Marlene,' mess? Huh? I will kick your natural—"

"Grounded? I'm grown. What the hell—"

"Don't you speak to me like that! And, everybody *stop cursing*!" Marlene pointed at Rider who now occupied a stool. Outright fury burned in her eyes and her voice dropped to a lethal octave as she spoke through her teeth. "You almost got a valuable member of the team killed!"

"Correct," Rider said. "Shark bait, right under the pier—"

"I handled it, and also got a bunch of them tonight." Damali leaned on her sword and glared at Marlene.

"No more solo acts. Period. We're not looking for numbers—we're looking for the source—the quality of the kill, not the quantity. That's the part you don't get yet. We can do topside vamps for a lifetime, and still wouldn't make a dent. Strategy is what you're lacking, and common damned sense!"

Damali studied her blade and looked up from it with a sideways glance. She respected Marlene, but she was sick of her telling her what to do. Who put her in charge, anyway?

"Mar," Shabazz warned, "drop it. She was doing what's natural, and there comes a point where you can't fight nature. You know that. A vampire huntress's job is to hunt."

Shabazz's comment made Damali relax a bit as a brief feeling of vindication swept through her, but the way Marlene glared kept her on guard.

"A Neteru's job is to hunt, but her job is to also work within a team. It is not to imperil the lives of team members in the process—just like our job is to protect. And just because she's smelling herself does not mean she can disrespect—"

"What!" Damali could not believe Marlene had gone there. She was practically hang-jawed, but that state lasted about two seconds until indignant rage kicked in.

"That's right! Smelling yourself." Marlene's tone was sharp enough to cut. "Getting Rider to steal a sword that's over seven thousand years old, given to me to give to you when *I* say you're ready. I *let* him take it—just to see what you'd do!" Marlene's eyes narrowed. "You're not ready for this power, because you have no respect to go with it—and just because you *can* do something, doesn't mean you *should*. Lesson number one, as a huntress."

Damali threw the blade on the equipment table, and the team pulled back, each standing slowly as Marlene circled her.

"Mar, you are fifty years old, and she's—"

Marlene's glare cut off Rider's words.

"This has been brewing for a long time," Shabazz said under his breath, moving to a neutral position out of the way.

"You can't let them go at it in here," J.L. said fast, incredulous. "C'mon, Mar, D, we're family, and this is very uncool. Chill!" His eyes darted between the would-be combatants, worry tensing his expression.

Marlene pointed her finger at Damali as she turned and addressed J.L. "You think I will not deal with her in here? Huh! I will not have a mutiny in this team, and whether she knows it or not, she's still got a few things to learn. She almost cost Rider his life tonight." Marlene's attention snapped back to Damali and held her with a hard stare. "You just try me."

The challenge ignited a level of defiance in Damali that was nearly intoxicating. But as she looked at Marlene's stricken expression, seeing fear, hurt, and concern, she forced herself to relax. Yeah, she could take Marlene in an all-out one-on-one, but there was indeed this thing called respect. And she did love this woman. . . .

"Look, I'm sorry. And I shouldn't have cursed at you. I didn't mean it like that," Damali said, forcing herself to take a deep breath. "I picked up the trail, then all this weird stuff started happening to me, and I couldn't turn it loose. I didn't mean to put Rider at risk. It won't happen again." She watched Marlene lower her arm and steady her breath.

"I'm tired. I'm going to bed." Damali cast a disparaging look at the team. "Yeah. At night. And no, I'm *not afraid*," she added sarcastically before they could speak—then snatched her sword as she left the room.

"Okay, that was fun," Rider said after they heard Damali's bedroom door slam.

"It's gonna get worse before it gets better." Shabazz sighed, finding a stool again. "We've got two queen bees in this hive."

"Oh, brother," J.L. mumbled on a long breath, going back to his computers.

Marlene wrapped her arms around herself, closed her eyes, and leaned her head back. When two tears slipped down her cheeks, Shabazz stood, went to her, and hugged her.

"Baby, you know our job is almost over, right? She's ready to fly now."

Marlene allowed her forehead to rest against his shoulder. "But she's *not* ready, Shabazz. Her body is changing—she's going through Neteru physiology spikes, but it's not a stable transition . . . hasn't locked in. The girl is a woman by society's standards—but by guardian and vampire huntress standards, she's just a child."

"I know, baby. It's tough on everybody. Like living with a teenager, times ten."

"Mar, exactly what's up with Damali?" J.L. asked, watching them from his station. It was obvious that he had been just sitting there, staring at the screens.

"Her bone structure, while light as a feather, gains flexibility, density—as do her muscles and skin as she matures." Marlene let her breath out in a long, weary sigh. "Can't really tell the difference between a Neteru and a normal kid until one of two things happen—either they are in a life or death situation, or they reach maturity."

J.L. stared at Marlene. "She could've killed another kid, just in a schoolyard brawl . . ."

Marlene shook her head. "No. It's adrenaline-activated. A normal schoolyard fight wouldn't have kicked this off. But something serious . . . yeah. She could have hurt somebody. It never got that bad for her, except once."

Shabazz looked at Marlene, then down at the floor as he spoke, remembering how they found Damali after she'd fought and run away from her foster father. "The physical structure is to make her an even match to do battle with a master vampire. If the vamps throw her, she won't sustain a fracture as easily as we would. If they try to bite or scratch her, her skin will give, long enough for her to defend against it. She'll be able to withstand a bite, and once she's fully matured, won't turn. She'll be faster, stronger than all of us—will have everything to match up against a vamp . . . telepathy, night vision, silent stealth, the nose to track them, the ears to hear the slightest register of sound . . . and lightning quickness. It's all sending her through these . . . these bursts. Even her voice is a weapon, it's a frequency that the males draw to, given their heightened hearing capacity. That's why she gravitated to the music industry."

Marlene shook her head. "By instinct she was seeking out experiences to ready her—to strengthen her skills . . . even if we had never shown up, she would have still been what she is now."

Marlene backed away from Shabazz and walked, glancing at J.L. "She's becoming a walking fighting machine . . . but, there's a flaw, or, I should say, a vulnerability."

"What else, Mar? What's the vulnerability?" Rider studied Marlene, and glanced at his teammates. "That female vamp made her crazy."

"Yeah. I know." Marlene went to the window. "She'll make the females attack. The inner core forces around a master vampire are generally females, for some reason. But, for the males, Damali's scent is like a drug; an aphrodisiac . . . makes them go nuts."

"Get the fuck outta here." Rider rubbed his hand along his jaw.

Marlene remained calm as she spoke. The time had come; the team needed to know. "The female Neteru can then draw the males out, and this drug she emits will make them hesitate to kill her—making them have to choose to kill her or take her, but it gives a vampire huntress the split-second blade advantage."

Shabazz nodded. "The same scenario holds true for male Neterus—they emit a pheromone that weakens the female vamps that guard a master, and will make them hesitate to attack him, leaving the master vamp they guard vulnerable. The master male vampires go postal at the scent of a male vampire hunter, and won't hide, will fight with pure emotion without strategy."

Marlene sighed. "Master males are highly sensory creatures—

within the hierarchy of vamps. But, they can . . ."

"Mar, tell 'em," Shabazz murmured, as J.L. now stood with Rider.

"Her telepathy is going to lock in on a master very soon to pull him out of the safety of his lair, and . . ." Marlene walked in a circle now, wringing her hands. "I've tried to do the best I could . . . You all have no idea the worry. She might have already locked in on a master—which could be why she's blocking me as her guardian seer so I won't detect it, because she's so anxious to go after him that she doesn't want to risk having any of us block her hunt. Or, it could be just plain old defiance—her wanting to do this solo."

"You know that's a natural thing, too," Shabazz said quietly. "The most difficult thing for all the Neterus, male or female, is to learn to work within a team. Half of their mind wants to keep the team safe by rushing into battle alone, the other half of their mind isn't totally rational when the blood lust hits them. That's our job as guardians, to teach the slayer how to temper those impulses and refine her strategy."

"Whatever it is, her power is fluctuating from the strain of sensing and blocking before she's ready. There are days when the kid is wide open, and I can read her like a book. Then, other days, I get a blank page. It's so frustrating—you all have no idea what I worry about!" Marlene whipped around and held Rider in her stare. "Rider . . . what if you had been out there with her, and her power dipped—even for a split second? Do you understand the magnitude of this? Don't you all see why I'm so upset? I'm not the bad guy. The closer she gets to her twenty-first birthday, the more vulnerable she is until she crosses over that line of transition. I only allowed you to give her the sword because I didn't expect that she'd have to use it."

"Marlene, these are significant changes—but what does a couple of days have to do with—"

"Marlene, spit it out." Shabazz held her gaze, but his eyes were gentle.

"She'll go into . . . there's no delicate way to put this." Marlene sighed and stared at the wall. "She'll go into heat. She'll want a master to come to her, and she'll be giving off a scent that will bug him out. It's in her DNA. She'll also broadcast erotic telepathic images." Marlene gave a dry laugh. "Funny how she'll use one of a vamp's greatest strengths—seduction—against him. But unless that huntress is seasoned, she'll be dancing on the edge of her own *very powerful* desires. That's why we, as guardians, are supposed to keep the Neteru in our care away from a central lair until she's ready. That's our code, our rules of the game."

Marlene looked at each guardian, her gaze connecting with each pair of stunned eyes before she spoke again. "Now do you gentlemen hear me? Damali found a nest perimeter too soon, and days can make the difference. It wasn't supposed to happen like this."

"Oh . . . shit . . . ," Rider murmured. "A fuckin' catch-22, if ever I heard one."

"It's deep," Shabazz said, rubbing his jaw and studying nothing on the floor. "When Marlene told me, I didn't want to accept it. But after what I saw tonight, Mar ain't overreacting."

J.L. muttered, walked in a slow, dazed circle. "Damn, Mar."

"In the meantime, you're telling us that until she's one hundred percent through this Neteru adolescence, we have to be sure she doesn't roll some master vamp?" Rider wiped his palms over his face. "Geez, Louise!"

"She'll be testy, evil, and wearing us out." Shabazz sighed.

"That's why ever since the heavens aligned, Mar has had this place under total lockdown. Tomorrow, we've gotta fill in Mike and Jose, assuming Jose is strong enough to come home."

"Would you all explain this planets thing you've been tripping about since May? What the hell? Might as well put it all out on the table now, don'tcha think?"

Marlene nodded, found a stool, and sat down. "We started going on the offensive because she needed to totally conquer fear and get ready for a battle with a master vamp. Think of these other minor skirmishes as going up against sparring partners. I just didn't want her to take unnecessary risks on her own until she was fully prepared." Her eyes were sad, as though she'd been defeated before the real fight had even begun.

"That much I'm stringing together," Rider said in a weary tone. "It's the astrology I'm drawing a blank on."

Marlene used her finger to mark invisible points on the table, and the crew gathered around her. "There was a five-planet array that happened in the heavens in May . . . Jupiter, Mars, Saturn, Mercury, and Venus—they made a straight line for the first time in several hundred years, and in the next hundred years, this will only occur three more times." She glanced at the blank expressions each guardian offered her as a response. "Don't you get it?"

"Duh-uh, noooo . . ."

"Rider, people, the planet Jupiter is known as the planet of expansion. When it shows up and transits, big things that are either very good or very bad on a major scale occur. A vampire huntress being born, and then going through a Neteru heat in a new millennium is a big thing that is good, but it's also occurring at a time when some major bad stuff is happening on the planet."

"Deep."

"Right, J.L." Marlene paused for dramatic effect, satisfied that she now had the group's full attention. "Saturn is the planet of karmic lessons—its lining up in direct alignment with Jupiter means that some very big lessons will be taught by the unforgiving taskmaster of the universe, Saturn. Then comes Venus—the planet of love, combined in alignment with the planet of war, Mars, lining up with Mercury—the universe's messenger."

She let her breath out hard and crossed her arms over her chest. "This constellation won't happen again until 2040, then again in 2060, and 2100. If we count this alignment, with the others, it means it will occur three times within a Neteru's lifespan . . . she's dealing with huge issues—good or bad, karmic lessons, war, love, hinged on communication. And, it just so happens that our huntress has a window in which to conceive during this first alignment." She stopped speaking for a moment when they all gaped. "Something else happened, too, after the initial alignment."

"There's *more*?" J.L. whispered.

"Three of the planets most influential in this particular alignment subsequently formed a giant pyramid in the sky. Mars—war, Venus—love, and Saturn—lessons, broke straight-line formation to create a spectacular celestial gathering. *That's* when I knew. This first transit is forming a triangle in the sky, a trinity. The pyramid shape told me this thing we're dealing with was raised from old Egypt, Kemet. There will be three sides to the battle, a trinity of forces our slayer will have to cope with—love, war, and her old lessons."

Shabazz just nodded. J.L. stared at her without blinking. Rider didn't say a word.

"We're in for the ride of our lives, gentlemen. That's why we cannot afford any slip-ups, people getting drunk, off somewhere unaccounted for. This is very, very serious."

For a moment, no one spoke, but allowed the silence to help

them absorb the bomb that had just been dropped on them. Their expressions were a combination of awe and fear.

"I have a confession to make. . . ." Rider cast a sheepish glance around the table, even as he avoided Marlene's gaze. "When we were on two-by-two detail, I sorta told her to go ahead and get her run out—get the Carlos thing out of her system."

Marlene closed her eyes and shook her head. "Some human boyfriend is the least of my worries. The only reason I object to that knucklehead is because he's a distraction, and his lifestyle is so negative."

"But I thought—"

"I'm not worried about her *virginity*, Rider!" Marlene fought to steady her breathing. "I know you all think I'm just some uptight old bat, but let me inform you that, I, too, once was young and had a life."

Marlene held them all in a glare for a moment before speaking again. "Damali can still die from a gunshot wound, or a car accident, or a stab in a bar brawl—if she's not paying enough attention to avoid it. Our huntress could wind up in jail, where she'd be isolated from the team without a weapon, and anything could slip through the bars at night."

"I hear you," Shabazz murmured. "Lotta stuff comes in the lockdown wards." He smiled. "Ask me how I know."

J.L. and Rider let their breaths out in unison, causing a combined whistle.

"That's right," Marlene said flatly, her hands now on her hips. "Somebody like Carlos lives in the streets, primarily at night, where they both could get jacked by a vampire posse while out clubbing and *having fun*, as you call it, and all his militia won't be able to protect our slayer. Or they could roll up on her while she's in Carlos's bed, with all her defenses down and no blade on her; something could slip through a window or a vent, and trust me, that girl wouldn't see it coming—she'd be distracted! Been there. Trust me."

"Damn, Marlene, I'm sorry . . . I didn't—"

"You didn't fucking think, Rider!" Marlene began pacing. Even Shabazz looked at her with trepidation. "I want the very best, and only the best, for that girl. I want her body cleansed of all toxic substances, like chips, and preservatives, and other crap—so her physical transition can happen as quickly as possible. I don't want her high, or drunk, or love-dazed—I want her to be a lean, mean, fighting machine so she can ward off whatever's coming for her! I want her consciousness raised, her spirit focused—it's a trinity transition, fellas, a mind, body, and spirit thing she's dealing with." Marlene was breathing hard, but as she paused, her eyes dared anyone in the room to speak.

"*That's why*, until she's ready, she needs to be with us. Got it? After that, she can go where she pleases, sleep with whomever she wants. She'll be able to protect herself. Until then, I will rip out the throat of any member of this team who sabotages my authority as her primary guardian again."

"We've *all* been practically living like monks for a reason," Shabazz finally said in a forceful tone. He glanced at Marlene and waited for her nod as she calmed down. "Marlene hasn't been tripping for no reason."

"Damn, Mar. I'm sorry," Rider said again. "I just didn't know."

"Me neither," J.L. said quietly. "Sorry for giving you the blues."

"Now you've been schooled, so no more team dissention. We clean up our act until Damali fully transitions. Right now, she's vulnerable to a master vamp attack. She's wide open, sensing everything in her environment . . . learning, cataloging, growing so fast internally it's wearing her out."

"You mean *we* brought on her outburst earlier?" J.L. asked in a near-whisper. "When we were all feeling rammy, and needed to get out . . . and she started ragging about everything?"

Shabazz held the team enthralled with a steady gaze. "Yeah, brother. And what that means is, if you feel something, Damali will inadvertently pick it up from you. You go out and indulge in *anything*, you bring the vibration back to a Neteru in sensory transition. Get drunk, she's slightly lit. Get pissed off, and start cursing and causing chaos, her fight instincts kick in. Get—"

Marlene held up her hand. "Oh, Shabazz . . . don't even say it."

Alejandro leaned his weight against his front door as he inserted the key in the lock. Giving the unmarked squad car the finger, he entered his beach house, and began taking off his suit jacket. It was all fucked up. Everything about the situation. Carlos was tripping, was about to start a war on three fronts—blaming the Asians, the Russians, and the Dominicans, possibly even the Jamaicans, without proof positive, and their ranks were too thin to bring it on. They couldn't bury their boys until the police were finished with the bodies, then it would be a closed casket deal for all of them. This was no way to live.

Pure disgust filled him as he passed through the foyer and stepped down, into the sunken living room. Spanish tiles echoed in complaint under his heavy footsteps. They had made their money, and had come up from the bottom. Now it was time to go totally legit and chill—but Carlos was always pressing for more power, more territory. Alejandro crossed the living room to his private bar and poured a drink, and then stood before the sliding glass doors that led to the deck. His gaze scanned the horizon. Beach was in front of him, a pool to the left, a Jacuzzi to the right, white on white was behind him, leather everything, a sound system to die for, and a fine woman upstairs in his bed. He sipped deeply from his glass, allowing the fumes of the fifty-year-old scotch to burn the back of his throat with bitter sweetness.

Life was bittersweet. He took off his tie and threw it on the glass coffee table behind him. Was a time when he couldn't have dreamed of owning a seventy-five-dollar tie, let alone all of this. And Carlos wanted to start a war? To what end? Their cousin and their best friends were already dead. Enough was enough. He was out.

Alejandro finished his drink, considered the stars, then pulled a small package out of his silk pants pocket. He took a hit of coke, allowing the sting of the drug to blast his nasal passages with a burn that became another bitterness on the back of his tongue. Good product. He made a sound and cleared his throat with it, setting the glass down by his tie as he left the room to head toward the bedroom. He hoped Sophia was awake, and wouldn't start no shit. Tonight he didn't need to hear a bunch of bull—just needed to get laid and go to sleep.

Thank God. She was sleeping quietly on her side. In the dark he could tell that she was naked under the sheets when he'd entered the room. He glimpsed her briefly and turned to take off his clothes. Alejandro went to the chair and kicked off his leather slip-ons, and began undoing his belt when he heard her stir.

"Glad you're home early," she whispered.

"Yeah, me too," he murmured, noting that the sound of her voice was unusually smooth. That's why he kept this one around—she knew how to read her man.

He walked to the side of the bed and sat down, slipping off his pants and placing his pager/cell-phone on the nightstand. She rubbed his back and he closed his eyes. God, her hands felt so good, and her breath was so warm against his cheek. Tension drained from him as she stroked away the stress in every muscle.

"Come to bed, baby," she whispered. "Whatever it is, you won't solve it tonight."

He covered her hand at his shoulder with his eyes still closed, feeling the softness of her skin under his palm. "I know. Cops are outside, and Carlos . . . well. A lot is going on right now, and you're making me forget all about it."

He could feel the bed shift as she moved against his back.

"Take off your jewelry, baby."

Her breaths were coming more like rasps, her tone wanton, sexy—yes, that's why he kept this one around.

"I never take off my cross," he murmured, allowing her kisses down his spine to send a shudder through him. Yeah, she could do that down the front, too, in a minute. His body was ready for her, just from the thought of it.

"I don't want it to break when I ride you." She laughed from a low place in her throat.

"You plan to rock my world hard enough to break my chain?" He chuckled.

"See for yourself—you be the judge," she whispered. "I know that piece is special to you, because it came from your brother when you joined his squad . . . but if you want to really see what I can do, take it off. It's your choice."

He smiled, sitting up just enough to reach behind his neck, find the clasp, and open the thick chain, dropping the silver jewelry on the nightstand without looking at it. "I don't do this for everybody, you know."

"I know. That's what makes it all so special."

He moved around her and laid on his back, smiling up at her pretty face as she straddled him. The moonlight coming through the window gave her an aura like that of an angel. Wet, hot woman surrounded him and made his eyes roll to the back of his skull. He shuddered as she moved against him in a low, grinding circle.

"It better be worth it," he murmured, admiring her naked breasts that jiggled ever so slightly each time she circled his groin.

"Oh, it will be, I promise you." She chuckled, throwing her head back.

"Yeah, work it, baby," he breathed, his eyes closing to slits as he glimpsed her riding him in the wall of mirrors by the bed—and froze. *No fucking reflection?*

A scream lodged in his throat as he watched her head tilt forward and her jawbone unhinge under its skin. Her fingers dug into his flesh, her French manicure becoming retractable claws surrounding his arms with an iron grip. His member was locked in a freezing, slimy cavern, and then acid began to burn away the skin of his groin. Pain so intense sent him into immediate shock; he shook and gulped air, eyes wide, and a silent scream strangled him as he watched massive incisors rip through her gums like they were giving hideous birth.

She smiled. An acid drool ran down a fang, burning his chest where the drop splattered it. Her pupils began to glow red, the shape of her eyes changing to slits . . . and a low growl emanated from deep within her chest.

"It's worth it," the thing on him hissed, slowly lowering its face to his. "Bring me your brother. I have my own debt to settle with Fallon Nuit, and you're perfect for the job. I need Carlos. I plan to ride him like this, too."

The last sound he heard was his own cry for mercy as his Adam's apple left his throat.

CHAPTER EIGHT

IN THE distance she heard the phone ringing. The sound of it carved a hole into her skull, and she flopped over on her belly and jammed a pillow on top of her head, trying to keep the sound out along with the sunlight.

Judging from the sun's position, it had to be past noon. Ravenous hunger drew her out of bed, as well as the fast footsteps coming down the hall. She could tell by the weight of their fall and the stride that it had to be Marlene. Damali's stomach growled. She needed something salty. High carbs. Chips. Health food was out this morning.

She got up, holding her head with her hands as she found her secret stash of contraband. The sound of the bag ripping open sent another shard of pain through her temples. This had to be the absolute worst hangover she'd ever experienced in her life. Not even after a forty of Old E, when she was a teenager and had tried her hand at drinking, did she wake up like this! Damn.

The door opened and Damali cringed as she shoved a handful of chips into her mouth. Her own crunching made pinpoints of light form behind her tightly shut lids. Marlene's inhale to speak became another blade through her brain. Damali held up her hand, tears beginning to form from the agony.

"In the equipment room. Now. Carlos is on the business line."

For a moment her stomach did a flip-flop and she could feel her pulse quicken. All she could do was open her eyes and stare at Marlene for a second, and then follow her.

With her hand deep in the open bag of chips, Damali paced behind Marlene, munching and squinting, and ignored the assembled team's stare. She gulped down the salty flavor, which was staving off the nausea, wiped her greasy hand on her yellow robe, leaving an orange trail, and accepted the telephone while her crew continued to stare at her.

"They did Alejandro," the deep male voice on the line murmured. "I just wanted to tell you—before it hit the papers. But then, it probably already has."

"Oh, my God," Damali whispered, not caring that members of her team were still staring at her and listening to every word she said. She set down the bag of chips slowly and walked in a circle, clutching the receiver. "How?"

"In his own home." Carlos's voice quavered and then became steady upon a deep inhale. "My mother has taken to her bed. . . . We have to close the casket. My grandmother . . . there are no words."

She heard him breathe in deeply, and she covered her mouth with her hand.

"I can't even explain what they did to my brother. Blood was everywhere. His throat gone. He'd been disemboweled. His forearms, shoulders, chest ripped to shreds like he tried to fight them off him. Even his . . . they used acid to burn away what made my brother a man—left a bloody, black hole. *Madre de Dios.* . . ."

"Whaaaat?!" Damali closed her eyes, images flashing through her head so fast that she weaved where she stood, Shabazz catching her under her elbow. She shrugged off his hold, her grip tightening on the telephone. She'd seen it last night. The one that got away on the beach. "Where are you?"

"Just left the morgue."

"I'll be there."

"No, Damali," Marlene warned quietly. "No."

"Tell me where you're at, Carlos. I'll be there," Damali restated, ignoring Marlene.

"I gotta go," Carlos murmured. "It's on, and where I'm going ain't no place for you to be. I just wanted to tell you good-bye—and to ask you to make sure my mother and grandmother get everything I own . . . my lawyer has been advised to break you off something, too, baby . . . but you never know how these things work out. Can't trust a soul—but maybe only just you."

"Carlos, wait!" The phone went dead in her ear. Damali glanced around at her crew's expressions.

She started to run toward her room to change, but four pairs of hands grabbed at her, and she could feel Big Mike's arms anchor her waist.

"Slow your roll, li'l sis," Big Mike drawled, his tone soothing. "This could be a setup, and we all need to keep a cool head to protect brotherman."

It was his mention of protection for one outside of the group that made her cease struggling. Each of them slowly removed their hold on her, and Shabazz pushed her down to sit on a stool.

"Make her some green tea, Mar," Shabazz said, keeping his gaze on Damali.

"I am not going to sit here wasting precious daylight drinking tea!" Frustration beyond her comprehension gripped her as her gaze tore around the room.

"You woke up feeling like you had the worst hangover of your life, didn't you?" Shabazz kept his gaze steady on her and his voice mellow.

"Yeah," Damali finally admitted, bringing her hands to her temples as Shabazz backed away. "Feel like I just got hit by a Mack truck."

"Aftermath. You're coming down. Your metabolism is shifting back to normal levels after a sudden hunt surge. All the neurotoxins in your body are flushing, and your system is regulating. Sugar, salt, fatty carbs are just quick fuel—and will make you hit bottom harder later. Your body needs a slow burn to replace what just got stripped from it last night. Won't always hit you like this."

"Okay, okay, whatever." Damali wiped her hand against her robe again, glanced at the chips, but heeded Shabazz's warning. If this was anything like the next-morning jitters, then she *knew* she'd never do drugs.

"This is the crash and burn part, baby," Rider said too loudly.

Damali squinted at the sound of his voice and reached for the chips despite herself.

"Ahhh . . . trying to bite the snake that bit 'cha. Always works for me."

"Shut. Up. Rider." Damali let her breath out hard and tried to focus on Shabazz, then threw the bag across the room when he shook his head. "What is going on?"

"First hunt," Shabazz replied as Marlene slid a cup of green tea beside her on the weapons bench.

"Bullshit. I mean . . . aw, y'all know what I mean. Sorry, Mar. I've been on how many *hunts*, though, as you call it? We've been kicking vampire butt for five years, and I've never felt like this in the morning . . . even the body blows hurt worse than before."

The group stared at her.

"Better have that birds-and-bees talk with girlfriend, Mar." J.L. stood. "I'm going to see how Jose is feeling."

"Jose's back?" Damali tried to stand but thought better of it, and reached for her tea instead. She sipped it slowly and grudgingly. It then dawned upon her that Big Mike was in the room. "He's okay, right?" Her voice caught and held the rest of her question.

"That's the only reason I'm here," Big Mike said in a mercifully quiet voice. "They said to monitor him, keep plenty of fluids in him, and if his condition dips again, bring him back. He's on oral antibiotics, so he could come home."

Damali nodded and relaxed, bringing the tea to her lips.

"What did Carlos say?"

Damali tried to focus her attention on the original subject. It was like her synapses weren't firing on all cylinders. It was hard to stay focused on any topic at one time, plus there were too many issues that required her brain to assimilate. Vibes and tension were zinging around the group, but she couldn't put her finger on why.

"They did his brother—horribly," she finally whispered. "Carlos said good-bye, like he was going on a suicide mission. We've gotta go get him before he either kicks off a war by blowing away the wrong people, or goes out alone and gets himself vamped. I just can't figure it out. Why is vampire activity beginning to concentrate around our people, our biggest competitor, Blood Music, and Carlos's operations? It doesn't make sense. I didn't really start to notice it until they went after his people, too. I thought they were just going after artists. What's the link? None of us even speak."

"Big Mike, go see if you can help J.L. bring Jose in here. We all need to talk," Marlene said.

Mike nodded and left the room. Marlene cleared a space on the long table, and rolled out a map in the center of it. When Jose walked in slowly, Damali stood and went over to him to hug him, holding his hand to bring him back to where she'd been sitting, giving him the stool. He closed his eyes and leaned his head against her waist as she smoothed his hair back from his forehead.

"I'm sorry," he murmured.

"Don't talk crazy," Damali said softly, kissing the top of his head. "Woulda went to Hell and back to get you back."

"Might have to one day," he chuckled sadly, squeezing her hand.

The group passed nervous glances between each other, studying Jose's frail condition. He looked like he'd dropped twenty pounds in twenty-four hours and his eyes were beginning to sink into the dark circles around their sockets. Damali just stroked his hair.

"We all have a story . . . ," Marlene said in a faraway voice. "When this first started for me, it began in New Orleans. I was just a young woman. Then it spread to South Carolina, Gullah country. Then it was cool for almost twenty years after."

"That was just before I was born," Damali said in a quiet voice. She glanced around as everyone else nodded.

"Last night," Rider said, his voice now quiet, "you went after a female vampire."

The group went still again and each of them glanced at the others in the room, their line of vision terminating on Damali.

"Mar, I'm sorry about how I treated you," Damali whispered. She looked at Rider. "Sorry that I might have put you in harm's way, too."

Marlene shook her head and sent her gaze beyond the group toward the window. "Wasn't your fault. Only a first- or second-generation vampire can bring on blood lust like that in a Neteru. Instinctively, you'll go after the head of the hydra."

"Mar," Damali murmured, glancing around the group to try to better understand, "I've never done anything like that before." She looked at Marlene who held her with a concerned gaze, her expression unusually tender. "In all our battles, I've never flipped like that."

"You'll stabilize soon."

"Stabilize?"

Rider began to pace. "Isn't there anything you can do, or give her?"

"What's wrong with me, guys?"

Marlene glanced up at Rider, and then returned her focus to Damali. "What did . . ." Her voice trailed off, and Marlene sucked in a deep breath. "What did the female vampire say that made you follow it like you did?"

Damali closed her eyes and took her time, her breaths steadying her. Marlene hadn't answered her original question, though. "It said, 'You can't have him.' Then something inside me snapped. It said, 'You can never take my place.' Whatever that means."

"A queen second," Mike murmured. "Just as Marlene suspected."

"Oh, boy. Here we go," J.L. said on a hard exhale.

"Jesus H. Christ." Rider sat down heavily on a stool, shaking his head. "Already?"

"Yeah," Marlene agreed quietly. "We've got one in our territory and the vampire huntress picked up the scent . . . and it's defending her own territory. Damali won't stop until she gets it, or the contrary. The female vampire's aggression is a sure sign that we've got a master male vamp in this quadrant. It just confirmed my suspicions. Until last night, I was just playing a hunch."

"I don't understand." Damali slowly pulled away from Jose and wrapped her arms around herself, intently watching her team.

Shabazz looked at the map and traced it with his finger. "The energy a guardian team casts will draw weaker members of a vampire line—because the perpetual hunger is not only blood, but power. The blood of a guardian is like a drug hit, too. So, from time to time, we get sniffed out, is the only explanation. But as Neteru energy matures, it throws a scent to a pack that's stronger than anything a guardian team can throw off."

Shabazz looked at Damali, his gaze softening as he glanced away. "When we found you, you were still a little bird . . . you didn't leave that much of a trail, or a marker."

"Wasn't long before a couple of 'em came for you, then we turned the tables on the situation, and went on the offensive— per Marlene's wisdom," Big Mike murmured. "The idea was to flush out the nest and wipe out that line before you came of age and had to deal with all of this." He looked away, and his voice dropped so low that Damali had to strain to hear it. "Marlene will tell you about why we had to clear this nest, or at least back it up, before your time." His eyes met Marlene's. "Right, Mar? You'll tell her today."

"Tell me what?"

Jose nodded to the map, his trembling finger touching the edge of it. His gesture temporarily drew Damali's attention away from her question, and it stilled the group. They let him talk uninterrupted in a weak, scratchy tone.

"My grandfather's people, the Creeks, believed that night feeders divide territory and mark it like wolves. Shamans say if one outside their line is caught hunting in the wrong territory, the others will attack it. Told as legend, the old ones say the night feeders migrate and are nomadic—but travel within the same route that they've been following for centuries."

Jose wheezed and straightened himself, and then leaned on the workbench for support as Damali's hands fell away from her sides. She folded her arms in front of her and waited with the rest of them for him to continue.

"There's at least one known vampire line on every continent—but like all predators, we're not sure how or why, but something limits their growth. Most times, they snap the victims' necks first, and then immediately feed, while the blood is still warm, fresh kill. Usually that just leaves a corpse, and there's no problem. Their numbers remain stable that way."

Rider let out his breath hard and rubbed his palms over his face. "Yeah, but we've got mugs jumping up off morgue slabs now in record numbers—so they're building in ranks like I've never seen before—not that any of this is normal, mind you. But comparatively speaking, something big is brewing."

"Okay," Damali said, taking her time. "So, Marlene was originally attacked, and like all of us, had a run-in with one of them solo, but made it out alive. Then, we somehow got guided to each other to form a team, right? That part I get. You've all told me this before, remember. Tell me something new."

"Divine intervention, how we all got together," Jose whispered. "We were shown, were blessed with the gifts to keep us out of that vampire line, and that light force drew us together by what others might call strange coincidences—but, by now, we know there's no such thing as a coincidence."

"True dat," Big Mike whispered.

"Okay. I know that. So what would make them move on a coupla record companies and a club—and not just feed and leave, if they have this growth limiter? And, what's this queen thing?" Damali's question hung in the air, and the group shifted nervously.

"We don't know what supernatural laws limit their growth," Marlene said softly. She glanced at the team, her expression tense. "Or, what specifically has sent them into a feeding frenzy . . . at least not all of what may have."

"Oh, shit, Marlene," Rider yelled, frustrated. "Just tell the girl!"

"Tell me what? Somebody talk to me!" Damali was now pacing, and no longer looking at the map. Her gaze was singularly focused on Marlene.

"When you guys all went out, and while you were asleep, Damali, I investigated the last known site of the master vampire—who was supposedly vanquished years ago—in New Orleans. I looked up the property records, and that same house is within what was then Fallon Nuit's holdings. It's now listed under Blood Music, and after you peel back the layers of owners, Nuit's name pops up."

"Why didn't you tell me this before, Marlene?" She stared at her mentor, and Marlene's gaze slid away. *"You know the master vampire's name?"* Damali was incredulous. Her group kept something this important from her. Now she was more than stunned, she was pissed!

"If you knew where the lair was, you'd go after it, before you were ready. Our job is to protect you."

"What is this 'ready' thing? Please, Marlene, fill in the blanks."

Marlene's expression was tender as she took her time to speak. "You had to clean out your body with organic food in preparation for the ripening, and to keep your body a temple—*that's* why we wouldn't let anybody near you. Then, the stars aligned, and—"

"Wait!" Damali screamed, putting her hands in front of her, and then digging her fingers into her scalp. "Talk slower! Ripening?" She felt like she would retch as everyone's thoughts simultaneously entered her skull. Information beat itself into her brain. Terror seized her. She was changing like that? They were all clamoring inside her mind about her bones, teeth, skin . . . Her body would do what? Oh, my God . . . she was a freak. Not just a sister who could kick ass. All the training made sense, all the weird shit that had happened to them. Damali squeezed her eyes shut, and tears streamed from the corners of them. "Don't even say it," she shrieked, and then blocked the rest of their garbled thoughts. "But why didn't you tell me this would happen?! You're telling me that I can hear and smell things like a damned bloodhound, and it'll only get worse? You call that ripening? Shit!"

"She's hearing thought before it's uttered," J.L. murmured. "You all have to take it easy. She's just hit a wall. This was a lot of data and you're crashing her mental hard drive."

Damali was breathing in shuddered bursts. Tears were streaming down her face. She didn't wipe at them, just let her gaze land on each face.

"We couldn't afford to break your confidence," Marlene said gently. "You needed time to accept this part of it all. You might have gone into battle unsure, in every fight you might have second-guessed yourself, or worse, been overconfident—and that split-second of hesitation, or a misplaced blow, could have cost you your life."

"How do you know?" Damali could barely ask the question as another sob threatened to choke her when she swallowed it down.

"I'm the seer, remember?" Marlene went to Damali and gently held her hands.

Damali dropped Marlene's hands, not in anger, but in abject despair. "Then why am I here?"

"Have you watched the audiences when you do your concerts?" Marlene whispered. "You were gifted with oratorical skills that mesmerize. How many great people changed the course of history, just by words? Think about it, baby. Even your name—Damali—means *beautiful vision*. You must now learn to see the path better."

Damali's gaze tore around the room again. She didn't know where it should land first. Silence stood among them, but she could still hear parts of their thoughts. The reality was disorienting. She closed her eyes to get her bearings.

"Every thousand years a Neteru is born," Shabazz said. "A vampire huntress. This millennium, you're it. And at least seven of us, usually twelve, come with the package to bodyguard a Neteru while they wipe out a predator's line that's getting too thick. There must be one hundred and forty-four thousand of us on the planet at any given time to hold all manifestations of evil at bay—an army of twelve times twelve, representing the twelve original tribes. Guardians are made and lost every day."

Shabazz walked around the table, his arms open, sweeping past the group.

"Twelve. Each guarding the sections of the ancient sacred texts. In Tibet, in Rome at the Vatican, in Egypt, in Asia, in the U.S., in South America, in the motherland, in Hopi country, you name a region or continent, we are hidden, but there."

Damali opened her eyes and just stared at her team. This was definitely new information . . . just as she'd requested. But it wasn't what she'd expected to hear.

"The Holy City and the Church of the Nativity has even been under siege with all three of the major world religions at war with each other—watch the news," Jose murmured.

J.L. offered him a confirming nod. "The planet Earth is out of balance, it was time for a Neteru to show up. Don't you think the recent world events would cry out for the need to return the balance of peace? Think about it, D. Evil has a stranglehold on mankind, making us wipe each other out . . . culture-by-culture, race-by-race, tribe-by-tribe, and religion-by-religion. You think that's an accident?"

"Like we told you when we first found you—music, art, draws people together across these invisible, ridiculous lines. That's why it's sacred, baby. Remember what we told you? Connect the dots. The artists cross the lines; music is universal, like other forms of art. It touches the soul, can make people feel emotions past ideological rhetoric. Can blend, bond, fuse, and heal the rip in the human family. It's powerful. You were gifted with the voice. So, here we are," Marlene added and then gave Shabazz the floor.

Shabazz accepted his turn to speak again and released a slow breath with patience. "But what we didn't tell you was that guardians are secreted away to preserve the balance within *every* aspect of human interaction. We didn't just coincidentally roll up on you and then band together."

Shabazz paused, and then pressed on when Damali remained silent. "Sure, we told you we were guardians, and loosely described that you were a vampire huntress, a Neteru—a slayer—but never properly defined what that meant. It wasn't the time. First we had to protect you, gain your trust—which was hard for you to give us, coming from your life on the streets. We needed to earn your respect, and you needed to emotionally mature enough to listen to us without running away again to avoid the inevitable. Today, you're ready to hear us. Clarity is required."

Damali nodded, and Shabazz continued. "There are more of us out in the world than just this team, that's what we never explained. Some guardians are dispatched to work with the spirits to close tears and fissures in the veil between worlds. Some work with world leaders to bring wisdom, justice, compassion. Some work the streets. Some work the schools to develop young minds. Some to unearth demon nests . . . and some of us, from every culture represented, get selected to guard a Neteru. None of us wanted to freak you out with too much knowledge too soon. Until last night, we had been able to pass you off to the vamps as just another guardian . . . until you went into your first real blood lust. Now, your energy is strong enough for them to find you. So, I am a Neteru guardian, as are we all. I am honored."

A collective "*Ashé,* Amen," rippled through the group, as they yielded the floor to their team's most learned philosopher, Shabazz.

"Those that guard the sacred texts, and the Neteru guardians, have the most dangerous mission, but the highest honor of the sets of twelve—and the most difficult," Shabazz said, his tone unwavering. "Everything we taught you was to keep you safe, our Sankofa, until you could fly like an eagle on your own. Last night, you tested your wings. Now, it's on. You *have* to fly."

"*A hundred forty-four thousand* guardians in secret armies?" Her head was spinning. Damali found the sofa and sat slowly, needing to breathe.

"How many vampire colonies do you think are walking the planet, sis?" Rider shook his head and paced away from the group. "There's at least five or six that we know of. Now let's add in werewolves, demons, not to mention just your regular schmoes who do bad shit in the world. Okay? There's plenty enough to keep divisions of us busy down here, along with all the companies up in Heaven. We are at *war* with the dark side. It's a war, not just one battle in the night. That's why Mar flipped out on you. She had reason. You need to listen to the general, until you get your stars, kiddo."

Damali's line of vision searched the deadly serious faces around the table.

"We let you have time to be a kid," Jose murmured. "Because we love you."

"Yeah. Information like this sorta blows the groove, doesn't it?" Rider let out a weary sigh. "Hell, after the first attack, Marlene didn't even want us to explain it to you, because she wanted you to still have a little more time."

Shabazz nodded, and then pounded Rider and Big Mike's fists.

"The forces of light came to Marlene in a vision. That's why Marlene, a guide, found you. Seers are always the ones to locate a Neteru and form the circle of protective guardians around him or her—and that's why during religious purges, seers are the first to be put to the stake. Kill the visionaries—the seers—and a slayer can be lost in the mix. But the Divine always knows where you are. The planetary alignment signaled when you will come into all your powers—three inner planets signaled three months from the alignment." Shabazz used his hands to speak, drawing out the constellation for Damali as he tried to get her to understand.

"One outer planet signaled the lesson that must be learned in one month—your birth month. The last large planet, Jupiter—a massive planet signaled a massive event soon to come. But it's also the planet of good luck."

"Then, let the chips ride on the big Jupiter bastard, then," Rider said, letting his breath out hard. "Man!"

"Rider, your mouth," Marlene warned, shaking her head. "I know it's hard to change, but please. We are trying to school a Neteru."

"Sorry, Mar. Old habits die hard. Been cooped up for months; I have a slight verbal aggression issue." Rider chuckled as Marlene raised an eyebrow and Shabazz let his breath out slowly again.

Damali couldn't focus on Rider's sidebar commentary. Instead, she just shook her head as she stared at the team. Too much had come at her too fast. Yeah, she knew there were these things called vamps. Yeah, she knew there was above and below . . . a lot she'd learned, but that was more abstract before, and today it was applied science—the mathematics of it, the planets, the physics, secret armies. The logic. Whew . . .

"How do you guys *just know* all this stuff?"

"Unfortunately," Big Mike said with a weary sigh after a moment, "we had to research it—some the easy way, some the hard way. Each one of us went through our own personal trial by fire. We each survived an attack, and were then led to another person like us, who had also survived an attack. Baby girl, you aren't the only one who grew up feeling weird as a kid."

Mike glanced at the team and received nods of confirmation. "Heck, when I was younger, I thought I was crazy. I could hear things nobody else could hear. Scared the heebee-jeebies out of me, most times. So, I didn't tell nobody, never. It was my secret, until one day something rolled up on me and I had to deal with it."

"Word," Shabazz muttered. "I could be out in the hood playing B-ball, and brush up on somebody, and feel when they were gonna die. Or give an aunt a hug and know her time was limited. We've all been there, Damali. Everybody's had their own private wake-up call. We all have a long story, and we wanted you to have as much time being a kid as you could."

"Yeah," Big Mike agreed. "We didn't find you until we were readied, either. You had to be in a place in your head where you were ready to be found, had seen enough stuff on your own to accept protection—just like we all had to."

"Right," Jose agreed. "And we all had to be ready . . . it took us time, too, to learn to accept the cosmic laws of reciprocity. We would teach you and be taught by you. We will hunt and be hunted. We will guard you and be guarded by you. We will defend you and also sustain attacks from the vamps. Whatever we all do follows the natural and supernatural laws of energy exchange, Damali." Jose labored as he spoke, and his body slumped from the mere exertion of his statement.

"Here on Earth is the gray zone; it's both light and dark here," Marlene said as everyone nodded. "In this war, the good and the bad pull from the casualties of that war—the choice border, Earth. That's what we defend."

"Last night, your metabolism changed," Shabazz said in a matter-of-fact tone. "Second sight, olfactory and taste awareness, tactical sensing, increased audio capacity strength. When the seventh one hits . . ."

Damali kept Shabazz's gaze trapped with her own as his voice trailed off. So much had come to her at once that she could no longer get inside the group's heads. Part of her didn't want to. Before today, she'd never mentally probed them—but it had been a reflex when it happened this time. But now it was almost as though they'd thrown up a mental barrier to her thoughts, and when she looked at Marlene, all she saw was blackness. Why would Marlene block her that hard now? "What's the seventh?"

Thoughts, emotions, and an ache so deep that she couldn't move, battered her—her heart hurt. She just stared at the people around her, listening, trying to make sense of the insane. But they were forcing her to grow up overnight and fast-forwarding her awareness. The shift in tempo of the group was dizzying.

"Later," Shabazz said, shaking his head. "Marlene will go over that one-on-one. We need to look at the map." Shabazz went to the weapons table and gave Damali his back to consider. "Our people are going down, as are Blood Music's and Carlos's—forming a triangulation of activity between here, Carlos's hub, and New Orleans where the bullshit began."

"The vamps have eyes everywhere—normal joes who do their bidding . . . think this big worldwide concert has anything to do with it?" J.L. fired up one of his computers, and clicked on the attached projector, shining a map of the world on the wall whiteboard. Using a laser pen, he drew a line between the five selected continents, marking the cities where the concerts were to be held. "It looks like a giant pentagram. Anybody want to bet that the dark realm has claimed all the space between the points as the place where their major attack will be mounted?"

Marlene sent a glare so sharp and with such warning embedded in it toward J.L. that he looked away. If Damali didn't know better, she would have sworn Marlene wanted to cut the man's tongue out. Deep. Later, like Shabazz said. However, this time when the group fell silent, the quiet horror they shared was audible. No words were needed.

"We've been following the attacks happening to Blood in the papers, just like we've been following what's up at Carlos's joint. We can probably rule out that his performers are vampires, because to perform, they have to cast an image," Jose rasped, countering Marlene's glare as the group's peacemaker. Despite his weakened condition he appeared to be desperately trying to restore civility. "Their artists are doing music videos, interviews, traveling on planes during the day, whatever."

"Have you seen 'em lately?" Big Mike argued. "They look like walking death, too. Might drop and turn any minute. Never can tell, if this old master vamp, Fallon Nuit, runs Blood Music."

Shabazz shook his head. "Vampires have normal business operations to keep them rolling in capital. They don't feed on everything around them; that would be stupid—and the last thing vampires are is stupid. The only reason this world concert made us sit up and pay attention is because J.L. showed the team that the locations formed a pentagram. That part is not a coincidence. So what if their artists look like hell? Plenty of goths look like death warmed over, too."

"Drugs will do that to you," Rider said with a sigh. "We can't go staking what we think are negative artists on a hummer—even if they can't play a lick of music and their act reeks. I believe cops will call that Murder One." Rider made little quotes around the word "negative" as he glanced from Big Mike to Damali.

"No," Rider added in slow contemplation. "If they're casting an image, they aren't a part of the equation—except as possible master vamp helpers. Hell, we've had presidents that were surrounded, and they were even guarded by Secret Service from a master vamp's groupies. Every part of the world has had a leader that was either surrounded, or compromised, at one juncture or another. A coupla hot music artists doesn't stress me. Vamp traitors gotta make money, too. That's part of the deal—your soul for millions, power, and fame. Basic. Once the deal is made, a human is marked for that master vamp. However, vamps don't generally do their marked human helpers . . . so it might be safe to say that wherever bodies are dropping might just be happy hunting grounds."

"No, listen," Damali said, finding her voice as she approached the map. "Didn't you all say they stake out territory like wolves and fight if lines are crossed? Well, this concert is being simulcast—which means that they had to form an alliance across competing vampire borders. If what you're telling me is true, they're not supposed to do that, right?" She glanced around and then wiped the perspiration from her brow. "Either there's been a weird alliance, or one master vampire has taken out a lot of competition to be able to cross vamp borders worldwide."

"Li'l sis has got an excellent point," Rider conceded, finding a stool and sitting down again. "Damn. Maybe the bodies dropping had to do with some war we didn't see coming, some subsurface event that was hiding in plain sight—just like this slayer is. What if that's why the killings were all so brutal, and not the normal, smooth, two-hole bite? Ever think of that? A vampire version of a drive-by, maybe?"

"We're still not sure it's pure vamps, though. What about what Marlene said earlier about that revenge demon?" Damali shot her attention to Marlene, who remained silent.

"Let's not jump to conclusions, though. Like Carlos's shop and ours," Shabazz interjected, "the Blood Music team is probably just a feeding ground for a line—grazing lands." He shook his head as he walked away from the board, kicking a metal stool out of his path.

"Yeah, but Shabazz," Damali argued, "the concert is *worldwide*. That's a lot of territory. It would be different if only artists from L.A. or New York or whatever had dropped. Think about it. They've had to cross their lines. Kids have been dropping after *all* of these concerts in the last few months. Now they're linking those cities with one label doing a megashow? Uh-uh. Something ain't right."

"The Blood Music label draws kids from all walks of life— lost souls, and seducing good souls, too." Shabazz leaned over, his fingers tracing and retracing the steps. "Anybody without a strong spirit is susceptible to the negative vibrations and can be hypnotized by the violence in the music. It's real easy when the concertgoers are in altered states, partying under the influence of drugs . . . like in the clubs. Shit happens, nobody finds out why, or really cares. They're just teenagers going down from drugs and violence. Parents grieve. Whatever. Concerts get shut down for a little while, just like a club that has had an incident and then reopens in a matter of weeks. Authorities can't shut down a venue if some junkie kicks off there—and it wasn't the organizer's fault."

"It's a perfect cover for a vamp operation," Rider admitted. "Right out in the open, like I said."

"You're right, though," Shabazz finally conceded, turning toward Damali. "The artists that have died were all linked to the same company by contracts, but they haven't just been dropping in L.A. How our people, and an unrelated club network that Carlos runs, fits into that is the thing that's nagging me. We have to find the epicenter of activity. Something big is definitely going down."

Jose's frail voice held the group enthralled. "So, if it was just feeding grounds the vamps were after, Blood Music's regular concerts gives them plenty of opportunities to eat. Why are they *turning* our people, and possibly Carlos's people? If vampires want to eliminate a threat, they can easily just kill it, then feed off of it. But if they're increasing their ranks, then Damali has a point. Something's up."

Rider nodded with Marlene. "Yeah. Who knows? Maybe they only went after us because they thought we'd get in the way of their ability to feed when the *Raise the Dead* simulcast concerts go down. I have no idea why they went after Rivera's posse."

"But," Jose argued, "ours *and* Carlos's *are turning*."

"If they're turning, and building in numbers, then they could be getting ready for a vamp war. I think this goes way beyond feeding grounds."

"Was I the only one left out of the loop on this Nuit character?" Damali suddenly asked, not needing her team to answer her. She already saw what she needed to know in their eyes.

Damali's skull felt like it was splitting. Her focus went to Marlene, who had to be the one to give the hush order. "Why didn't you just be straight up and tell me who owned Blood, especially if you had a run-in with this Fallon Nuit years ago? Why'd you give me some bull about some millionaire in Beverly Hills?"

The group looked at Damali and then Marlene.

"I needed to be sure myself, first. Blood Music *is* listed under some high roller in Beverly Hills, who's probably just a vamp helper. Fits the profile. But, when their artists started dropping, I started researching and digging. I found out that Blood was under a dummy holding company in New Orleans. Once I dug through the layers of publicly traded holding companies, and waded through the boards of directors, and dredged deep enough, the same company kept popping up," Marlene said quietly.

"That still does not explain why you didn't tell us once you found out."

Again the two women's eyes met.

"Simple. I didn't want you to go to New Orleans."

"Why, because you don't think I'm ready to clean out a lair?"

"Partly."

"Then what's the other part, Marlene? What's the damned address in New Orleans?!"

Marlene's eyebrow arched in a challenge, but she kept her voice even. "When you're strong enough to get through my psychic block, then you'll know, because then you'll be ready. If you can't read it on your own, then, baby girl, your stubborn behind ain't ready to deal with what's in New Orleans. Perhaps none of us are."

Tension thickened the silence that surrounded the group. Finally, Jose tried to stand, but couldn't. It made everyone start, as though they wanted to catch him before he fell, but they allowed him his dignity by keeping their reactions in check.

"You know, Blood Music has this whole *Stars D'Nuit* PR thing going—the stars of the night. Their whole goth motif—even the recent murders around their bands—have been drawing kids in like flies to the mystery and danger of it all. Marlene, I know you had your untold reasons for holding back the info from the Neteru, but *we* should have known that part about a master vampire's presence. You and Shabazz should have told the rest of us sooner. It might have saved Dee Dee."

Jose's angry whisper made Marlene and Shabazz look away. No one wanted to think about Dee Dee and the pain of that loss, but it was impossible not to. Damali went to him and touched his arm, and then her unanswered touch fell away. She understood where Jose was now. The vampires had driven their own kind of stake right through Jose's heart and had impaled him with a level of anguish that maybe a lifetime wouldn't erase. The only thing she could think of to help him cope with his grief was to not allow Dee Dee's death to have been a sacrifice made in vain. She would take up her argument with Marlene later, and get answers then.

"So, his artists are possibly vampire helpers covering for vamps? Or just unaware pawns, right? Maybe a few of them were even turned, who knows? At least three incidents got reported about Blood Music concert victims not being in the morgue the next day, so we can assume they're undead." Damali walked and talked, rounding the table and staring at the map.

When her group only nodded, Damali kept brainstorming out loud. "Okay, so we have a master vampire in our midst. But then, that only explains the teenagers murdered after the shows—which has become this dare to attend the concerts, the stupid rites of passage that is PR hype. Most of those kids died and didn't turn, and weren't left in a state to turn—like our people and Carlos's people were. And it still doesn't explain this international thing, which wouldn't be possible if only vamps were running it—because of territorial lines . . . unless something major was going on in the vamp world that would make them galvanize across borders."

"Yes. Something like that." Marlene stared at her, then glanced at the guardians.

"There's a significant piece missing," Damali said in a low voice. "They could have fed from the edges of Carlos's team, or ours—but they went for his inner core. Doesn't make sense."

"Brotherman, Carlos, rose in the ranks awful fast, D," Big Mike replied. "How many dealers you know get to his level by twenty-three without being shot, or locked up? Feeding from his edges might have been the original plan, but he also could have reneged on a part of the deal . . . like the mob, vamps have ways of making their helpers pay with severe interest—if something goes wrong."

"Fine, Mike, but then there would be bodies that wouldn't be in jeopardy of turning."

Rider nodded. "Point well taken."

"That's why we don't want you over there, especially not alone," Marlene said, her voice firm. "We just don't know completely what's up—and not having the full story is a dangerous position for any of us to be in. I'm opposed to the idea of even doing the gig at his club, and the only reason I agreed to go along with it, is because we'd *all* be there as a fighting unit."

"I say we go to New Orleans, then, and get this done." Damali stood and stared at the telephone console. She sensed that Marlene was about to say something more, but Marlene had cast a glance that quieted the group.

"The choice is hers, Mar. Back off," Shabazz warned.

"She's not ready," Marlene said quietly. "Neither is the team.

We need to curb our language—the cursing has to cease. I've said it a million times, if ever. All thoughts have to be *pure*. Our bodies need to be cleansed out and inviolate. We're in the last phases—and words, thoughts, and actions all have power. She's a lightning rod, now."

"You have one choice, Marlene. Give me the address, or I'll get on the Internet, or go to New Orleans alone and find it. Either way, whatever you're supposedly protecting me from is gonna come out in the wash. So, if you want to help, try finding out if we're dealing with vamps or demons or both! Research that." Damali stared at Marlene hard and then glanced at the telephone again.

When the phone rang, everyone looked at Damali. She crossed the room, and calmed herself enough to sound nonchalant before she answered it. "Hey, Dan. What's up?"

CHAPTER NINE

"HEY, DAMALI," Dan said in a cheerful tone. "Check it out. I know you guys don't need my services anymore, but I was wondering if you could hook me up with a reference—if you think my work was all right . . . I mean, Marlene said it was only a financial thing, but—"

"No, no, Dan. It *was* a financial thing," she lied, glancing at the team. "Sure. We can give you a reference. Let me put you on speaker—I'm working and need my hands. Talk to me, dude. What's up?" She placed the phone on speaker and gave the team a look to remain silent.

"Great. But, uh, look, no offense, and I know they're your biggest competitor and all, that's really why I'm calling, but, uh, Blood wants me to do a little work for them, and I was wondering if that was cool—especially if I promise not to—"

"Dan. Blood Music asked you to work for them?" Damali forced her voice to remain calm, even though pure alarm was cascading through her system. The members of her team froze. She could feel the stillness that came over them, could feel their worried gazes pressing down on her. She ignored them. She had to, in order to coax Dan into divulging more.

"It was the weirdest stroke of luck. I floated out my resume and work samples, and started making calls, and then this guy from Blood called me right back and said they needed me. So, I was like, yeah, sure, but let me talk to the folks I used to work for first—because we all left on cool terms. He was like, 'Cool. Make it happen.' So, really, D, I'm just trying to earn a living, not hurt you."

"Daniel, listen to me," Damali said, quietly but firmly. "Do not go over there, and not just because of us. Those guys are . . ." Her gaze searched the group for the right word. "Barracudas."

Dan laughed, his upbeat voice pouring through the speaker of the phone. "Aw, D, I know you've always got my back, but the whole industry is infested with sharks. I can handle myself. This is a once in a lifetime opportunity."

As he continued to laugh, Damali shut her eyes. Her mouth spoke before her eyes or brain had a chance to get a sanctioning nod from the group. "Dan, if it's the money, we'll figure out a way to pay you—just don't go over there by yourself, especially at night."

A quiet gasp came from Marlene, who paced away from the table. Big Mike shook his head no and folded his arms over his huge chest. J.L. pulled back from his computers and sighed. Jose's shoulders slumped as Rider slapped his own forehead and Shabazz slowly shook his head no. She knew the team was sending a silent warning to keep Dan clueless, and to also keep him as far away from their operation as possible. But the poor guy was about to walk into a possible vampire pit, and she wasn't about to let an innocent go out like that.

"See, I knew you were cool people from the moment I met you, D. That's why it was so hard to leave the team. All those guys at Light are cool. But don't worry; I'll be fine. In fact, I was kicking this idea around with the guy who wants to hire me. It could represent a real opportunity for you guys, too."

The team became very still and all eyes were on Damali.

"Talk to me, Dan," she murmured, putting her finger to her lips to remind them not to interrupt.

"Like, this feud is silly. I mean, it loses money for both sides. They haven't been able to find a female lead to challenge you, D, and for whatever reasons, they've snubbed one of the biggest, hottest club networks in entertainment out here in L.A.—Club Vengeance—but I told them you had an inside track there, and already had a gig lined up in a coupla weeks."

"What did you propose to them, Dan?" Damali could feel her blood pulsing so quickly that her ears were beginning to ring.

"Check it. They have this worldwide concert, right?"

"Yeah." She looked at the team hard as they became restless, the nervous anxiety almost making the air around them crackle.

"Well, what if you moved up your gig date, and one of the big Blood concert sites was broadcast from Club Vengeance—as one of the highlights? That would put you on the international map, heal the feud, give both sides crazy audience share, you'd hit places around the world, the club would be fat paid, Blood would have their needed female star . . . all artists' differences and BS aside, we could all go home fat, dumb, and happy. Then, later, if you guys want to go at it again, you could. Whaduya say?"

"Whose idea was it, Dan—yours, or this guy's?"

Dan laughed again. "Okay, okay, so Blood proposed it to me, and said my ability to get you to consider it had a lot to do with my condition of employment. You outted me. But I was just trying to—"

"The idea has merit," Damali said, holding up her hand as Shabazz almost lunged for the phone. "Tell them that we are seriously interested . . . but do me a favor."

"Wow, Damali, that is so cool of you. Just name it," Dan said fast, his excitement blaring through the speaker.

"I want you to put on your Star of David that you were bar mitzvahed with, go to the synagogue, and I want you to stay away from there at night—they've had a few police-related incidents."

"That's it? No problemo! But . . . uh . . . why the—"

"You know how spiritual our crew is over here, and I'm sure by now you know our way of making deals . . . some things, are uh—"

"You don't have to explain, Damali. I know you guys anoint everything and anything. Guess you wanna be sure I won't end up a turncoat. Hell, for this deal, Marlene and Big Mike can splash me with holy water any day."

"We might need to when he comes back," Mike whispered, ignoring Damali's stern glance.

"What was that?" Dan asked, still chuckling, and sounding overjoyed that he had the group's support.

"Nothing," Damali sighed. "Bye, Dan. You're good people. Stay that way. I'll get back in a day or two after I run this by the team."

She hung up the telephone and the group erupted at once.

"What, are you crazy?" Rider hollered, toppling his stool as he leapt from it.

"Too much of a risk!" Shabazz boomed, walking in a circle around her.

"I won't allow it," Marlene said.

"She's lost her mind," Jose said. "Gone completely loco."

"Go into the belly of the beast—are you insane?" J.L. pushed back in his chair and unfolded then refolded his arms over his chest.

"Are you all finished?" Damali sat down on a high stool and looked at the map.

A collective, angry "No!" returned to her.

"It gets us inside during the concert," she said in a controlled voice. "It allows us to possibly get close to figuring out what's going on."

"No," Marlene cut in. Her expression was so tense that Marlene's complexion had practically gone ashen. "Do you know the date of the concert?"

"It doesn't matter, Mar, we were already going to do a gig at Carlos's—"

"It does matter!" Marlene was breathing hard as she rushed to Damali and grabbed her arm. "The damned concert is on your birthday!"

"What does that—"

"If not now, when, Mar?" Shabazz stopped Damali's rebuttal with a deadly glare aimed at Marlene.

Marlene dropped her hold on Damali's arm and walked away. "Not now."

"Why not?!" Shabazz was on Marlene in a flash, and the two squared off. Everyone seemed to hold their breaths.

"Because *the choice* is hers! You know that is the law. The Neteru must choose, and must fight that *first* battle alone, so it resides *within her* to know how to have the ultimate gift of discernment. If she doesn't learn the lesson well, she'll be at risk for second-guessing her own judgment for the rest of her life! She makes that choice. Not me, not you. Got it? And *I'm* in charge of such highly volatile lessons—it's a woman thing, and you just wouldn't understand, brother."

Shabazz dropped Marlene's arm, and he grudgingly walked

away from her and went back to looking at the map.

"If the choice to find the lair is mine, then I can't think of a better birthday present—to end all of this," Damali said in a sarcastic tone designed to bait Marlene.

Shabazz cast a glare at Marlene that was so intense, Marlene looked away.

"She's a baby, and doesn't even know what she's dealing with." Shabazz began looking at weapons choices, and shoved a pile of stakes off of the table. "We need more than this. J.L., Jose, this shit is pitiful. Make her something she can go down swinging with—with some pride as a Warrior of Light. Fuck this!"

Marlene nodded but didn't speak. Damali peered at Shabazz, awed at the way Marlene hadn't flinched when he, *of all people,* lost his cool and used the big "F" word that Mar hated so much. Okaaaay.

"Look, you guys, I'm grown—and while I may be just coming into my own as a Neteru, so to speak, I want this done with, finished once and for all, for everybody's sake. I want to help Carlos. Don't ask me why, but he doesn't deserve to get eaten . . . and I don't know where he is right now. I want to keep Dan safe, but he—"

"—Might already be compromised as a new recruit for the vamps." Rider spat on the floor and shook his head.

Big Mike shook his head. "Rider, I know you gotta clear your sinuses, as a nose, but can you give the compound floor a rest?"

"No, Rider," Damali said with conviction, ignoring Big Mike's comment. "I don't think Dan's compromised, not yet. I didn't sense that from him. We can't keep anybody truly safe, though, unless we get to the root of it. And that's my point. I say the sooner we get to New Orleans, the better. If we clean out the lair, then the concert won't be a problem. If we miss in New Orleans and get back home safely, then the concert gives us another run at them. Plus, agreeing to do the concert could make them think we have no clue about a possible lair in New Orleans. Is everybody following me?"

When a series of disgruntled replies followed her questioning, Damali folded her arms. "The sooner we start flushing the nest, the better. If the choice is mine, then let's do this."

When still no one answered, she let her breath out hard. "I'm going to get dressed, and while it's still daylight, I'm going to try to head off Carlos. I promise to take Madame Isis with me, and I'll be back way before dusk—if I can't find him, I'll have to just live with that."

Again, none of the team challenged her when she left the room, and she made it down the hall with a thousand thoughts on her mind. If it was going to be bad, so be it. Bring it.

The mountains north of Beverly Hills were always his favorite place to think. It was where wealth and its owners secluded themselves and did their unseen little deeds. The temperature even dropped here, and darkness was a cloak. Trees stood like giant pillars. Crickets and other things of the night made their own music.

He'd gone everywhere, and threatened every council, and had probably brought a war upon himself. But his weapons remained unfired. Carlos looked into the blackness as he sat alone in the northern hills listening to the night. A double-barrel shotgun leaned on the floor and on the gear shaft beside him, and an AK-47 nestled in the passenger seat like his favorite sweetheart after a night out on the town. He held his custom-made, silver-plated magnum in one hand and the steering wheel of his black

Lexus sedan with the other. He would drop a body tonight or be damned.

The Asians had been traditionally gracious, as expected, and even offered to professionally assist him—of course his hundred-thousand-dollar bounty helped raise their pledge to help in his search. They understood the situation was a matter of honor; that was their way. Their territories didn't encroach—they moved heroin and women, he moved everything else. What had happened was bad for everyone's business. It was a cool truce; all wanted it kept that way—better for business. Small bills, one briefcase. Easy money for info to turn over a few bodies—the law of the jungle, done for lesser offenses, albeit smaller payouts. Let the bounty and the punishment fit the crime.

He'd told them all that, with each day that passed now that the offer was made, the bounty figure would decrease by ten grand. Expediency was, therefore, in everyone's best interest. The Russians had shrugged, and he'd almost taken one of them out. Their blasé demeanor had been disrespectful—then he'd reconsidered it, since that was their style . . . besides, a lower henchman was not worth jail time. He needed to be on the outside to exact his revenge. The Italians, Dominicans, Jamaicans, and the brothers, all had the same response—for a hundred Gs, they'd do the Pope. So, he waited—without a weapon fired. This would take time.

He thought of sending a message the old-fashioned way. Just flat blast a few establishments his competitors owned. Take out several lower levels and wait like bait for the fight to come to him. But he needed to get to the dons to tell them what was interrupting business at the lower levels, rather than have his message diluted by a level below them. That had been the message. He wanted a meeting. This situation warranted a breach in protocol. He had a right to come before them to state his case. Someone had done his brother and his inner circle. Someone would pay.

Carlos breathed out slowly and watched his breath turn to steam in the frigid night air within the car. Patience was not his virtue. It never had been. But shrewdness had argued with him as he sat calming himself in the quiet. Money—the root of all evil—always turned evidence and he knew how to grow a tree from it.

"Yes, Alejandro . . . I pledge to avenge your death." He closed his eyes and let the sound of his own voice echo back to him. They didn't just take his brother's life. They'd mutilated him.

Carlos thought over the options. A shootout would not only send the slime scattering and into hiding, it would also create new vendettas against him, clouding the issue, making the perpetrators harder to find. Word was already on the street that he was looking for those who'd committed the unpardonable sin of killing his family—and he'd bankrolled the hunt, very publicly, within the circles of those who needed to know. He just wanted to see the look in the man's eyes who had done this, and had ordered it. His bounty would have to draw out the offenders to his brother's honor. Then he would hunt them down, and give them a slow death.

He sat with the plan, frustrated, shivering from the cold and hatred, but blanketing himself with the satisfaction of the horrific tortures he'd visit upon the ones that would be finally given up. He'd unearth them, and make them know that there were things worse than death. His cell phone rang and he let his lips curl into a cold half smile. The digital display showed the code he had given to the hunters in order to collect their bounty.

"Speak to me," he murmured in the darkness.

"We have your man—a meeting is in order."

"You will be handsomely rewarded."

"We'll bring him to the designated place we discussed in the northern mountains—bring the money."

Carlos smiled again. God was hearing his prayer. Something had led him to sit here in the darkness where he often came to think and wait.

"You know the location. Keep him alive until I get there, or the bounty will be cut in half. I want to look into a dead man's eyes."

Driving deeper into a more secluded area of the mountains, Carlos turned his sedan off the winding, single-lane road and his wheels connected with orange clay, bumping the vehicle chassis as he drove further into the new section of woods. Following the rows of taillights that slipped beyond the tall pines and redwoods, he felt another transition as his wheels sank and moved against dark, moist earth.

Yes, this was a perfect place to finish a kill. He loved the woods, even more so than the beach, for it offered the cloistered environment of secrecy . . . it was where wolves hunted and the true force of nature could be felt.

His every nerve ending was on fire; anticipation made him lick his lips. He breathed in the forest, allowing the scent of pines, raw earth, and broken blades of grass to enter his nose— along with a hint of sulfur.

Carlos narrowed his gaze at the semicircle of black sedans. Pure rage made his hands tremble as he gripped the wheel. Sulfur. If they already did his kill, there would be a price. He glanced at his AK-47, and the thought of taking them all out in a spray of bullets made him breathe faster. If they did his kill . . .

All senses painfully heightened, he watched the configuration, studied the ritual. Five black Mercedes sedans had come to a stop first, dousing their lights. A long black stretch Mercedes limo made the sixth vehicle. Carlos eyed his shotgun, wishing he'd brought something with a heat-seeker mount. If this was a setup, his magnum and the automatic could get him back to the car. He was the last one in, so he could be the first one out—and the shotgun could take out a pursuing driver, blow an engine, ignite a gas line—maybe enough to blow and flip the first vehicle if it gave chase, blocking the others behind it. So he waited, to see what package they'd brought, then turned off his headlights.

Slowly, one by one, the doors of the sedans opened, and he watched through his black tinted windows, using only the quarter moon as light. An eerie mist seemed to exit the cars with the passengers. One bodyguard got out of each driver's seat, and each went to the backs of their cars to open a door for a higher-ranking boss. Cool. They had brought the upper levels. He stared at them intently, and began recognizing faces he knew. But he waited.

The Italians were represented, then the head of the Asian mob who he'd never met—he had always conferred with his underlings. But if the don had come, then perhaps he was in trouble. Carlos pushed his magnum into his waistband and watched, taking up the automatic in its place. A high-baller Dominican got out, and then a Russian, and a Jamaican. He knew these men. Their bulky guards stood beside them. Still he waited and stared at the headlights of the limo that were aimed at him, but he relaxed when they went out. All right.

It was odd, but even in the darkness he could see. The moon cast a blue ray into the clearing, and owls could be heard hunting, sending their mournful call out into the trees. The limo had a series of small flags, making it appear to be a diplomat's car. What the fuck—high-level government? Carlos kept his motor running. Suddenly a hundred Gs didn't seem to be enough money, and a setup felt like it was in the offing. He couldn't identify all the countries on the tiny flags. He squinted. Southwestern states and European countries? What was the one with a five-pointed star with an emblem in the center? The assembled team smiled in the darkness. His eyes had to be playing tricks on him as the strange moonlight seemed to made their teeth whiter, longer than normal.

He was about to put his gears in reverse when the limo door opened and two men were thrown from it. They hit the ground with a grunt so he knew they were still alive. Excellent. Their hands were bound behind their backs by nylon tie-strips. Carlos breathed out slowly, steadying his impulses. He continued to study the situation as a tall, light-skinned brother got out next without assistance, looked directly at his windshield, and then nodded and smiled.

"I have the beginning of your hunt, Rivera," the man he didn't know called out. "We are all invested in this, like you are. Bring your weapon, if you'd like—but also your money."

Carlos opened his car door, and carefully got out, packing two weapons, and reached for the silver metal briefcase in the backseat to bring with him. But he left his doors open, and his car running.

"Speak to me," Carlos called out, leveling his machine gun at the men on the ground, and then swinging it up toward the unknown man.

The others in the circle raised their hands, stepped forward to show they were unarmed, and made a half circle around the mystery man, who grabbed the two struggling forms on the ground—bringing them to their knees.

"Carlos, let me formally introduce myself. I am Fallon Nuit. I own Blood Music—and these men here," he said, nodding to the dark suits surrounding him, "are my associates, my brethren—and yours."

Carlos nodded and lowered his weapon, glancing around at the faces he knew.

"The problems with your organization are bad for everyone's business."

"Yes," the aged Russian said. "It makes people wary to go out at night. Makes it hard to make a killing, and drives down profit."

"Makes people ask unnecessary questions," the old Asian said.

"We cannot have that," the elderly don said with a sinister half smile. "Especially in the music and club industry. We need bodies at night."

"As do we all," the graying Dominican agreed, casting his gaze to the Jamaican who nodded. "We need them to keep coming like cattle."

"Ayree."

"So," Nuit said, as he walked around the two kneeling men, coming closer to Carlos, "we are all here to form an alliance. Your cause is our cause. A very simple matter of practicality and business. We heard your call to arms, and responded—the way family should when there's an outside threat."

Carlos nodded. He appraised the man who had spoken with a smooth, controlled voice. His vibe was one of pure confidence, arrogance. He liked his style. He couldn't place his race, though, as he looked into the blackest pair of eyes he'd ever seen. It was like staring at a very tall version of Prince . . . could be Latino, could be black, could be a mixture, skin as pretty as a woman's, no matter. The man named Nuit smiled as though reading his mind, and a flash of brilliant white escaped his lips and caught in the moonlight. Carlos had to shake off the eerie tremor that

staring at this brother produced. He had an almost feminine quality about him, but at the same time his vibe was cold business
and very male. Wealth and power oozed from his pores. The
man put one finger to his lips, just as Carlos was about to yell a
question, and smiled a half smile.

"I'm unarmed. Let's discuss this with finesse," Nuit crooned
as he slowly came nearer. "I'll come close enough to hear you,
but not close enough to make you draw your weapon, *si?*"

"A hundred Gs seems too little to split amongst so many,"
Carlos said across the clearing to Nuit, and gestured toward the
group. "But that's the bounty."

Carlos studied the headman's smooth, relaxed demeanor, and
the way the silk of his voice had more easy threads running
through it than his black, custom-tailored suit. The wealth that
surrounded the brother was in the billions, and yet it was evident
that this relatively young man was in charge. Intrigued, Carlos
lowered his weapon and stepped forward two paces—drawn to
his sheer power.

"Oh, no," Nuit said with a wave of his hand. "We can't claim
this bounty. We came to add to it, and offer you ten times that
to finish the job for us." The man nodded as one of the black-
suited guards retrieved a leather briefcase from the limo, walked
forward, and handed it to Nuit.

"I prefer skin—leather," Nuit said with a smile, his manicured
hand stroking the case. "Silver is so . . . passé. You keep it. I bet
what's inside my black bag is bigger than what's in yours anyway." Then Nuit laughed.

A million dollars? Nothing came for free. Carlos lowered his
briefcase to rest beside his leg and studied the group harder,
noting their every detail so that he could remember each one if
this shit went down wrong. Moonlight glinted off Nuit's gold
cuff links and huge ring that also held the same crest as the flag

he couldn't identify. Without a word, the men behind Nuit held up their hands showing their rings as if to answer the unasked question again. The others had the same ring. He hadn't noticed that before. The shit was beginning to spook him.

"What's the deal?"

Carlos felt suspicion riddle him as he looked at a henchman grab the men on the ground by their suit collars and thrust them forward before Nuit, then step back in line with the others who were watching the transaction.

"These two," Nuit said, putting a foot on one man's back, "are from the FBI. They used to be our helpers—then made some foolish decisions. We still have others inside, and the Minion is inviolate. Not to worry. These are ours—so we cannot accept your money in good faith. Fair exchange is no robbery."

"What's that got to do with me and my bounty?" Carlos asked the question across the small divide between them. "I have one fight—the FBI isn't on my agenda."

A million dollars or not, he was out. Carlos reached down to pick up his silver case, keeping his eyes on the group with his finger hovering on his gun's trigger. To accept their money meant taking up their battle, and he only had one—to avenge his brother and family's deaths. Going after feds was way over the top, and very bad for business. The police were already sniffing around his operations too much. And who the hell were *the Minion*? This wasn't his fight!

"But it is. These men took out your family."

Nuit's words stilled Carlos, and he set down the case slowly, stood and walked forward, ignoring the protest and pleas of the men on the ground. Either this rich, suave motherfucker could read minds, or he was tripping. When Nuit threw back his head and laughed, Carlos wanted to bitch-slap him.

"Bullshit. Federal agents might whack one of us, but they don't do ritualistic slayings."

"Oh, no?" Nuit challenged. "What's the best way to start a territorial war? What's the best way to make us all come out of hiding, create distrust amongst the group, and make us begin to turn on each other? Make it seem like one of us did this. Like I said, we have friends on the inside who delivered them, and their weapon."

Carlos remained very, very still. He could almost taste blood in his mouth as a new level of rage claimed him. Nuit stared at him, and oddly, as the two remained in a quiet standoff, Carlos could practically feel uninhibited power run through him.

It became difficult to breathe as he watched Nuit's face intently. The feeling was nearly indescribable, and Carlos soon became aware of something else he hadn't expected to feel. This brother was almost swaying him, making him step forward a pace. Something sensual was claiming him, and he shook off the strange reaction. The fact that something almost erotic was drawing him to a man gave him the creeps. Carlos held his ground and stopped moving forward.

"Feels good, doesn't it?" Nuit murmured, as he watched Carlos. His voice dropped an octave, became richer, more seductive. "Hatred is such a pure emotion—intoxicating. And when it finds release . . . there is no greater satisfaction."

Carlos nodded. "You should have seen what they did to my family. Have you any idea?" His own voice surprised him. It was gentle, sad, a confession of pain like he'd surrendered. What the fuck . . .

"Yes, I do. It was unspeakable," Nuit replied softly, the tone of his voice drawing Carlos closer to the center of the group where he stood.

"I swear to you, we didn't do it," one of the kneeling forms pleaded, tears streaming down his face.

"Make it fast," the other man sobbed. "Have mercy!"

Carlos's gaze went to the begging men, and he took in the dark brown face of the one and looked at the ashen white complexion of the other. Their cries had broken his attention away from Nuit. He now felt semi-dazed, but totally enraged.

"Did you have mercy on Alejandro? And you dare to beg me for mercy?" Carlos spat on the ground. "You will die so slow and so horrible a death that your mothers, too, will not be able to bury you in honor!"

Nuit tsked, making a little clucking noise with his mouth. "Don't spit out that taste of vengeance," he said as the others chuckled. "Let it coat your tongue with its bitter flavor and fill your heart. For they have broken our code and have visited great pain upon one of our rising stars."

The last part of Nuit's statement made Carlos shift his focus from the bound men to Nuit's face.

"One of *your* rising stars?"

"Be realistic," the Italian don said. "You don't think you rose so fast from a street-level dealer and gangbanger to all that you are now without a dark angel on your shoulder, do you?"

"Ever since you made the decision to choose this path, we have watched over you—because you were destined to be one of our own," the Russian added with a half smile.

"Hombre," the Dominican said, "your territory is already marked for you—just claim it."

"Power beyond your imagination," the Jamaican said. His expression was stone behind his dark sunglasses, but his tone was deep and seductive. "Feel it. It is electric."

" 'To be able to topple an empire that is heavily fortified,' " the Asian murmured, " 'requires a quiet battle from within. Then that empire will feast upon itself, and you can walk with the spoils of war'—from *The Art of War*." He put his hands together and bowed as he smiled.

Nuit let out a long breath through his nose, closed his eyes, and acknowledged each one of the Dons' comments in their native language. When they nodded, Nuit opened his eyes and smiled. Carlos had understood what had been said to the Dominican . . . *Give him a moment, this is all new*. That was cool, if that's what had been said to the others, but not knowing the other languages worried Carlos.

"Relax," Nuit crooned in a voice that made Carlos begin to feel safe.

Carlos considered what he was being told as he studied Nuit. "And, if I want to continue solo?"

Nuit sighed. "It's your choice. But you will no longer be under our protective aegis. One day the police will come, or you may meet an unfortunate end. That is the natural law. We have crafted very different laws that guard our own. You tried to protect your family. They perished at the hands of your enemies. It doesn't have to be this way . . . unless you prefer to turn the other cheek?"

Carlos listened, and slowly nodded. Turn the other cheek, fuck that.

"Take off that emblem of your old life and cast it away. We will give you a family crest to replace it."

Carlos fingered the cross at his neck with hesitation. With this squad, he'd be stronger. Invincible. He could feel it as he stared at Nuit.

Nuit smiled. "Yes . . . you will be invincible."

The voice had rippled through him like a lover's touch, stroking every dark desire he'd ever held in his heart. The man before him was showing great patience, his smile knowing; Carlos could hear him talking inside his head. Something was telling him it would be so very, very good. A life like he'd never even dreamed of was within his reach. Two FBI agents were groveling at his feet, and no one standing in the clearing even had a flicker of worry on their faces. All he had to do was say yes. All he had to do was cast off an old gang cross, and take their ring. He'd never have to worry about dying again. Carlos couldn't even blink as he stared into the depths of Nuit's pitch black eyes.

A chance at revenge, protection from a powerful group, a million dollars . . . Juan's cross in his pocket weighed heavily. His boys and his brother will not have died in vain. Steadying his weapon in one hand, Carlos found the other hand slowly reaching up behind his neck, opening the clasp with his nail, and holding his cross out to the side of him by the chain. Then he flung it—casting away all of his mother and grandmother's silly prayers that had not saved any of those dear to him, not even his sister. There was only one law—the law of the jungle, which required consummate power.

"Very wise choice," Nuit said on a heavy breath. He closed his eyes briefly and laughed from deep within his throat. "The weak ones don't understand that a man must do what a man must do. But you have always known the true laws. Welcome."

"We didn't do your people, I swear to you, Rivera," one of the crying men wailed. "We wanted in; we were supposed to get made, too!"

Nuit's fine leather shoe connected with the man's cheek, splitting it. Blood oozed from the gash and Carlos noted that it seemed to make the group lick its lips—then he heard a growl coming from the limo. His gaze tore to the vehicle and back to Nuit.

"What the fuck?" Carlos whispered.

"The perfect weapon—and she's quite beautiful," Nuit said with an easy grin, studying his manicure. "They used her on your brother, and the others in your family. It was a nice cover—made your Alejandro's death appear to be the result of exotic animal betting . . . where your brother didn't last long in the ring. They used it on a few of my artists, your people, a few agents that wouldn't comply, and another record label that has been marked by our family. Created chaos. Fear. And this weapon is so blatantly horrific that no one would associate it with an inside job from human authorities—no bullets, no knife, very creative."

Fury took Carlos's reason as he thought of his brother's body, Juan's, and the others. "Then these two will die the same way!"

"Is that your choice?" Nuit smiled.

"Yes."

"Hand the man the briefcase. Put it beside him so he can get a sense of what a million dollars in small bills feels like—sitting beside his own paltry offering. And so he can have something to add to his choice to watch these men die."

Carlos waited as a dispatched guard flipped open the case and walked toward him showing stacks of bills. The breeze made the ends of the dollars ruffle—the smell of new money permeated his nose. Nothing but the Benjamins. Damn. He nodded and the guard stopped, closed the case, and slid it on the ground. Carlos stopped it with his foot. If this family had already given him a quick rise to power, and only wanted him to take out the rest of the traitors, what the hell? Resources were always appreciated.

"I assume that you accept this offering of your own free will, then?"

Carlos nodded to Nuit. "Let's do this."

"Come, Raven," Nuit called toward the sedan.

"Shit!" Carlos backed up two huge paces and clutched his gun preparing to fire as a large black panther jumped down from the limo, snarled at him, and loped toward the men on the ground who were now screaming.

"She won't bite you—if you don't make any sudden moves while she feeds," Nuit assured him while laughing. "She's just hungry. Poor thing. She's practically starved."

Even with all of his rage, the sight of the animal approaching the men gave Carlos pause. Adrenaline made him watch the panther, an eerie intrigue keeping his gaze upon it, but another part of him deep down in his soul had to fight not to cringe.

The animal sniffed the first man, and Carlos stared as the pleading man lost his bowels. His eyes were shut tight, tears streaming down his face as the panther licked the cowering soul's neck and cheek and hair. Then it happened too fast.

The man emitted a whimper, and just as suddenly, his throat was gone. The other prisoner tried to scramble away on his knees—but Nuit's henchmen held him. Carlos stared in horror at the ragged, gaping, bloody hole. Terrible sounds of ripping flesh made Carlos take in air in short sips. The pungent stench of fresh blood surrounded him, making him want to retch as the beast put one paw in the center of the dead man's chest, lowered its head, and began to gorge.

Then it looked up at Carlos, its eyes narrowed to gleaming slits, entrails momentarily hanging from its mouth as the big cat gulped the bloody tissue. Licking the open, empty chest cavity, it lapped up thick wetness, and then sat back on its haunches. In a very calm fashion, it licked its paws clean, began to purr, and stood again, circling Nuit's legs like a giant house pet.

Nuit's hands rubbed the beast's head as it showed massive fangs, closed its eyes with an expression that Carlos could only liken to ecstasy, and nuzzled Nuit's groin. The sight of his pending fate made the remaining man vomit. Nuit chuckled.

"Soon this poor, abused creature won't have a master. She only did what she was told, no reason to kill her. She's useful to our purposes." Nuit stroked the panther tenderly. "She's gorgeous, beyond comprehension—and is only doing what is natural . . . and she does it so well."

When the animal turned its attention to the second trembling man on the ground, Nuit yelled, "No! He's for our guest."

Stunned, Carlos could only stare as the well-trained creature backed away to simply stand at Nuit's side, giving its master a grudging glare with its growl.

"This is power, my friend," Nuit murmured in a deep, sexy tone. The brother had an expression on his face like he'd just ejaculated. "Are you with us?"

Carlos nodded. This was the most powerful shit he'd ever seen in his life. To take another man's weapon and turn him on it like that. Images of his brother, however, made him look away from the carnage to the man who was still alive. Damn, just watching the fear in the one who was still living, who had pissed and shitted himself, and vomited . . . the smell of fear made Carlos spit again. The grisly sight of the remains had given him enough of a taste of revenge. This was some twisted bullshit.

"Just do the other one, the old-fashioned way," Carlos said, breathing hard, bile creeping up his throat with an acidic burn. "Two shots in the back of the head. Clean. The panther is over the top, *hombre*. Even for me."

"Like I said, he's new," Nuit told the others who were intently watching the still-living man on the ground. "Soon he'll have the thirst. Give him a few days."

The others nodded.

"You want this man killed clean, then?" Nuit's smile broadened.

Again, Carlos only nodded.

"You don't want to do it? After all, they murdered your brother and your cousin and your friends."

"Just do it. Or—"

Before Carlos could lift his gun or finish his statement, Nuit had reached into the man's back with his bare hand. An awful, bloodcurdling scream came from the victim, and the sound of bones and ligaments tearing echoed past the trees as Nuit's hand came away from the body dangling an entire spinal column. Carlos was paralyzed by the gruesome sight, his voice lodged in his throat as his eyes quickly shifted from the twitching body on the ground to the dripping cord of bones in Nuit's fist. A deep gully had been carved in the back of the jerking dead man, his glassy-eyed stare fixed upon Carlos's shoes.

Carlos could not move as he watched Nuit break sections of the spinal column off and toss them to the headmen who were now panting as they grabbed the dripping bones. Nuit glared at the big cat again as she tried to approach the fresh kill, and the panther backed away with a sullen growl. The henchmen were sucking the bones, licking between their fingers. They now gathered around the body, knelt at the open gully in it, and lowered their heads. Only slurping sounds could be heard. Carlos turned away, and dry heaved.

Listening to it without seeing it was worse. "What the fuck was that shit?! Oh, goddamned . . ." Carlos's voice failed him as he turned around again, unable to keep his eyes from watching the grisly sight. Transfixed, all he could do was hold his gun. No, fuck it. This was too ill. He was out. Panic claimed him. He'd never seen no bullshit like this in his fucking life!

"Calm yourself," Nuit crooned in a reassuring voice. His eyes were steady as they held Carlos, his voice alluring.

For a moment, Carlos couldn't move. To get out of there,

he'd have to mow down the big cat, then what? These moth-
erfuckers might eat him!

"No one will lay a finger on you, my friend, I assure you,"
Nuit murmured, his eyes closing to half slits. "We have much
bigger plans for you than that. Plans that involve an increase in
territory, much more money than you could ever spend in one
lifetime." Nuit chuckled. His voice now held a seductive reso-
nance, like the way a man might speak to a difficult woman to
talk her drawers off. "Think of the money that is out here in
the woods. These men might have a perversion, but they are
filthy rich and very protected . . . not even the feds can touch
them. You want that, and you know it . . . to travel the world
with a seal of protection . . . to operate with impunity, laughing
at the authorities." Nuit stepped closer to him and leaned his
head back with an expression of ecstasy. "Tell me you don't want
that," he whispered. "Tell me . . . from way down in your soul."

Perspiration soaked Carlos's nylon jacket and made it stick to
his skin. Beads of sweat on his brow became a quick trickle
down the sides of his face. His hand trembled from gripping his
gun so tightly and his fingers twitched as they remained glued
to the trigger.

Nuit lifted his head, opened his eyes, and allowed his gaze to
rove over Carlos, sending a ripple of carnal pleasure through
him. "You can't even find the words to tell me . . . because it's
not in you. You want what I've described, and you covet what
I have, *n'est pas?*"

"But, goddamned . . ." Carlos's sentence derailed as the words
lodged in his throat.

"It is damned, and it is power." Nuit inhaled deeply.

As each of the bosses stood and wiped their mouths, Carlos
stared at Nuit, paralyzed by the grotesque, transfixed by the se-

ductive, while this madman licked blood from his own hand, and sighed.

"You ripped a man's back out . . . then—"

"Martial arts." Nuit smiled. "Did you know that many old cultures ate of the remains of their enemies after a battle? To the victor go the spoils. It is an old custom, designed to give you the power that the other side once had over you. Just a small ritual—you don't have to participate, unless you are so moved. We accept diversity, as you can see." Nuit chuckled. "And, we can teach you how to protect yourself from a gun, or anything else more dangerous . . . if you want to go to the next level— and if you want to really get to the bottom . . . or should I say, the top of who did your family."

Skeptical, Carlos didn't move, but also didn't nod. "I'm not doing the blood shit."

"But you are intrigued? Take your time. Think about it. We have all night."

He didn't answer Nuit. Two men that had done his family had indeed died horrible deaths. All these years he had been protected by these men and given safe passage. He had a million dollars sitting beside him, plus his own hundred Gs still intact. They were going to show him how to expand, gain more power, and be untouchable by the law. He'd never have to watch people close to him die at the hands of violence. He'd never have to worry about having children—his would be safe from what he and his brother and sister endured. He could protect *his people* and all that he'd built for them to enjoy. For the first time in his life, the madness would end and he'd be in a safe camp—a squad with unlimited power.

Nuit studied him with a sly smile. Carlos mulled over the options. He had everything to gain and nothing to lose.

Hmmm . . . Freaky rituals of revenge notwithstanding, there was some merit to the consideration.

"If I say yes, that I'll go after the rest of them—what else do you want from me? I want it all laid out, no after-the-fact negotiations."

"A true businessman," Nuit murmured, his voice cool as he continued licking the last of the blood from his hand. "I respect that." Nuit cast his gaze in the direction of the panther. "She's an excellent way to ensure that our way of life is preserved. She sends a powerful message to those that get in our way . . . tends to *turn* them to see things from our perspective." Nuit chuckled low and sinister. "So effective."

"You want me to keep *that* in my house?" Carlos laughed nervously and shook his head no.

Nuit chuckled from a place deep within his chest. "No. She's a lot to handle and hates the sun. We'll house her. I just want you to train her and control her."

"I don't know jack about training a beast like that." Again Carlos shook his head, and he laughed.

"We'll teach you how—just look how easily she came to me."

"So, when I do a hit, I'm supposed to make that thing—"

"Details, details," Nuit sighed, putting up his hand. "The creature is yours, but I'll keep her for now. In fact," he said smoothly, "I'll trade my pussy for the one you have under your control." He smiled. "Deal?"

Carlos shook his head and picked up the leather briefcase and stashed it under his arm, gripping the handle of his silver case along with it, while still holding his gun in his other hand. He'd heard about men like this—so rich that they'd lost their fucking minds and had gone freaky. "Name any woman of mine you want, and I'm sure she'll have no problem coming to you.

Money, power, draws women like flies. I'll send her to you," he called over his shoulder as he began to walk away.

"Wait!" Nuit said. "Say that again."

Carlos let his breath out hard, turned around, and watched as Nuit closed his eyes and seemed to inhale his exhale from across the clearing.

"I said, pick any one of them you want," Carlos restated impatiently. "Name her, and I'll bring her to you. The deal is a million for the men who did our people, and a woman—I get to own a panther, but you get to house and feed it. And I get crazy protection, with no bullshit attached. Period."

Nuit's eyes narrowed to slits, and he wrapped his arms around himself and trembled, breathing hard. "Come here. Seal this pact. Then you can go."

He knew the custom—seal it with a handshake or a don level embrace.

"Fuck you. Lock the panther up first, man."

Nuit smiled. "Yes, she is daunting, even for her master at times. But she is so good—even in bed."

"I don't need to know all that," Carlos muttered as a disgusted shiver ran up his spine. "Just lock the monster up, and then we can shake on it." Carlos set down both briefcases, but kept his automatic. These guys were whack.

He only stepped forward when the panther jumped back in the limo, and one of the guards locked it in the vehicle.

Carlos watched the men as they continued to lick the blood off their hands. Then they wiped them with dark silk handkerchiefs, then cleaned their mouths. The thought of shaking on the deal with them was abhorrent, but he had a cool hundred thou at his left side, and a million on his right.

Unconcerned that Carlos was still heavily armed, the Italian stepped forward first, but grabbed Carlos's face as he offered him his left fist to pound, pulling him forward in a powerful embrace, and landing a kiss on each cheek before releasing him. Carlos wiped his nose with the back of his hand—the stench of blood, sulfur, and death filled his nostrils.

"Grazie," the older man murmured, his eyes cold and his smile even more threatening.

By instinct, Carlos allowed himself to be subjected to each of them, as they grabbed his face, kissed both cheeks, and released him. However, their strength was the most perplexing aspect of it all. Each of these men, who were substantially older than him, had handled him like he was a baby—and he was a man in top form!

When Nuit stepped to him, he braced himself. The top man could deliver the kiss of death, or the kiss of passage. It was all in how one was released from the embrace.

Cold hands went to Carlos's face, almost stroking it with a chill. The black eyes that met his were so intense that he could not turn away. A strange current ran through him. He could almost hear his own blood rushing through his veins. His heartbeat became erratic; he could hear the sound of its thud in his ears.

"You are going to know a pleasure so profound, a power so vast that it will make your dick hard," Nuit whispered.

CHAPTER TEN

FALLON NUIT's icy palm cradled Carlos's cheek with a lover's touch. Yet his grip on Carlos was an iron hold. Immediately Carlos tried to pull away, but was held firm as Nuit's face neared his. The sexual connection, the sensuality that ran through Nuit's fingers and onto Carlos's skin fucked with everything he believed in. The combination of surrender in the wake of such power also made him high, dazed for a second, and drained any desire to struggle out of Nuit's grasp.

Then Carlos saw it in slow motion—paralyzed with horror. Massive eyeteeth replaced the ones that had gleamed in the darkness, a black tongue licked a trail of slime at his neck. His gun unloaded, firing rounds against the earth. His neck was forced to bend and expose itself, pushed by a cheek that felt like it was packed with steel. His voice was muffled by blood in his throat from Nuit's hold, then impact.

Searing pain made his whole body convulse and twitch, he heard his collarbone snap and felt flesh tear away from the bite. Something was siphoning him, pulling at the open wound. He couldn't breathe. Heaven help him! He was dying in a man's arms.

His grandmother's face flashed in his mind, he saw his mother weeping as she held the phone. Their prayers connected with the one his mind was screaming now, Por Dios, *not like this!*

Carlos immediately dropped and saw a distorted face hovering above him, retching and spitting out blood. He tried to right himself, tried to stand. Where was his gun? He'd pulled the magnum from his waist, but his body went limp. Then he was moving fast, careening through blackness as though he were a car without windows. Putrid air whizzed by him, making him feel weightless, traveling faster and faster. The wind tore through his hair, terrible images blurred. In the distance he heard a howl, joined by more howls and screeches that made him try to cover his ears—but he was moving too fast, centrifugal force made anything but hurling forward impossible. A pinpoint of white light was in the distance, and he fought against the force that bound him and desperately reached for it. The light moved away from him. He was dying. Damali's words flashed in his mind. *God in Heaven, forgive me,* his mind screamed.

Suddenly, all motion stopped and he came to a halt with a thud that sent shards of pain through every cell in his body. His eyes were shut tight, and he could hear voices around him. Angry voices. Hisses, growls, an argument. Something in his pants pocket was burning his leg—Juan's cross. Blind, he groped for the cross and took it out of his pocket. He gripped it and then screamed. It scorched his fingers, his palm, branded it, and he threw it. Carlos slowly opened his eyes.

"Sacrilege!" Nuit yelled, his voice cutting through the night air. He walked in a circle, spitting and hissing and holding his abdomen. "He died with a prayer in his heart! The blood is tainted! *This one was previously marked to be a tracker guardian.* This one had a slayer's prayers, and the prayers of the elderly over him! Even the slayer's team once prayed over this bastard. Why was I not informed?! I thought he was marked as one of ours!"

The others now bore fangs, their faces like demons. Weak, Carlos pushed himself up to a sitting position, and then he scrabbled with the earth to get enough of a hold to finally stand. The rows of vehicles vanished with a wave of Nuit's hand. All but his black Lexus were gone.

"Save your thought projection energy," Nuit ordered the men around him. Then he studied Carlos. "Mine is a master's bite. You shouldn't have immediately turned, yet you've healed," he said, circling Carlos. "Something is very wrong in the supernatural order." Concern flickered in the red glow of Nuit's eyes.

A strange calmness overcame Carlos as he felt strength enter his body. There was a weightlessness that he couldn't describe. He raised his hand to feel his throat and neck, and he was awed when he pulled it away—there was no blood, no gaping wound. He looked down at his hand as Nuit continued to circle him. All the pain in his body was gone.

"The bastard immediately healed. But we still have a deal. I made you!"

Carlos surprised himself by laughing. Instinct made him know that somehow in this weird transaction, he'd gained the upper hand. He studied the angry and worried expressions of the group. Yes . . . he may have died, and might even now be in Hell . . . but if that was his fate, well then, he'd make the best of it.

Another wave of strength poured through Carlos. He looked at the night with new eyes. In the darkness he was able to make out even the veins in the leaves high above . . . *In the dark?* He trained his ears on the distance, and focused on a mouse scurrying from an owl. He rolled his shoulders, let his head drop back, and howled. Power. Infinite power made him drunk, and he laughed again.

"So, you did make me," Carlos finally breathed out. "So much for so little."

Nuit held up his hand to the group that appeared ready to lunge at Carlos, and then he smiled. "Gentlemen, gentlemen. Is this how we treat a new brother who has a marked territory? You cannot kill him anyway. He's stronger than you. Did you witness how fast he turned? I'm more interested in how—lost guardian. Whom did you do a deal with? You had to form another alliance in order to heal so quickly, to turn so fast."

Carlos looked at Nuit and shrugged. "We all have allies," he bluffed. "It's advisable for business. And you can't kill a dead man twice. If I'm in Hell, then so be it. Knew that I was going there when I died—now or later. What difference does it make when?" His voice trailed off as a renewed current of energy swept through him. "I just never knew it would be like this," he breathed, feeling an erotic pull to the sensation. "A much underrated place in the universe."

Nuit laughed. "You will make the adjustment just fine. Now bring me the girl."

Carlos fixed his gaze on Nuit. "Being one of whatever we are gives you a rush, doesn't it? I can dig it." He ignored the request. Nuit could have any of the women he screwed from the groupies that hung on him at the clubs. A woman from his club harem was incidental. Nuit had gotten the short end of this deal. Carlos felt a chuckle of satisfaction threatening his composure but secreted away his victory.

"The correct term for our race is vampiri. We are vampires." Nuit snarled, and began walking away.

"You are bullshitting me, right?" Carlos tried to play it cool, but there was no way to keep the panic from his voice. He'd tried to offer one of his usual, blasé sneers, but the comment had come out more like a question than the sarcastic blow-off he'd intended. No, he couldn't just blow *this* off. Vampires? This *had to be* pure bullshit. Impossible. They were just jacking with his head.

But before Nuit could respond, Carlos stooped and grabbed his stomach. His insides suddenly felt like they were on fire. His guts moved as though snakes infested them, and a hunger gripped him that made him cry out—his agony ending in a wail. Wolves in the distance cried with him, and he dropped to his knees, digging his fingers in the dirt. Retractable claws came from his nail beds, and he could feel his ears lay back against his skull as his jaw unhooked itself. A burn filled his mouth, and he leaned his head back, panting. Soon his teeth began to rip through his gums and fill his mouth. His whole body convulsed and trembled.

"Hmmm . . . painful, I know. Pity," Nuit said in a calm tone, looking at Carlos with an evil grin of triumph. "It doesn't have to be this way, however."

The agony that seared Carlos's abdomen made him stare up at his tormentor for mercy that he knew would not come. A deal was in the offing; instinct told him that much. But with his insides crawling, he couldn't think, much less respond. Fallon Nuit grabbed his shoulder with an air of disdain, and the mere touch temporarily abated the pain.

"You have no idea who you're attempting to negotiate with," Nuit said coolly. "Perhaps I should show you, and then you'll stop struggling against your fate. There is a much more dignified way to proceed than this." Nuit shook his head and made a little clucking sound with his tongue. "Arrogance is laudable . . . but not against me."

Too weak to even brush off Nuit's hold, Carlos again felt himself moving fast—but not falling. It was as though he was instantly airborne. A rush of night wind slapped his face and blew back the sweat-soaked hair that had clung to his scalp, sending a cold chill against it as the scenery below him became a blur of dark green forest, and then buildings, lights, followed by a hard crash against a smooth surface. Rock music made him cover his ears for a moment. Dazed, he was staring at a pair of expensive black shoes, and without looking up he knew he was at Nuit's feet. The piped-in music made the floor beneath him pulse. Nausea consumed him, and he nearly dry heaved to the beat of the acid rock sounds.

For a moment, Carlos allowed his cheek to rest against the coolness of the black marble floor. Drenched with perspiration, his clothes stuck to him, and soon mild laughter entered his ears. Too disoriented to immediately stand, he peered around his new environment, and was met by a scene that his mind could not comprehend. Never in his life had he witnessed such a decadent display of pure wealth.

"This is all mine," Nuit said proudly, waving his arm as he spoke toward several well-dressed henchmen. "Just like they are all mine. But there's more."

Pushing himself up to a sitting position on the floor, Carlos stared at the luxurious black leather sofas, marble and gold-chrome furnishings, and the huge marquee that said BLOOD MUSIC, INC., which took up half of the walnut walls by the elevators. The receptionist's area alone was a massive twenty-foot semicircle of marble with the company's logo engraved in it, and a stunning blonde with ruby-red lipstick gave him a sly glance, her smile widening just enough to show a hint of fangs. She toyed with a gold chain at her throat that ended with a crest at her voluptuous cleavage. Mounted gold and platinum records in heavy chrome frames lined the wall behind her, but she cast no reflection in their glass casings. Nuit chuckled, and pulled Carlos to stand.

"Just one of the many benefits of this lifestyle, *n'est pas?*"

There was no other response but to nod. Carlos's gaze ricocheted around the lobby. Although surrounded by windows on three sides, he had no idea how high up he was. The only thing he was able to tell was that there was no other building blocking his view. A pounding headache pierced his temples, stabbing his brain with the artificial track lighting.

"You like?" Nuit pushed Carlos forward without touching him, but by simply waving his hand. "Sixty-six floors, L.A. earthquakes notwithstanding, with six hundred and sixty-six employees who all belong to me. However, this is only a paltry example of my holdings. Why don't we take a little tour?" Nuit rounded him to lead the way.

Again, Carlos felt his body moving from an external force as against his will he stumbled behind Nuit down a wide corridor bustling with activity and crowded with expensively dressed employees. Modern art, murals, and Grammy replicas encased in Lucite collided with awards, mounted covers of *Rolling Stone* magazine, Teen Choice Awards, and MTV Awards, the glare from platinum and gold records making him squint. Photos of top Hollywood stars alongside recording artists and a who's who in the entertainment industry created a veritable wall of fame as they walked while all the while hunger clawed him.

Each busy female they passed looked better than the last, and each woman gave a sly, deferring smile toward Fallon Nuit as they made their way deeper into the Blood Music terrain. But what Carlos couldn't figure out was, why in the world would Nuit want any woman from his clubs? It seemed like the entire *Baywatch* set had been emptied into the Blood Music offices. Brunettes, redheads, blondes, sisters with braids, and every male that walked by was buff, wrapped in designer gear; no one appeared to be over thirty-five in the whole joint.

"You've noticed my substantial evening staff," Nuit announced over his shoulder, pride oozing from his voice. "While we have a significant day-presence in the building, I'm sure you can appreciate that a considerable number of those in my employ do their best work during evening hours—so we have flexible scheduling to accommodate such necessary preferences. Diversity."

Staffers quickly nodded at Nuit, moved out of his way, practically genuflecting as he passed and ignored them. With a wave of his hand, the double onyx-and-chrome doors to a huge conference room opened. Nuit crossed the threshold and sighed.

"Permit me to introduce my marketing team," Nuit added with bravado, motioning toward a large ebony table that had a backlit, glass-etched world map in the center of it, and then toward a huddle of three men and three women—each bearing fangs when Nuit pushed Carlos forward. "Ladies and gentlemen, meet our newest employee, Carlos Rivera."

A series of disgruntled snarls met Carlos, and Nuit laughed.

"I know, don't worry. Once he feeds he won't still smell so human. But please, show him our holdings."

A tall, angular blonde sashayed from behind the table and nearly purred as she sidled up to Nuit. Her black sheath clung to her gaunt hipbones, and her nipples hardened beneath the semi-sheer fabric as she neared them. She licked her lips and stared at Carlos.

"Has he been broken in yet?" she murmured, her gaze narrowing on Carlos.

"No, love, this one is for Raven," Nuit intoned with a smile, cupping her face with his hand. "Next time."

She let out a sigh with the pout, and walked back toward the table and picked up a red laser pointer. "We have the entire North American territory, with expansion throughout the Caribbean." She eyed Carlos with a bored expression reinforced by her equally weary, disgruntled tone. "We have the Pacific Rim, and Europe to the old Czech Republic—"

"That includes Transylvania, one of the most historic landmarks, I might add," Nuit cut in. "My dearly departed mentor brought fame to that region. Now I own what he owned, and then some."

The blonde nodded. "We've recently picked up Moscow, Brazil, and a section of East Africa. We have a lock on five key locations for the international concert, sir."

"Carry on," Nuit ordered, dismissing the team as he turned to face Carlos. "Some of the other territories are still in dispute, but that is a mere temporary inconvenience. Shall we go to my office and have a drink?"

Carlos hated the way his body was forced to move, and the satisfaction of power that Nuit lorded over him. Each question Nuit proffered was rhetorical, teasing Carlos as though he had an option to do anything else but follow. His legs walked against his will down another bending corridor and another female smiled at him as she stood up behind her desk.

"Mr. Nuit," the sexy, dark-haired secretary murmured, "the senator called while you were out, and I have three CEOs that would like to book a late-dinner appointment with you."

"Isabella," Nuit crooned, "tender my regrets to the CEOs and have one of my vice presidents handle those nominal social affairs. Smooth it over by sending the yacht for them with a nice assortment of the girls on it. But do get the good senator for me on line one, won't you, darling?"

When she smiled, Carlos felt the immediate erotic pull that arced between the two. Nuit chuckled low in his throat.

"Forgive me. I have been rude. Isabella, Carlos Rivera . . . my newest hire."

She studied Carlos with an assessment that made him feel

naked. "Will he have direct access to you, Mr. Nuit, or should he go through any particular screen?"

"No," Nuit replied with a half smile. "This one won't require a screen—I made him myself, and we have pressing matters that will require my personal oversight of his assignment."

She nodded and sat down, and began to carry out Nuit's previous instructions as Carlos found himself being ushered into an inner office.

Several artists that he recognized were lounging around on a wide, circular, black leather sectional sofa facing a half-moon-shaped glass table. Once more, Carlos could only stare for a moment. It looked like an entire neighborhood's shipment of pure Peruvian rock cocaine had been dropped in the center of the small table. Dazed artists passed the hose from a giant, six-foot water pipe to each other. Carlos sniffed the air while the pinkish-white smoke filled the pipe cylinder, and oddly he felt himself salivating for some unknown reason.

The artists gave him a cursory glance before going back to their get-high. Why was the burning sensation coming back to his stomach? Carlos glanced at Nuit who had an amused smirk on his face. The pain was getting worse, yet he hadn't said a word to further piss off Nuit! Hunger buckled Carlos's knees.

Crack, opium, heroin, hash, Ecstasy, acid, ludes, Vs, weed, and top-shelf liquor graced the table. Carlos didn't have to see it, he could smell it burning, taste it all in his mouth as it coated the back of his throat. He knew each product that he'd distributed by heart. Everything laid out was potent, pure, and stronger than anything he'd ever sold. But the hunger?

His line of vision became riveted on the thick, bubbling, dark liquid in the water pipe. Carlos watched the surface of it splash red globs of wetness against the Oriental design of a translucent dragon. The siphon of a smoker sent a rhythmic sound throughout the room beneath the ever-present music, creating a dense cloud of smoke within the pipe chamber before it was sucked out in a hit too large for one person to consume. Then he scanned the room.

Two large bouncers with dark, aviator-type shades stood by a food-service buffet table. The smell coming from it was as intoxicating as the contact coming off the pipe. Carlos felt a gentle caress at his back that made him spin quickly to stare at Nuit.

"Hungry yet?" Nuit asked in a teasing, suggestive tone.

One of the bodyguards walked over to the silver trays and removed the lids. Entrails filled one platter, and raw, bloodied meat that Carlos was afraid to guess at was piled on another. Small cordial glasses of dark Merlot-colored liquid were set on a third tray, and the others around it had tiny dripping hors d'oeuvres that sickened his mind but stabbed at the hunger in his gullet.

A new dampness crept down Carlos's chest and the center of his back. He briefly shut his eyes and then glanced toward the huge gurgling water pipe that sat on the floor within the arch of the half-moon table. A trickle of sweat rolled down the side of his face from his temple. Immediately he knew why the dense smoke that rose within the water pipe turned pink. Blood was in the base of it. Carlos felt saliva build in his mouth and he swallowed hard as a disoriented artist took a full hit of the substance.

A female vampire appeared out of the haze around the artist who was too gone to pass the hose nozzle without assistance. She took a hit from it, handed it to a person beside her, dropped to her knees, and opened the guy's pants. No one around the table even seemed to notice as her head began to skillfully bob above his lap.

"Let's allow the children to play. Step into my private office,"

Nuit said calmly, the display apparently holding little interest for him. "We have business to discuss."

This time, Nuit didn't have to thrust Carlos forward with invisible force. Thoroughly impressed, Carlos followed behind Nuit on his own volition.

A thirty-foot vaulted ceiling greeted Carlos as he walked in and then stepped down three wide, kidney-shaped onyx stairs toward Nuit's glass desk. All his life he'd dreamed of owning a setup like this one. Carlos glanced at a wall with sixty sections of black screen flanked by more industry awards and real Grammies. Nuit snapped, and the monitors came to life and flickered with disparate scenes.

"Villas and casinos in the vacation paradises," Nuit murmured with pride. "Electronics, pharmaceuticals, and bio-engineering firms in Europe and the Pacific Rim. Certain products that fly in under radar come from my Russian and South American holdings. East Africa has vast natural resources for more legitimate enterprises. Then, of course, there's Blood Music and all her splendor—from CD royalties, commercial endorsements, concerts, motion-picture soundtracks . . . the entertainment industry is one of North America's greatest global exports. We have reserved a piece of this for you, if we can come to terms."

Nuit sat down slowly in the plush, high-backed leather chair behind his crested marble desk and opened a crystal decanter, pouring himself a drink while Carlos stared at the monitors. The yacht on one monitor looked like it was the size of a Carnival Cruise ship. A jumbo jet with the Blood Music logo landed on a private airfield on another. Villas with outrageously rich appointments filled each screen, and then a mosaic of casinos entered the monitors, each scene in a different country, a different province . . . and Nuit owned it all. *Damn . . .*

But the smell wafting from the open decanter drew Carlos's

attention away from the screens. Nuit simply waved his hand to offer Carlos a seat before him. Carlos glanced around, noting the floor-to-ceiling windows, the built-in wall bar, and the heavy furniture that had to be at least twenty-five feet away. Ten of his offices could fit within one of Nuit's. Nuit smiled.

"I told you mine was bigger than yours," he said with a sexually charged smirk, taking a leisurely sip from his glass and rolling the liquid around on his tongue. He made a face, studied the contents of his glass, and let out a slow exhale in Carlos's direction.

The scent that flowed over the desk and toward Carlos sent a shudder of need through him. It was a pull that went beyond want or desire. Tears began forming in his eyes from the torturous seduction. The intercom buzzed just before he opened his mouth to beg for a small taste. He hated this rich motherfucker, but at the same time, he'd love to know how he'd done it . . . amassed so much, so young. Vampiri, huh? Yeah. Carlos studied Nuit as he reached for the black telephone console and pressed a button.

"I have the senator for you, Mr. Nuit, on line one," a sexy female voice intoned through the intercom.

Nuit's smile broadened. He pushed back in his chair, put his feet up on his desk, ignoring Carlos's agony, but never breaking eye contact with him.

"Senator . . . yes . . . it is also my pleasure. What can I do for you?"

Carlos watched like a hungering dog, swallowing fast as Nuit stirred the blood in his glass with a finger then sucked it clean.

"But I thought you needed to keep your lovely wife around beyond the election?" Nuit chuckled and let his breath out. "Cancer could be arranged. I know some people who know some people . . . Yes. Might kill two birds with one stone. You can be the dedicated husband, good for public opinion ratings, and she can succumb just after the election. Very simple . . . And, I'm sure, especially after such a heavy campaign contribution, my enterprises will have few problems with the Environmental Protection Agency. . . . Yes, it has been troublesome getting our nuclear plants certified. I know, I know. We always understand each other. Hmmm . . . we will have to do dinner one night soon—so you can pick out a new bride." Nuit laughed low and deep. "Oh, I always have a few you can choose from."

The call seemed like it lasted for an eternity, and all Carlos could do was wait and hunger and wonder. This was indeed the most power he'd ever seen manifest in one entity in his life. Smug satisfaction laced Nuit's smile as he ended the call, removed his feet from the desk, and stood, bringing leftovers within his glass around for Carlos to sip, but holding the tumbler just out of his reach. Carlos wanted a taste of it so badly that his mouth went dry.

"The yacht, I rarely use . . . as I prefer personal air travel," Nuit added, motioning toward the screens, still teasing Carlos with the glass, and using it to make his point. "The jet is for my human VIPs, artists, those with the human transport disability, and for less conspicuous business transactions. The villas are revenue generators, just like the hotels and casinos. Carlos, if you follow my lead, I will show you a life that will feel as good as a wet dream."

He handed Carlos the nearly empty glass, toying with him by snatching it back for a second then finally allowing Carlos to take it. "Who else have you cut a side deal with?" Nuit's voice was low and seductive. "As you can see, I can meet and beat their offer. Talk to me and let nothing stand between us."

Carlos's pride was in shreds as he accepted the glass from Nuit and brought it to his mouth with shaking hands. The smell coming from the liquid at the bottom of the tumbler was enough to get him high, and the sensation made Carlos close his eyes tight. But there was another part of him, the place deep within where his sense of self-respect resided, that made him take a healthy whiff and hurl the glass at the screens. "Then stop playing games, and nothing will stand between us."

Fallon Nuit's eyes narrowed as the fragile glass shattered against the monitors, creating a gash in one, and splashing red liquid across several others. Carlos pushed himself out of the chair, and immediately felt the sting of the bitch-slap Nuit issued against his cheek. He could taste the missed opportunity in his mouth. The sweetness of the blood lingered in his nasal passages. It felt like the snakes in his intestines were now slithering up his esophagus. Preserving his dignity was becoming a moot point. Carlos balled up his fists and clenched his jaw to keep from vomiting. He forced himself to keep his fists against his sides, and knew better than to swing. Not yet, but soon.

"I don't do sloppy seconds," Carlos said between his teeth. "And I don't do my own product—never did."

"This isn't drugs, it's blood," Nuit spat back, furious at the affront.

"My bad," Carlos hedged, his breaths ragged as the hunger continued to burn him from the inside out. "Thought it was tainted with product from the other room. That's the type of shit that will run your business into the ground. Become a junkie, and your days are over. I plan to be around a long time. Like you said, we have serious business to do—so let's stop jacking with each other and do business, *hombre*. You know more about this vampire bullshit than me. Think about it."

Carlos bent over, placing his hands on his thighs and gulped air. "Just didn't trust you at first. No good businessman goes into a situation on blind faith where I come from."

Nuit rubbed his hand over his jaw and paced to a window, giving Carlos his back to consider. "You are indeed an impeccable businessman. I just hope that you have the common sense to observe certain hierarchies that are in place. I would hate to lose one like you that holds so much promise. There are certain protocols that are sacrosanct. Perhaps your pure mercenary character is what turned you into one of us so fast, given that you were half predator when I made you. Nonetheless, if I ever find out differently . . ."

When Fallon Nuit turned around, his eyes were glowing gold and his fangs were slightly showing. For some reason, Carlos was concerned, but not afraid. Those eyes, gold, didn't seem as formidable as when they glowed red. The incisors were also at half the length he'd witnessed before. Okay, Nuit was pissed, but not enraged. That was cool. He could work with that.

Carlos watched Nuit open his fingers wide and press his hand against the glass, which instantly vanished. Now he was worried. Carlos could feel the night air blow against him in a silent threat. Then, without warning, a vacuum force snatched him from where he stood, sucking him just beyond the window's edge, and then dropped him.

A scream was ripped from his throat. The ground got closer and closer, and he grappled with the air, the nothingness in his hands, as he was hurled toward the parking lot on the ground. Porsches, Mercedes, Fiats, Jags, every car he'd ever wanted was now going to break his body into hundreds of bone-snapped pieces and splatter his guts on the pavement. Terror and anger were close companions as he realized he was going to die—again. Then calm resignation took over. It happened so fast, the end would be a second of pain then he'd be in black peace, he reasoned . . . and stopped struggling with the air. At least the internal burn would stop.

But instead of hitting a parking lot of high-priced cars, Carlos came to a thud on the grass in the woods, again at Fallon Nuit's feet where the entire travesty had begun.

"Feed him," Nuit ordered toward the newly reappeared limo. "I refuse to, until I find out exactly what happened here." Nuit cast a disparaging glance in Carlos's direction. "Her blood won't keep back the suffering for long, but will just keep him half alive until I make a decision. Next time he may not be so hasty to cast away a sip from his master's glass."

The panther slinked out of the vehicle, turning into a gorgeous woman as it walked toward Carlos. She smelled of blood, was tall, lithe, and dark, with huge walnut-colored eyes that glistened in the night. Her hair, the hue of midnight blue, swept across her shoulders, and she held out her wrists to Carlos as he remained on his hands and knees.

"I just ate," she whispered in a sexy tone. "C'mon lover—he gave me to you."

In one deft motion, Carlos was on his feet, and had pulled her to him, taking her wrists and slitting the veins in them with the side of a fang. Then he lowered his head and allowed the sweet elixir of life to fill his mouth. The sensation was so quenching, he had to close his eyes to drink. It cooled the burn, brought strength back to every tortured cell in his body as it slid down his throat, its sticky essence putting out the flame, stilling the worms and snakes in his gizzard. He groaned and heard her groan with him. Nuit had not lied. It made his dick hard.

"Do what you will with her," Nuit stated with disinterest as he slowly walked away. "If you survive the night, she'll teach you how to feed, and you will one day feed her. When your suffering for your master's blood becomes strong enough, I will return to claim you. Just remember your bargain . . . and stay out of the sun. Our deal is something you *can't* break with your silly prayers. But I will get to the bottom of how you could resist your first taste from me."

Upon Nuit's next footfall, he vanished. Carlos pushed the woman against the trunk of the tree and glanced over his shoulder. The group of dons and henchmen became one cloud of fluttering dark smoke, then dispersed into the night on leathery wings. Intense desire turned his attention away from the bats and toward the writhing cold form beneath him. He ripped at her black leather skirt, shredding it with his nails as her legs wrapped around his waist and her talons stripped away the damp nylon that swaddled him. An equally compelling desire made him breathe her in, and sink his teeth into her exposed throat as he entered her.

Carnal pleasure had never felt so damned good.

CHAPTER ELEVEN

HER SEARCH for Carlos had ended in frustration. Damali stood in the locked foyer of the compound allowing the UV light to pour over her as she waited for the second steel safety-door of the sanctuary to open. The crew was huddled over the design tables and the computers when she entered their haven at dusk. She was thankful that they only gave her a cursory acknowledgment as she briefly spoke to them before she went to her room.

Her insides ached with a growing despair, and she found her spoken word journal—the place where she poured out her soul.

Choices. Her mind wrapped around the beginning of an anthem. Damali sat slowly at her worktable in her bedroom, watching the sun go down, and the steel security gates come down over her windows with it. Choices—a road high and a road low. Such a narrow margin of error in between.

Her hand furiously scribbled the words that spilled from her mind:

They say do the right thing, easy words but a hard road to follow.
Grandmommas call it a tough row to hoe—like cotton country
and tobacco land madness, hot laundry rooms, buckets to wash

*other people's floors . . . while remaining pleasant—A rock and a
hard place—all sistahs know where that is. And they say the
words from the master wordsmith, explaining how life ain't no
crystal stair, I got dat part—but the splinters in this are a bitch.
People pulling me left, then right, shredding who I am. The gray
zone, neither right yet, or wrong—standing on the border, I
wonder. There but for the grace of God, go I. Really? Cool.
Who am I to judge, or cast the first stone when they judge me,
first . . . before they know who I am? But then, I'm becoming a
rock thrower myself these days, just to keep my balance—within
me—who is that, I ask?*

*Because you see, they have me standing between a rock and a
hard place, knowing what I know about all the women who have
stood here in the past. Betta recognize—I do, I feel you—but
yo, y'all need to give up props, too—'cause the new millennium
ain't no joke. Have you seen what's out here? What's left of the
slim pickin's . . . for a young sistah with wisdom, with purpose,
who wants more than splinters in her butt?*

*And I'm trying to get cool with this position that ain't changed
since Eve shook things up, girlfriend was ahead of her time and
said oh well—my choice. But then, that fucked things up, for
real, for real, and sistah went down hard. Been paying ever since,
and they called out her name behind it. So, I do have sense. I
am listening, I hear ya, but I'm still in between this funky position, when I want to feel freedom—which I hear ya, ain't free.
Prepared to pay the cost to be the boss just takes the hard place
to a new level, and I'm tired of analyzing the risk factor—just
wanna have fun. Just wanna forget for a moment that when I sit
down hard there will be splinters in my high, round Nubian ass.*

*I don't want to have to listen to the brothers call me baby, then
in the next breath bitch—when I make my choice and it's not in
their favor, and I want the old dolls to back up and give me space*

to breathe, to figure this complex shit out on my own—respect, notwithstanding. Naw, I ain't trying to be a baby's momma, when I'm just a baby myself . . . and I like my new power to turn heads, and make men shiver without touching them, I'm just playing—just seeing how strong my vibe is, but that don't give them the right to violate it. Naw. Don't give the old dolls the right to judge what's on my mind, neither, just 'cause my body's talking to me loud and clear—

The light tap on her door made Damali stop writing and look up. She murmured for the intruder to come in and then watched Marlene close the door behind her and cross the room. When Marlene sat on the corner of her bed, Damali turned her director's chair around to face her mentor.

"You're back to writing again," Marlene said quietly. "That's good."

"Yeah," Damali murmured. "It's all good."

The two women sat in strained silence, Marlene's gaze going toward the sealed windows and then to the floor as she clasped her hands in her lap.

"Damali, I'm sorry," Marlene finally murmured as she let her breath out slowly and then studied her hands. "I've been really tough on you for a long time, and I don't even know where to begin. There's so much to teach you, and so little time."

The silence made Marlene look up to connect with Damali's gaze.

"I'm trying so hard," Damali whispered, "to be what everyone says I am, or that I need to be . . . but I'm human, too."

"Yes, baby, you are," Marlene whispered back, and then glanced away.

"I don't understand everything that's happening. I don't even know how I feel about anything anymore," Damali admitted, making Marlene look up at her again. "Everything feels like it's spinning out of control, and like as a team, we're on the verge of another catastrophe . . . and I don't know how, or if, I can stop it."

The two women quietly stared at each other for a long time, until Marlene nodded.

"I should have told you everything earlier," Marlene said. "I just couldn't."

"Why now? That's the part that hurts so bad, Mar. You didn't trust me."

Marlene shook her head. "I trusted you. I just didn't trust my own fears." Marlene looked at Damali directly, her gaze furtive. "Fear is a terrible emotion. It makes you look at things from a very restricted point of view. I didn't want to lose you to the fallen night."

Damali's gaze softened and she could feel her body relax. "I know that, Mar. But where's your faith? You have to allow a person to figure out some of this stuff on their own."

Marlene nodded and laughed sadly. "From the mouths of babes come words of wisdom. When you live a long time, fear starts to make your bones . . . your mind . . . your spirit brittle to any change. That's because change always seems to have pain associated with it—and comes at a frighteningly high price."

Damali stood and went over to sit next to Marlene. Her arms found her mentor's shoulders and she hugged her. Marlene let out a long, exhausted breath. The worry laced within that breath threaded its way through Damali's heart, touching the core of her.

"I love you so much, Mar. I would never do anything to hurt you. Don't you know how I feel about you and the group? You're family."

Marlene nodded and pulled away gently so she could stare at

Damali while holding her hands. "You are so young and so beautiful that I guess I just wanted to wrap you up in a bubble of safety and keep you away from any of this big, bad world. I'm a mother. One day, God willing, you will be one, too. Then you'll know a level of fear that goes beyond your own personal safety."

Tears formed in Marlene's eyes as she spoke. "Even if there were no such things as vampires or demons, I'd still have this fear. I pray daily for each of you, but not as hard for the others as I pray for you, my baby girl."

Wiping at the tears that had fallen from Marlene's wise, aging eyes, Damali kissed her cheek. "I love you. Do you understand?"

Marlene nodded and smiled, and then chuckled in a tone so sad that Damali swallowed as tears threatened her own composure.

"I've taught you almost everything I know to make you strong, independent, and courageous, and I tried to pass on all of that—then, when you were ready to fly, I was the one clipping your wings. Like I said, it's insane, but real. I'm sorry."

"No, don't be sorry, Mar." Damali shook her head and pushed a stray lock off Marlene's shoulder. "Momma eagle, you have flown through storms, hunted and brought back food for the nest, and battled in the wilderness. It *is* dangerous out there, and I'm so new . . . just floating on air . . . while you have the eagle eyes that know there's a storm coming, there's a cliff nearby, fierce beasts in the night, and you did what you knew, screeched a warning for me to get back to the nest. Your eyes and instincts are still good, Marlene. Know that I respect that. Please."

Marlene chuckled again softly, wiping at her own tears as she broke Damali's hold to do so. "Then why did we both go blind for a moment . . . especially after that show in Philadelphia? That scared me, baby. And we haven't been on the same page since."

Damali stared at Marlene.

"It's like my gift is waning as yours strengthens . . . and it's the same with the rest of the group. But your gifts are so new and so untested that the warnings come in fits and starts—and I'm concerned about the times when your sensors are down— you understand?"

"Am I dredging you guys?" Horrified at the concept, Damali stood and began to pace. "What if I'm siphoning the group of its energy?"

"No," Marlene said quickly. "This is the natural order of things. You are getting stronger, our perceptions are dimming— not because you are a drain, but because you are coming to a point where you have to be able to make decisions, come to conclusions on your own. Our job has always been to protect and guide you until you come of age. We'll maintain our gifts in the long run, but while you are in this delicate transition, we cannot overpower your perceptions, your realities . . . your spirit. You must be your own guide." Marlene stood and went to the window.

"All of us are wondering, did she get lesson one-o-one? Did we transfer enough knowledge, did her mind absorb the concepts, what did we forget to teach her . . . what took root, what was left behind? Panicked, we started retracing our steps, going over the basics—things you already knew—not because you weren't sure, but because *we* aren't sure. I know it pisses you off. But we're bugging because we see a storm brewing and just want to know, will our baby be safe, will she be able to hunt on her own—and if she faces deadly challenges, will she make the right choice?" Marlene turned and looked at Damali with firm love in her eyes.

"Baby, every parent on the planet asks themselves this, and they quietly freak when it's time to let go and let God. Not just slayer guardians. It comes with the serve and protect cross to bear that all parents have invisibly on their shoulders. But in the end, we have to let go. We all hold our collective breaths when the time comes. Then we all beat ourselves up if our beloved child stumbles and falls . . . and we cringe at our own legacy of human error wondering if we had been more perfect, more righteous, could we have helped our child avoid a fall."

"Deep . . ." Damali's murmur trailed off as the impact of the burden became so clear. She thought it was all Neteru-related drama, but suddenly she could understand how most of this was pure love—and would not have been any different if she was just a normal young woman. She raked her fingers through her locks and let her breath out hard.

Marlene immediately let her breath out with a soft sigh, following Damali's exhale of epiphany.

"Truth is, we never know." Marlene held Damali in her gaze again and searched her face. "Baby, I don't know if my own mistakes will be a part of your legacy. I don't know if, or what, I could have done better. That's it—*I'm human,* imperfect, I have issues . . . and God help me, I never wanted to visit those things on you—so I tried to hide them. Just remember that, okay? No matter how all this goes down."

Marlene turned away as a sob caught in her throat. She covered her mouth with her hand and closed her eyes. "What could I have done? What have I left undone? That's the nagging question that drives a mother crazy—what if?"

Damali crossed the room, wrapping her arms around Marlene as she rested her chin on Marlene's shoulder and rocked her.

"Mom—Marlene," Damali said. "You gave me everything that you could. Now I have to figure this out for myself."

Marlene's hand touched Damali's and she squeezed it. "You called me Mom," she whispered.

Turning Marlene to face her, Damali traced Marlene's tears

with her finger. "Because, by any definition, that's who you are to me. You have given me *everything* you had to give, all from a good place in your heart. Don't you think I know what you're afraid of most? That I'll get bitten."

Marlene smiled. "I guess you would. You have the eyes, too. I just don't want you to ever hate me for the choices I've made, or had to make."

"I know you are not the enemy," Damali said tenderly. "I'm afraid of what's out there, too. I'm no fool."

Both women chuckled and held hands in quiet contemplation.

"Let's start again," Damali said in a soft tone, as she gazed at Marlene's accepting expression. "Me and you on the same team. I won't promise to do everything you say carte blanche—but how about if I listen while you teach me tonight?"

Again, Marlene chuckled. But this time the sound that came from her was richer, deeper, more at ease. "You want to know how to know when," Marlene said with a smile. "If I knew that answer, I'd book myself on *Oprah* and be done with the music scene. You know she's retiring in 2006."

They both giggled and shook their heads and sat on the edge of Damali's bed.

"You think I'm bad—wait till you have kids," Marlene teased. "A momma that can hear everything, smell everything, can see in the dark and carries a blade—man, I pity your kids already! You wait."

Damali laughed hard with Marlene; the thought of finding herself in the same position years later, however, trailed off her laughter. Damn, this was some deep shit.

"You know, Mar, I hadn't even gone there. You might have to visit me in prison for staking some poor heavy-breathing teenager who was trying to push up on my daughter."

"See, it ain't so funny, is it?" Marlene smiled.

"No," Damali admitted. "Not in the least. The predicament is a trip."

"Uhmmm, hmmm . . ."

Damali's gaze drifted toward the bathroom, and Marlene rubbed her thigh with a supportive, maternal touch.

"Carlos is in your system," Marlene murmured. "I know. I don't need second sight to tell—it's a woman thing. Knowledge, regardless. But I would never, *ever* violate that space in your head. Know that. Because it's private, and I don't want it done to me . . . or any of the guys."

Damali's gaze immediately found Marlene's. "How did you know I was concerned about that?"

"I'm a mom . . . and a woman. Remember? Plus, I can see some things written all over your face whenever the man's name is mentioned."

She could feel herself smile as her face began to burn with embarrassment.

"I want you to take a white bath every night. Let me put a ring of salt and sage around your bed, and hang garlic . . . even over the showerhead." Marlene winked at her. "Just a lucky guess. I wasn't prying."

Damali conceded with a nod, looking away, too ashamed to speak on the subject.

"Once you make your decision to be with someone, it will be difficult but not impossible to fight the pull. You will get to a place where your mind and your spirit will arrest your body," Marlene said in a quiet tone. "You get to a point where your eyes will see what is necessary to see before you act, and you will have the strength of will to garner patience—and you

will acquire a level of truth in your choice that will take away
the burn . . . but you will always simmer. That's life." Marlene
smiled. "Ask me how I know."

Damali studied the pattern in the gold bedspread as she spoke,
unable to meet Marlene's knowing gaze. "Some days . . . it's . . .
well . . ."

"I know," Marlene said. "You're burning too hot to even
think—your mind is frying. Look, even if it ain't a vamp pull,
there's stuff and people out there, these days, that can kill you.
Be prudent, despite the burn. Everybody needs to chill, and get
back to basics. The old way."

"But, Mar . . . for real, for real . . . I mean with everything
around you—and . . . How do you just chill, make it go away,
and move forward without thinking about it sometimes? Wondering, you know . . . even when you know it could be bad for
you?"

She cast her gaze to her finger as it made a new pattern within
the comforter pattern. How could she just come out and say it—
to a mom-person? How did you just tell a mother that this guy
was in your head, in your dreams, made you wet your panties
just thinking about him, and that every time you closed your
eyes you wanted to be with him? How did you explain that this
very basic instinct *was* the basics at the moment, that it rode
shotgun with the other things you had on your mind, and traveled with you while you did everything else necessary in your
life . . . that it was on you like a habit? Rather than speak, she
let her breath out hard again instead. Carlos wasn't a vamp, but
he had a pull like one.

Marlene sat quietly for a while, watching Damali draw invisible swirls on the bed. "I know it's hard, and I'm not going to
lie to you—I don't have a secret potion for that."

Marlene chuckled. "*You* have to do that. *You* know the life he leads, and *you* know the outcome of said life. If you think a pull to Carlos is bad, wait till a master vampire gets into your brain during a lair hunt. That's what I'm concerned about, baby. If you can't get a mere human attraction out of your head—when you know it's not good for you—then, I have my very realistic worries. It means you aren't ready. Carlos is . . . just a guy," she added with a sigh. "Coulda made something real positive of himself, had all the attributes to make him really an asset, a community treasure . . . in fact, he was guardian material, once. *But* for whatever his reasons, and we all have a long story, he chose to go down the wrong road—one you are very far removed from. Got it?"

When Damali looked up and gave Marlene a mournful glance, Marlene laughed.

"If it's that bad, maybe I can cook something up."

Damali chuckled and shook her head, blinking back sudden tears, not sure where they came from. "I'm cool."

"Yeah, right," Marlene scoffed. "Whooo boy. Okay. Listen. I want you to get to a very still place in your head. I want you to go past the primal, the physical level, and think about the future. What do you want—long-term? What is important—long-term? What can you build that is positive?"

Marlene sighed and forced Damali's chin up with a gentle prod of her finger. "If it is damaging to your spirit, to your mind, or your soul, I want you to fight it and step away from it with everything that we have all taught you thus far. I don't care if the pull is to something human, or otherwise. These are the basics, young lady. And I will trust that you'll do that, even though the mere thought of just stepping back and watching you decide all by yourself gives me white knuckles." Marlene chuckled softly. "Girl, I'm getting the hives from this mess."

Marlene continued to chuckle quietly as she stood and walked in a circle. "Shoot, if we only had to worry about a mere human on your trail, and just a hood, we'd react the same way! The fact that Carlos is a community predator—even if he ain't a vamp—we'd still trip. Shabazz has been itching to roll up on homeboy to call him out anyway."

Marlene took a battle stance, making Damali laugh hard now as she imitated Shabazz's deep voice. "Could you see your big brother rolling up on Rivera—'Yo, player, player, if you lookin' for a woman, Sleepin' Beauty will tighten you up. Don't get it twisted—my li'l sis is off-limits. *Chill.*"

The way Marlene swaggered around the room with an invisible Glock in her hand made Damali burst out in a new round of laughter as she fell back on the bed. When Marlene put both hands on her hips, Damali waved her away so she could recover. "Shabazz would freak."

"Yeah, and picture him and Big Mike meeting *hombre* in an alley. Okaaay."

"No, stop," Damali wheezed. "Okay, okay, okay, I get your point. Dude has issues. I know," she said, chuckling, "But . . . but he's *so fine* . . . God. Why couldn't he have just gone down the right road?"

"He wanted money and power, and wasn't patient to figure out another way—so pick a different guy. I don't care if he's not bearing fangs, and is *all that* looks-wise—sexy Latino voice, smooth vibe, *what-eva.* His lifestyle is just as dangerous as a vamp's. Carlos Rivera is not a good choice—not a smart one. Not for you."

"I know . . . been knowin' that. But, dang . . ." Damali shook her head; the mirth began distilling into despair again. "But I also thought it was my choice."

"It is—but you can't blame us for wanting to stack the deck

in your favor . . . which is to steer you away from guys like him."

Damali sighed and nodded. "You can stack the deck, but just remember I hold the cards. Okay?"

"All right," Marlene conceded. "But men are crazy."

"Mar, tell me something I don't know."

They both looked at each other and laughed.

"You think I'm lying, girl?" Marlene sucked her teeth. "These young men out here have no respect, no decorum, don't know how to run a household—wouldn't give a hoot about just stop, drop, and rollin' you. Pullease. I have issues, daughter. I have *serious* issues with the world today, and have no problem posseing up, as a mom, to protect my investment—you—from anything, or anyone, that might steal your joy, that might take the sparkle from your eyes, that might break your spirit and your heart. Brotherman doesn't have to be a vampire to do that—just an emotional predator. Oh, it's on, now, daughter of mine. I will kick his natural ass if he hurts you. That's why I'm doing heavy anointing tonight."

"Okay, okay." Damali laughed as Marlene began to chuckle in a peevish tone. "Go get the stuff for the white bath."

"Humph! The guys in the weapons room have no idea about the worries of a mother. Shabazz and Big Mike and them ain't got nothin' on a mother's mad," Marlene fussed as she walked toward the door. "Yeah, I got something for Rivera. I'm make you shave, too. And I'm bringing henna."

"Shave?" Damali was laughing so hard now that she had to wipe her eyes as she peered under her arms—which were whistle clean. "That's *out*, Marlene! No way! You are not putting a whoo-doo henna chastity belt on my stuff. You've gone too far!"

"Don't play with me, girl. You know what I'm talking about.

By the time I finish anointing and putting on symbols of protection, any man, dead or alive, is gonna need a battering ram to get through Marlene's work." She gave Damali a wink. "All right, if you feel that strongly about it, no henna. But all of us could use a renewed seal of prayer protection from a white bath. Just go with me on this one. Run a hot tub, and stop looking at me like that—and stop laughing."

He lifted his head from Raven's throat and pushed away from her with sudden disdain, spitting out the last swallow of the blood.

"What's wrong, lover?" she murmured, sounding anxious. "There's more. I'll just feed again, and you can have more—or we can go hunting together to bring down fresh kill, baby."

"Shut up!" Carlos stalked away from her, closing the front of his ripped pants, his hands roving over the tears in them and sealing their ragged condition with sheer thought. As he did so, a heavy six-pointed gold ring materialized on his finger. Amazing. After he'd fed, it appeared.

He walked a distance, leaving Raven behind, and tried to remove the ring that was stuck on the fourth digit of his left hand. Unable to get it off, he brought his hands to his head and then he covered his ears with the heel of his palms. African chants, bells, and drums pierced his inner ears. Thick smoke choked him—frankincense, myrrh, roses, garlic, sage—polluted his nose. His breathing became erratic, and he slapped Raven's hand away when it touched his shoulder, and then he moved deeper into the forest, angered that she'd followed him.

Carlos shut his eyes, and tilted his head to the side, trying to focus and hear beyond the drums and flutes. "Leave me," he ordered and turned on her abruptly. "They said they would house and feed you. That was the deal. Now leave me alone!"

"When you want me to come back," she whispered, snarling with disappointment, "all you have to do is call in the night." Her feet became thick, black smoke, and then she disappeared, leaving a sulfur haze where she had stood.

Carlos walked deeper into the woods. In the back of his mind, he could still hear his Lexus's engine running. The smells, the sounds, the sulfur, made him want to retch. He closed his eyes, a new fear coming over him as the awareness took root. He was damned. Heaven help him.

As the last thought echoed in his mind, the nausea suddenly abated. He kept his eyes closed and leaned against the trunk of a nearby tree, his balance unsteady. What was he going to do? What had he committed himself to? They'd tricked him—partly—and there was no turning back.

Damali . . . How would he protect her from himself? He could see her behind his lids. Naked, peaceful, but well guarded by the white light. Carlos dug his claws into the thick redwood bark as an old hunger overtook him with the vision. He breathed in deeply, and the scent now made him nearly insane. Her skin was damp, warm, golden bronzed by the light of the candles. Her face was serene, music and words were in her head and heart. Saliva built in his mouth, and he swallowed it away, the taste of her now on his lips. He could hear her breathing, watched her breasts rise and fall. The sound of her human heartbeat echoed in his skull, and the tiny brown pebbles at the ends of her small, perfect mounds were hardened by wafts of air . . . were that he was the air, brushing them. A shudder consumed him at the thought.

The sensation forced him to tilt his head, and he again inhaled deeply of the scent that was driving his torture. His breaths now frigid pants, he leaned his head back against the tree again, letting go of it to hold her in a phantom embrace—but immediately dropped his arms as the mental touch of her burned him. Fury ripped through him, and he took out a chunk of the tree with one swipe. They'd surrounded her, and not even his thoughts could get through!

"Hey, playa. Frustrating, isn't it?" a voice said from the distance.

Carlos spun and glared at the tall, black-hooded entity. Only gleaming red slits could be seen from a cavern inside the robe— even with his new powers, he couldn't make out a face. This thing had no face, just glowing orbs that hovered beneath its hood. Its crooked, skeletal finger pointed at him in a beckoning motion. It waited patiently for Carlos to respond, like a tall, thin harbinger of death. Were it not so tragic, Carlos would have laughed. This thing was too late. He was already dead.

On guard, Carlos circled the threat and snarled, bearing fangs. "What are you? If you came to collect the living, you're too late. I'm a dead man walking."

The entity laughed. "You have much to learn. . . . Soon you'll even be able to speak the old language."

"Where are you from? Who are you?!"

"From the same place you've been, recently. Hell."

The urge to kill whatever it was before him made Carlos's muscles twitch. "If you stay here, I'll gladly send you back—in pieces."

"Why don't we go together, my new brother?" it hissed. "The Vampire Council of old would like to have a word with you. I'm just a messenger. Let's take your complaint to them."

CHAPTER TWELVE

W HAT FELT like an unbreakable magnetic force held Carlos in place as the thing with no face came closer.

"When the council calls, you have no choice . . . for obviously your choice has already been made. Come. Stay near me as I guide you through the darkness—we must go past the demon realms of levels one through five, down to level six—and we cannot afford to lose you along the way." The thing let out a vicious serpentine hiss, and brought a sickle out from under its robe, wedging it in the earth and pulling a tear in the grass and mud before hiding the huge blade again.

The earth began to vibrate and quake, and a deep fissure opened, uprooting trees, releasing dense plumes of yellow and black smoke until where Carlos stood became a cavern. Instantly he fell as the ground beneath his feet gave way, the dim moonlight above moving farther and farther away—then the overhead fissure sealed itself with he and the entity within it.

Carlos couldn't even yell; the force of the drop was so swift, so brutal. Slimy things grabbed at him, but the bony hand of the entity dug into his arm. He could see the scythe hack at limbs as body parts fell in a blur and screeches and screams echoed behind them.

Then his motion slowed and he came to a crash landing on his feet. The thing beside him glanced up into the darkness above them and shook its head.

"They're getting stronger," it hissed. "Follow me."

Not knowing what else to do, Carlos followed the hooded entity before him, taking note of the soot-blackened rocks that studded the narrow passage. The dank floor and walls were littered with stalagmites and stalactites bearing symbols he could not fathom, along with bones, the smell of acidic bat urine, and the winged vermin that murmured as if they could talk—then screeched in a cacophony of voices that sounded suspiciously like laughter.

The being came to a halt and held up its hand as the heat around them intensified. "After the lava moat, place your hand on the door. My journey ends here."

Carlos looked over a wide embankment that was a red-orange-yellow swirling sea of volcanic heat. Only a thin path of rock extended from where he stood to the other side. The entity pointed to two large doors beyond a thin crag that were of a black shiny rock like marble. Each side of the double doors hosted a huge gold crest with brass fang-bearing, demonic knockers. The ornaments were so realistic that Carlos could swear the heads would bite.

"How do I cross?" he asked the entity warily, looking down at pure liquid Hell. He motioned to the bodies writhing and moaning in the swirling furnace. "I'm not trying to end up like them."

"Nor I," the entity spat. "Those who were not summoned, but were foolish enough to attempt a breech of the Vampire Council Chamber, go there—or, those that did not answer the summons. Step out and cross, or be sucked into the abyss . . . the corridor of perpetual agony is within the sixth realm."

With few options, Carlos stepped out onto the thin path, and only looked back once as it began disintegrating behind him, making him bolt to the other side. He reached the thin ledge full-throttle, his cheek slamming against the thick marble, and in reflex he grabbed at the brass rings. Immediate pain shot through his hands as the knockers sank their fangs into his flesh. A yell of agony came from him as the doors began to open, and he was forced to let one of the knockers go when it retracted from his right hand.

The left door had only opened itself a crack, and he swung his body through the thin margin between a black marble floor and an ocean of heat beyond it. Falling to his knees, he placed both hands on the cool stone, and drew ragged breaths. Adrenaline and fear gripped him. What had he done? Then a low series of hisses made him look up. Almost afraid of what his mind would encounter, Carlos raised his head slowly and stared.

Four pale, black-robed entities faced him, their heads clean-shaven, with no eyebrows or eyelashes, and skin so thin that he could see their blue-green veins. Only one of them wore a peaked, black hat that resembled a Pope's crimson pontiff cap. Carlos's gaze tore around the room where he'd landed. Highly polished black marble was beneath him, a five-point star-shaped table was before him, and its center and each point appeared to be threaded with shining red marble and gold. In the middle of it was a raised, ugly seal circled by cryptic letters that almost seemed to move and swirl around the golden-horned, fanged deity of the crest. Golden goblets sat on the table before each entity and were filled with a ruby-colored liquid. Carlos inhaled. Blood.

Saliva built in his mouth as the scent from their goblets wafted across the room. Pure awe battled with terror inside him as he glanced at the surrounding walls that were of jagged, black granite, and hosted massive, iron-held torches. He gazed up to the ceiling, but there was none. Above him was angry, swirling gray smoke that released intermittent screeches and distant howls. He slowly lowered his gaze. Strange inscriptions also covered the walls. Soon he could see the red veins within the huge table were not fixed. They throbbed, moved, and were fluid . . . more than likely blood.

The entities were seated in what he could only liken to high-backed onyx thrones, each bearing a different crest inlaid in gold. Thick black candles oozed tallow from tall, scorched iron stands that cast an eerie glow to their fanged faces. They sat before him like a row of judges. If his crimes in life were to be sentenced now, he was done for. Their long, willowy fingers were folded before them. But their countenance was calm, as though they were inspecting a bug under a microscope.

Vomit roiled within his chest, and he could not speak to even offer a plea for mercy. He was beyond disoriented. His heart beat erratically, stopped, and his hand immediately clutched his chest. Pain seared his ribs, lungs, and wracked his body with agony as the muscles around the dead organ within him constricted until there was nothing, no pulse. Yet he was still alive. Or still aware? What was he?!

Confusion and despair brought tears to his eyes. He could feel his body begin to cool as a hard shiver snaked through him. His breath now came out with a frosty mist, as though he were outside on a freezing day. He'd obviously been mistaken before. *This* was Hell.

"I see our messenger has been successful in bringing him down from the topside." The words seeped from the entity that bore the peaked hat.

"The demonic realms are getting out of hand, we must rectify this, Mr. Chairman," another intoned.

"It is hard to find good messengers these nights," the counselor agreed with a nod.

"In due time, Counselor, gentlemen. For now, our cargo is safe," the one identified as the chairman said. It smiled. "Do not be disturbed by our appearance," it added in a cool tone, staring at Carlos. "Down here, we do not waste our valuable energy with image projection to assuage delicate human sensibilities. We save that illusion for when we are topside. Down here, there is no need to cater to human deception . . . we are what we are, and if you have been summoned, you are what you are—lost." Then it threw its head back and laughed in a low, evil tone, drawing a round of deep chuckles from the seated group.

Their voices cut into Carlos's senses. Their harsh intent entered his ears and made them hot, feel wet. He brought his palms up to cover them, and came away with his own blood.

"He's new," the chairman said with a wicked grin. "Adjust your frequencies, so he can adequately hear us. We have much to discuss."

The seated entities offered the chairman begrudging glances and then nodded and complied.

"Welcome, Mr. Rivera. Our apologies for the abrupt and inconvenient mode of transportation." The chairman stood and smiled more broadly, showing an impressive set of hooked fangs. He put his withered hands behind his back. "Our elder council members are too valuable to take the topside risk more than once a year. We only come up annually to meet with the gray-zone world leaders that have been compromised. Come. Join our table—we have a proposition for you."

Carlos blinked, still disoriented, as he stared at the four black-robed figures before him. Each was seated at a star point around the table. One throne at one star-point was vacant. The creature called the chairman occupied the furthest point away from him.

He studied the pale, hideous things before him that were in full black regalia threaded with gold. He was mesmerized as he stared at their discolored blood moving within them, and on each of their hands they had a ring like his—but each had a different colored stone in the center of it that matched the long stole sash that hung down the fronts of their robes.

The one at the head of the star-shaped table hissed and began speaking in a brute-sounding tongue that was quick, complex, and totally indecipherable to Carlos. It set off a flurry of conversation between the others, and Carlos found his feet. This was power—consummate, infinite power. He could feel it enter him through the floor, forcing him to his feet. They had done this. Knowledge of that was evident when the eldest-looking one in the group fixed his gaze upon Carlos, and flicked a serpent's tongue, making Carlos feel the acidic lick across the room.

"Step forward!" it commanded.

Slowly Carlos complied until he was directly before the massive table. He could feel an electric current run through the length of his body, and immediately a metallic taste registered in the back of his throat.

"Very good," the head entity murmured, then relaxed and sat down.

"He's strong-willed," one of the others at the table whispered. "Could pose a risk."

"Or a distinctive advantage," the eldest one said, returning his penetrating red gaze to Carlos.

"You have been summoned and offered much. Be prudent," another warned. It had been the counselor who spoke. "Mr. Chairman, you have the floor. The Vampire Council comes to order."

The chairman nodded, then smiled. "Carlos Rivera."

It had whispered Carlos's name like a lover and briefly closed its eyes. An erotic waft of sensation ran through Carlos's body as the entity deeply inhaled. Disturbed beyond reason, Carlos's hands made fists at his side.

"Do not fight it," the one identified as the chairman murmured. "Pleasure goes with the pain. Enjoy the encounter—always."

"Look," Carlos interjected quickly, bringing the horrific thing out of its violating assessment of him. He could feel it touching him, groping him, stroking his skin with an icy palm . . . licking him as though tasting the salt from his skin. "I don't know what the hell is going on, but—"

Screeching laughter rang out in the room as the entities around the table stared at Carlos and shook their ugly heads in unison.

"Mr. Chairman," one said. "Point of order. He's new, but time is of the utmost concern."

The chairman chuckled. "To be sure. My apologies to the council . . . it has just been so long since the topside has sent one such as this."

The bald heads around the table nodded in agreement, flashing powerful incisors with their sinister smiles. Then each picked up a golden goblet and sipped at a thick, dark, ruby liquid. Carlos breathed in, hungering from the scent of fresh blood.

"We are an old race," the chairman said, his glance roving the other entities beside him. "Our council was formed to ensure peace and order, and we are the most powerful of the realms of Hell." He let out his breath slowly, and took his time. "Our methods are subtle, unobtrusive. Our bite is clean, only two puncture wounds to efficiently drain the human body. It avoids unnecessary alarm. It is accomplished with finesse. We leave no scent, no trail. We are highly evolved, and have mastered telepathy—brute force is rarely our way." The chairman sighed, and his expression became almost philosophical. "We blend in with the human world, and relieve it of its more unsavory characters, so in that respect, we perform a vital service."

All Carlos could do was stare and listen as the creature before him spoke. How was murder of innocent people *a service*? There were no words. Hundreds of questions slammed into his brain, but as long as the creatures before him appeared peaceful, he didn't dare move a muscle or ask a question. However, as the thing continued to talk, he became less disoriented, and his senses felt more keened.

"Good . . ." the chairman said and chuckled. "You are beginning to adjust, and let's not quibble over the fleeting merits of a human life." He stretched out his arm and motioned to the seated group. "Let me introduce our Parliamentarian—council member, Senator Vlak . . . an attorney, and once a member of Caesar's Roman inner circle of advisors. He handles our contracts and our worldwide business negotiations with the humans, but has been having great difficulty with our clerical invasions . . . albeit we are pleased with his infiltration of the North American Roman Catholic Church. Pedophilia. Pure genius. Creates such chaos . . . much like the old days of the Inquisition, Counselor."

The one entity designated by the chairman's hand nodded and offered a smug look of satisfaction. "Thank you, Mr. Chairman. I will have forces in the Vatican again soon enough. I urge patience."

"Very well," the chairman crooned and then looked at Carlos once again. "Council Member Chu deals with another delicate balance of topside power . . . he minimizes the light within the dark sector of the yin and yang—he has Asia, and all within the Pacific border. The others"—it pointed with a bony, clawed, hook finger—"have their specialties in war, famine, disease, and human lusts on every continent."

The group smiled as the chairman acknowledged them.

"You are too kind, Council Chairman," one said.

"But our Dark Lord is so eagerly watching the progress of your possible destruction of the Church of the Nativity in Jerusalem. We shall monitor your success closely."

The eldest entity bearing the hat put his hand on another's shoulder as he began walking behind the seated members to denote each one by one.

"European and African council member, who led our transatlantic slave trade, conquest of the Americas . . . I must commend you on the recent topside wars in Rwanda and Bosnia. Oh, yes, and the modern plagues of rampant diseases visited upon impoverished, developing nations that cannot combat them. He does outstanding work. But as you can see, we are still missing a seat at our table, which means a sector goes vulnerable to peace. We cannot have unspoiled virgin territories in our midst—which present unacceptable environmental hazards."

The chairman stopped walking and held Carlos within a riveting stare. "You see, we have a family member on each continent. Each reports to one of our council members. Each helps to keep the chaos of humanity in full strife, which is how we remain undetected. Until recently, all was in balance." The entity smiled at Carlos. "You have a question?" It closed its eyes and opened them slowly. "You are granted permission to speak."

Carlos glanced around and nodded, but kept silent. Fear began to edge away as the slow awareness entered him; he had not been summoned to the slaughter. There was obviously a problem topside, as they called it, and he had been brought to an even higher council than the one in the woods. Otherwise, why was he here and still whole?

Every instinct within him coiled itself tightly, readying his mind to spring at the first hint of opportunity to bargain for his own safety, if not his longevity. Survival was imperative. An alliance had to be forged; it was the way business was done—and again, he was the youngest man brought to the feet of the most powerful.

Readying himself to pose the question, Carlos forced confidence into his voice as his line of vision continued to sweep the group. He watched their expressions, body language, and every detail of their reactions before saying a word. He'd heard them speak. He'd picked up the way they strung the language together. Like being in court before a judge, you had to quickly learn the vocabulary—and one thing for sure, you had to show deference.

"I'm here, then, because you have a proposition for me, as you said upon my arrival, most notable council members?" He was no fool. He wasn't going to allow a lapse in showing respect to get him killed. Carlos told himself to just play it cool, and find out what they wanted. So he waited.

The chairman grinned and poked a long, gnarled finger into his goblet, stirred the contents, and withdrew a bloody digit and sucked it. "I like his style. He learns quickly. He shows the council the required demonstration of submission. He has finesse, unlike our rogue. This is a man who recognizes opportunity and craves power. One must give credit where credit is due—after all, he did offer his soul for power, and thus, must give the Devil his due as well. Interesting."

"He's eager," the attorney murmured. "Impatience can be a good or bad thing for us."

The chairman nodded. "We have a concern, Mr. Rivera," it said in a slow, even voice. "As I stated earlier, our world is a very orderly one, a balance of discretion and strategic aggression.

Twenty years ago—a moment in time, comparatively—one of our most gifted council members went rogue."

"He went after a cleric and turned him," one of the other members snarled in anger.

"Yes," the chairman said in a smooth, even tone. "We may kill clerics, as they understand, as do we, that there is a hereafter. To kill one only adds that soul to *their* side of the spiritual equation. It is even foolhardy to kill them, for they only become stronger in the spirit form, and we try our best to avoid such casualties. But to turn one that had not been seduced properly is heresy in our world. A clerical turn requires that human to willingly give in, barter away his salvation for one of the lusts like power, money, fame, or another carnal desire, which properly compromises the cleric's soul—instead of sending his soul down here from a mere bite *after the fact* . . . which then attracts battalions of warrior angels. Our rogue member did not properly seduce his intended cleric victim; he stunned and bit him, but the cleric never gave his soul of his own volition. There was no willing exchange. As I said, we try to remain very subtle in our tactics."

"Not to mention, this rogue almost ruined *the opportunity*, and almost sent our nations into a return of feudal law," the attorney spat.

"It could have been chaos, so we doomed him to the corridor of unrelenting agony—where he could not feed," another said.

"At his appointed time of incarceration, he was to be tortured in the sea of agony, and then banished to travel the fifth realms and upward—demon country," the one at the far end of the table added. "He was locked from topside, could not feast on fresh human blood. But within days of his sentence, he escaped. We'd left him to perish in the upper levels; demon meat is all that's up there." The thing shivered and spit on the floor with disgust. "Yet the punishment was never exacted. Providence unlocked his prison."

"And he was wise and formed an alliance," the chairman corrected. "He was always a brilliant military strategist, I would have been disappointed if he'd done less. We must offer credit, where credit is due." The chairman sighed and shook his head. "Brilliance gone rogue, however, is dangerous in any empire. He must be eliminated. We cannot sustain such variable risks to our way of life."

Before he could censure himself, a question had rushed past Carlos's lips. "Why don't you just send a messenger to whack him?" Carlos waited as the group became still again and their focus went to the chairman. He instantly realized that he'd spoken out of order, and fear crystallized in his veins as the vampires gave him a disapproving glare.

"Our rogue got out under the most fortuitous circumstances," the chairman finally chuckled, making Carlos relax a bit. The old vampire shook his head and then laughed with a bored sigh. "Stroke of luck, mixed with a stroke of pure genius." The entity looked at Carlos with an open, direct gaze. "See for yourself," it murmured. "Nuit killed a cleric and turned him twenty years ago. We immediately sealed his lair . . . but the man's wife, a church woman of all things, went to Nuit's mansion assuming her husband was having an affair, and did a ritual that an old, jealous witch had given her."

At the mention of Nuit's name, Carlos's eyes locked with the chairman's. As he gazed at him, the chairman's eyes siphoned breath from Carlos's body. He felt like he was moving into the image that was cascading before him. Suddenly, he was no longer witnessing the image; he was inside the scene, feeling it all. The illusion made him experience the brief sensation of floating as in a dream. Then the dream structure around him became solid. He could see the past as though it were the present. He was in a mansion, walking with a beautiful, but frightened, woman down a flight of basement stairs. She looked so much like Damali that it made his lungs hurt for her.

He could smell her perspiration; he could feel her anger driving her beyond her fears. He reached out his finger and touched the flame of her black candle and it burned him. This was real.

He watched her make a five-pointed star symbol on the dirt floor, saw her cast herbs, watched her lips move. He oddly understood the language. Bile rose in his throat as her hatred for her husband's lover grew. He could see above and below her. The woman's feet were planted on the dirt floor just above Nuit's sealed coffin. He could see a pair of glowing eyes open within the casket. The woman's voice was getting louder, the floor began to give way, and she cried out. Tears streamed down her face, and something else, not Nuit, but equally hideous, began swirling in an awful black cloud that came up from the dirt, toppling wine racks, obliterating shelves, unearthing Nuit and the casket at the same time. The woman covered her face as shards of glass from broken bottles exploded toward her, splinters of wood scored her arms and stuck in her hair. She was shrieking as two forms appeared.

Carlos was panting as the vision abruptly ended. Yet his mind was still sensing images, putting together the details, fitting the jigsaw puzzle together. He gaped at the chairman, who nodded with a wise smile. "Her husband was hiding his vampire hunting activities from her to protect her," Carlos choked.

He looked at the council and shut his eyes tightly. The images would not stop careening inside his skull.

"Yes," the chairman murmured. "Compelling drama, isn't it?

Lesson number one: dissolve the image; get it out of your system once you've tasted it. Remember that."

"She was pregnant when it began." Nausea and anger from the woman's hurt still laced his system as Carlos kept talking. He had to get it out, to say it out loud, lest it stay in his mind. The more he talked, the dimmer the images became, and the less he felt the woman's agony. "Her husband's lies that he was with parishioners got found out. All the people he'd claimed to be with, when she checked, hadn't seen him. The first clue came as an accident, and some people began acting strangely, which made her start digging."

"Correct," the counselor said in a weary tone. "Hurry. Purge, so we can get to the matter at hand."

Carlos shook his head. "She had the baby, and one night she saw a man, Nuit, seduce her husband in their living room. She was upstairs, the child had awakened, she heard what she thought were lovers . . . Nuit carried her husband out the door in his arms to finish the bite—her husband didn't seem to resist, and she made assumptions. . . . The minister disappeared for three days. She found an address. His car was parked at Nuit's house. She went there on the third night." He wiped at the trickle of sweat that had run down his temples. "She didn't know what she was walking into."

The chairman sighed. "The foolish woman did not understand that what was seducing her husband was a master vampire. The pastor had stupidly gone into a master's lair alone during the day, leaving a trail, which Nuit later followed. The cleric's penchant for heroics, and not wanting to have another of his human folk hurt, allowed him to be led there on a suicide mission." The chairman drew a deep inhale and let it out slowly as though garnering patience. "Alas, his wife thought her husband was having a male liaison." Now it laughed. "That was before such things were in vogue, so the poor woman lost her mind and sought out an old hag to work roots, of all things, on the situation. Country bumpkins, spare us all!"

Carlos nodded. "She went in there with vengeance in her soul, and to get her man back."

"Correct. We've dealt with the root worker long ago. That is of no consequence. But what is perilous is the fact that, by her giving the dark ritual to the minister's wife, our seal on Nuit was compromised. The wife released a revenge demon right above a master vampire's crypt—*in his lair*. Unheard of." The chairman's laughter immediately dissipated as he stood again and began to nervously pace.

"Do you have any idea of the irony of this event?" The chairman paused, looked at Carlos, and resumed his complaint. "We *never* cohabit with demons. It is unthinkable. They are locked to locations—which we avidly avoid. They, unlike us, can only be summoned by an entity possessing a soul, which we do not have. Hence, those compromised humans within the dark arts are very careful to never commingle them with us—they perform their rituals elsewhere, and all remains in balance."

Suddenly the chairman whirled on Carlos and slammed his clenched fist against the table. The throbbing veins within it splashed blood against his fist. "*A church woman*—an innocent released Fallon Nuit *and* a revenge demon—stupid bitch! If we didn't know better, we'd swear that the warrior angels had a hand in this atrocity! And because she knew nothing of the dark arts, she did this . . . this . . . *ritual* without understanding the ramifications. Fool!"

"But—"

"Listen!" the chairman bellowed, cutting off Carlos's unspoken question. "Nuit bit her, and half turned her in his lair. He was overconfident, and wanted her to suffer slowly while he and the demon made plans. The demon would get to have free access to movement within what Nuit calls *the Minion*—his own made, now rogue vampires . . . humans who have willingly traded their souls for something they want, which also now bear an ugly signature bite like a revenge demon, an Amanthra. The legions of Amanthras merged with Nuit's Minion, using the vampire bodies as hosts to freely move about unbound by locations, and have thus created a hybrid. That possession demon type is prevalent, as it lurks just below the surface and is drawn by human emotions of jealousy, vengeance, and blind anger. Those that could not find a vampire host, await more vampires to join Nuit's faction to inhabit.

"It is an ugly, *ugly* demon—because it has no finesse, no subtlety, and is not strategic, it acts without thinking, something that is totally contrary to our highly evolved vampire species. We do not consort with any demons, but especially not *that one*." The chairman's breaths were now coming in short bursts of fury as it circled the table. "Nuit got released from our prison and was offered protection from our hunters. The Amanthras allow him to use their tunnels; they get to use his bodies. That was the barter."

Carlos stared at the chairman, then let his gaze slowly appraise the concerned expressions of each powerful council member. This was some heavy shit. . . .

The counselor eyed Carlos. "*An innocent* performed the ceremony, and she still had purity of heart . . . her husband, who still loved her, heard past Nuit's call, came to her in that basement, and interrupted Nuit before he could finish the wife off. Nuit struggled with the minister, and committed the second grievous act in our world. He picked up a piece of wood from the shelving and drove a stake into the heart of his own second-generation made vampire!"

A collective shiver went through the group.

"He turned *and* killed a cleric," the chairman stated, breathing heavily. "The woman, realizing what she was about to turn into herself, and that before long she'd die from rapid blood loss, committed suicide with a prayer on her lips and love in her heart for her infant child."

"A baby girl," the counselor whispered. "*Neteru*. A vampire huntress. . . ."

For a moment, no one spoke. The council members passed nervous glances among them. Finally unable to stem his roiling curiosity, a question formed in Carlos's mind without censure. He watched as the group seized upon it.

"Other humans rushed to the scene and tried to contain what they thought was a demon, but their incantations didn't work, because the alliance had been formed. The bite signature on the wife and the way the husband's body had been mangled in the struggle, threw them off . . . how would they know a hybrid had been created? They never staked Nuit—they used a ritual— which had no effect on a vampire. The one Amanthra within Nuit perished, but as I said, they have legions. Another simply took its place. Nuit disappeared from the surface and bided his time . . . trying to locate the Neteru. And another human seer— a younger one, female—secreted the baby away. We have been looking for that infant for twenty years." The chairman sat down heavily in his throne and took a deep swig from his goblet.

"We have also been searching for a way to stop Nuit," the counselor said in a distant voice. "But he is too strong, once having a power seat at our table. Our brethren outside his marked territory cannot get close enough to him to do the hit. With his alliance, he can now travel freely using the demon realm's high-speed tunnels near the surface, something they have province over which gives them access to the gray zone to possess bodies, enter households, and claim souls. Those areas in levels one through five are heavily fortified.

"Our portals are few, since we are so deep and close to our Dark Lord. Only our lairs give us access to the topside—and any lair not in the Minion is heavily watched by the Amanthras to be sure we do not breech their tunnels. His lair is impenetrable by our forces, as the Amanthras far outnumber us and guard it day and night—they are impervious to sunlight, our one evolutionary flaw. Topside, Nuit is like a phantom. His senses are keen; he is an old vampire with many skills. The moment we attempt an abduction, Nuit vanishes into an Amanthra portal."

The chairman glanced at the counselor. "We are at the top of the food chain—and our human helpers above both feed and protect us . . . it is, shall we say, a symbiotic relationship. But even they cannot get to a master's lair, past demonic protection in those numbers." The chairman paused. "On your way out, our messenger will show you the levels of Hell—just so you can familiarize yourself with the new environment . . . unless you'd care to stay?"

The others around the table nodded and murmured. Carlos sensed a thinly veiled threat. Hmmm . . . this was becoming interesting.

The attorney gained a nod from the chairman and stood. "Your maker, the head of your bloodline, has not only violated our basic policies, but he's been on a dangerous feeding frenzy above."

Carlos stared at the counselor, whose eyes immediately offered the truth; Fallon Nuit had been the one to take out his family. He'd been double-crossed. Vengeance slithered through him. Raven had to be the one that did Alejandro and the others. He'd seen her work. He'd eaten from her veins and had fucked her—now he could feel her presence as he witnessed how she'd murdered his brother and posse in the chairman's knowing gaze. The attorney nodded as soon as the thought of Nuit's deceit crossed Carlos's mind. He could feel his brother's death and hear his screams within his head. Tears of bitterness rose to Carlos's eyes and burned away. Fallon Nuit would pay.

"Yes. You catch on quickly. So, we have a proposition for you that will aid us in capturing Fallon Nuit, and will allow you to avenge your family's demise."

"What comes with this proposition?"

"Oh," the attorney smiled. "What's in it for you?"

The council members glanced at each other, seeming amused as they murmured, for a moment, among themselves.

"Sit in Nuit's chair," the head of the council ordered, holding out a hand toward a high-backed black throne.

Taking his time, Carlos complied and sat down, but the sensation of power was so overwhelming that it made him shudder with devastating ecstasy. He had to close his eyes to suffer the wanton pleasure of it. Images, knowledge, history, languages entered his skull so quickly that he thought it would fracture. Information he'd never dared to conceive slammed into his cranium, made his tightly shut lids flutter. A moan escaped his lips as he writhed in the bath of power and knowledge.

"Awesome, isn't it?" he heard the chairman say.

"Yes," Carlos whispered.

"Let the dark energy fill you. All of this could be yours, if we can come to terms. We don't offer this to every made brother . . . never to a second. If we allow you to keep it, you will instantly become a master."

Carlos leaned his head back and behind his lids he could see the past fate of nations that had risen. Empires and armies marched into armed conflict. Near delirium, his hands felt electrified and his ears buzzed. Blood was in his mouth. Tears of pleasure rolled down his cheeks. He felt on the brink of orgasm. He cried out from the sheer pleasure of it all.

"Stand," the chairman ordered, his harsh tone and steely gaze bringing Carlos around. Immediately the power ebbed and the throne went dead.

As soon as Carlos stood, he could feel his knees buckle. "What do you want?" His question came out on a weak whisper, his gaze still affixed to the throne.

"You were turned immediately—which is not our normal policy. It was a risk we took to snatch your spirit in the death throes, to essentially hijack it while Nuit was siphoning you. There was a split-second window of opportunity caused by your internal struggle and, ironically, the slowness of your soul's descent because of, all things, a prayer and a crucifix you still had on your body. An interesting paradox. However, this poses a risk to beginning another all-out war with the other realms above, as it temporarily violates our ecosystem. But, desperate times called for desperate measures."

Dazed, Carlos could barely focus his attention on what he was being told. The chair he'd just sat in was whispering to him, calling him, and he wanted more of what it contained.

The counselor appraised him hard; his impatient glare finally forcing Carlos to look at him. "When a vampire delivers a bite, according to supernatural law, it takes three eves before the dark power enters the victim to raise it and mark it into an existing territory. However, Nuit has been running amuck. We normally only allow a certain number of second-generation bites. Only masters can come below—the lesser vampires . . . second and third generations, remain topside, six feet under in graves, or in dark hiding places. We have to keep the territories within pragmatic growth parameters. Second and third generations must kill the victims, then feed. No turns are allowed, as it will make the humans grow wary . . . much like the natural order of things, where wolves populate more slowly than deer, the supernatural ecosystem must be kept in balance. Nuit has violated even that basic principle."

"Yes," the chairman concurred. "Our way keeps our numbers low enough to avoid detection, and the power within the individual vampire family lines diffuse enough to disallow a potential coup. We cannot go back to the old way before the Vampire Council was formed." The chairman folded his hands in front of him on the table and leveled his gaze at Carlos. "You have been spared, and made immediately—and given immunity to Nuit. You are his equal. You are a master . . . should you accept our proposition."

"We'll break the hold on Nuit's ring," one creature near the chairman said in a hissing whisper. "You can remove Nuit's crest at will, but it is advisable that you wear it, lest he become suspicious. Keep it concealed from human eyes as well. Simply project the thought, and it will not be seen."

"All right," Carlos said breathing hard, looking at his hand and extending it to them, "but I still don't understand what that has to do with me. Why not use an older vamp? You could have easily dispatched any of them."

"In Nuit's haste, he bit a guardian's child, mistaking it for a Neteru—and made Raven, after his escape. A female. She, a second-generation vampire, has been making thirds. We know this because each new vampire is entered on our docket and is registered, just like every vampire slain is registered. He overstepped his bounds, topside, in search of the millennium Neteru. We could not let the older vampires in the territories know about the extent of the breech, or what was actually driving Nuit, because each would have searched for the vessel that was previously believed to be mere myth." The chairman's stare raked

Carlos's mind. "The millennium bridge vampire huntress is no legend. She exists. But our regional masters do not need to know this information."

Incredulous, Carlos tried to get words to form a simple question that might answer the hundreds of questions stabbing into his brain. "A millennium bridge vampire huntress?"

"It is a female human vessel that is made by the heavens once every thousand years. These warriors are deadly to our kind in particular, and they also exact a heavy toll of losses on the demon realms as well. *Neterus are rare.* She has a ripening time where her womb can either bear another slayer, a guardian, or a daywalker—one of our vampire seed that is impervious to light, and that can breed. At any other time, we can only breed through the bite. However, daywalkers have the ability to impregnate . . . their seed is not dead. This Neteru's presence was made known to us by the alignment of the planets. Only high-ranking council members like those you see currently seated know such information. Nuit used his seat at our table to gain access to our information vaults and crafted his own rogue plan."

Carlos allowed his gaze to settle on the chairman. "But I still don't understand—"

"As above, so below," the attorney said, jerking Carlos's attention toward him. "The vampire empire is held together by an evolving, but fragile thread. Each line master hungers for power, but to date, none have been so bold as to challenge this council. We needed an unregistered new blood. You were dark enough from your life, had been marked as a member of the Minion . . . when you were bitten we seized the opportunity. Nuit's impatience, no doubt from his demon influences running through his system, led him to make a fatal mistake. You're a hybrid, but with a third element running through your veins now—*ours.*"

Carlos looked at the attorney hard.

"You died with a prayer of sacrilege in your heart." The thing shook his gruesome head. "And *a crucifix* on your person?" The beast had an expression of total disdain. "*A crucifix*—a direct channel conductor to the realms above, anointed, christened on a human *baby*, an innocent, and still on the personage selected by a master to turn? Unheard of. We *do not* conduct business that way! This is of the new breed—no sense of decorum, which is why we are at war with this heresy. I am offended beyond description. This Vampire Council is deeply, irrevocably offended!" The counselor spat, and the others growled their agreed discontent.

Now Carlos stared at the chairman. How had his call to God—

"Not here! Not even in your thoughts!" the chairman bellowed, setting off a round of hisses at the table. "Never think of He who shall remain nameless in our realm."

"All right, all right," Carlos stated quickly. "I'm new. My bad."

The chairman paced behind the table, agitated. "You want to bring upon the end of our empire? Do you want our Dark Lord to come up from the last realm to begin an inquiry? Are you mad?" Breathing hard, the chairman wiped his forehead and looked at the group. "We must educate him quickly. He has no concept of the potential wrath."

"Who is the huntress?" Carlos glanced around the table, trying to read them but came away with no image. Instinctively he knew they'd locked him out of their minds as they conferred among themselves for a moment, intermittently speaking loud enough for him to hear scattered fragments of their conversation. But he would chill. And *no*, he didn't want to deal with, or have a run-in with the Dark Lord. Common sense took over. His conceding thought seemed to make the tension in their bodies drain away.

"Our territories are already running rampant with rumors. The demons no doubt have fueled the dissent. Their alliance with Nuit gives them leverage to become transformed into us, but above us, if the vessel is filled . . ."

"Yes," the attorney agreed, speaking to a council member beside him. "Rivera's prayer sacrilege and carrying *that thing* in his pocket—I can't even say it—gave us a slight window of opportunity. Nuit's full venom could not take root." He looked up at Carlos. "We were able to circumvent Nuit's full authority over you and give you enough strength in the moment in between while you fell. But in three eves of moonlight, the very thing that opened you to the gray zone of choice, will close. If you die to us, you will awaken to him—and he will not be pleased with you. Need I say more?"

"And?" An eerie confidence filled Carlos. Yes, this was indeed becoming interesting.

"And," the attorney said quickly, "although Nuit made you, we dispatched a messenger immediately to collect you, just like we immediately turned you—as well as gave you access to a knowledge and power throne. In a few hours, you will adapt in mental capacity as a master vampire . . . we won't have to tell you things, you'll know. This is another indication of our generosity. A good-faith offer, and a vital weapon you'll need to deceive Nuit and get past guardian forces to bring us the Neteru."

"But if all you want is some chick, then another master vampire could have—"

"No," the attorney spat. "Not possible."

"You haven't told me her—"

The chairman smiled. "We know." He took papers from the attorney and slid them across the table toward Carlos. "We have a time-frame issue. Our council gave you all the powers of a master so you could combat a master—an immediate turn without the wait."

"He has to do it before the vessel ripens with ova," an ancient council member whispered from a far point on the table. "We only have a few eves. Her twenty-first birthday approaches."

"If he does not comply, all five of us, if we count in Rivera, will not be able to collectively fill the vessel—offering us a share of equal power. Nuit will have her to himself." Another member of the council made a tent with his hands before him and stared at the counselor.

The attorney pointed to the papers. "Sign."

Carlos looked up. "Why?"

The council members leaned in toward each other and conferred, then assessed him. It was also becoming apparent, and quite intriguing that, since he'd sat in the chair and some time had elapsed during the tense meeting, they now seemed to only have the ability to pick up part of his thoughts, not all of them. Maybe it was the only thing that Nuit's double-cross had afforded him. A modest advantage. It was in that moment that Carlos became clear that while they had *almost* infinite power, he still had a few aces in his hand. The problem was, he didn't exactly know what the sum total of his leverage entailed.

"You drive a hard bargain, Rivera," the attorney finally said through his teeth.

"Tell him," the chairman ordered. "We are losing precious moonlight."

Carlos cocked his head to the side in confusion. Again, the mention of a woman. He remembered Nuit's unnamed request.

"Bring us Damali Richards," the attorney whispered.

A part of Carlos froze, but he kept his exterior cool. As the vampires bickered among themselves, he could feel their claw-hold on his mind recede. Damali? A Neteru? A freakin' vampire huntress? In the midst of all of this? The only woman that had ever made him feel? Panic aligned itself with anger and remorse. No. They couldn't have another one of the people he loved. But there was only one way to play this. He had to be strategic and stay business-cold.

"Let me ask you gentlemen a simple question," Carlos said, now pacing slowly in front of the table with his hands behind his back, watching their faces. "Why couldn't you send a messenger for her, or why couldn't Nuit—who is formidable topside? Anyone with power could go get her, correct? In fact, when Nuit told me to bring him a woman, he didn't name her."

The chairman let out a long, death-stench breath. "None of us, not even the topside clerics, ever know when a female Neteru will be born. But, Nuit was the protégé of a true legendary member of our legions, Dracula. Nuit's mentor uncovered a partial scent years back—he had only followed the trail to uncover a carrier of the recessive gene, not the actual vessel. The Neteru wasn't even born, yet. But Dracula was on the trail of the human line that might produce her. His quest also became his demise—but he was from the era prior to the Vampire Council's formation. This madness was passed on to Nuit, the master that was made from Dracula's line . . . we just never suspected Dracula's madness would have been passed. Our error in judgment, indeed."

The counselor cut in upon the chairman's glance. "For years since Dracula's termination, Nuit had secretly hunted for the Neteru his mentor had foretold—we all believed it to be legend. We did not see evidence of a Neteru having been made in the millennium in which Dracula searched . . . until the stars aligned in May."

Carlos smiled. "Mr. Chairman, Mr. Counselor, Council, forgive me, but you still have not answered my question. Why not send in your forces to bring her in, since you've now identified her? Why me?"

The chairman hissed and leaned forward in an open threat. "After the planets aligned we sent out topside sniffers—third and fourth generations too weak to fulfill the prophecy alone!" He banged his fist on the table again, making it quake and bleed onto the floor with his rage.

"Don't you understand by now how valuable a Neteru is to our realm?" The attorney walked around the table to stand before Carlos with the papers in his hand as he continued his snarling argument.

"For centuries we had been locked in feudal struggles within the vampire nation. Each territory battling for control of the other, and adding to their domains with unregistered turns. The Vampire Council was formed to bring order—lest our own anarchy propel humans to hunt us to extinction. Fear of demons and vampires and ghosts, what they term monsters, draws the humans to hallowed ground in panic, strengthens the houses of worship."

Another council member was on his feet. "We needed the humans to go into a false malaise of spiritual apathy. If our empires did not form an alliance and cease battling, the humans would have redoubled their faiths—giving over too many souls to the light. One redeemed sinner is worth the soul-weight of one hundred holy men, and one compromised holy man is worth the soul-weight of one hundred sinners. This has been the equation of the struggle between darkness and the light since the dawn of time, when our Master fell from Grace. Each time their side garners one of ours, we must replace it with one of theirs, or more. Our Dark Lord was very, very displeased that our regional activities were sending people into the arms of faith in droves—it was come together or perish. Thus, the only logical alternative."

Now both beasts were circling him, and Carlos remained very, very still. Even the chairman and the fourth council member had stood slowly and leaned forward from behind the giant marble pentagram. Carlos eyed them as they moved, their robes wafting behind them as they walked. The swishing sounds from their black velvet robes had a hypnotic effect, and he understood how close he was to the edge of this delicate negotiation.

"If any one master vampire were to know where to track the scent of a ripening Neteru, and find her to use her as his vessel, then he would become a singular empire ruler. The new emperor could shift the balance of council power," the attorney pressed on. "Power would concentrate, and not be diffused. That is dangerous to order."

The second council member hissed, his eyes going to slits. "That ruler would have sanction over us. Only his territories would prosper, and all others would become second-class citizens—Nuit would never state her name in front of his second generation, as they might attempt a coup, like he is attempting now. He violated the council oath. We were to all simultaneously mount her through temporary incorporation in one virile body, and send our collective seed to produce one heir from many; we would all be the new heir's master, thus assuring the equal distribution of power amongst all territories."

Carlos studied his fingernails and began cleaning flesh, dirt, and tree bark from under them in a nonchalant gesture, then sighed. "Interesting history. But, I will ask again. Why didn't you send one of your own to claim her?"

The two entities walked away from him in frustration and returned to their seats. The chairman sat down with the fourth council member, as the attorney cast the papers on the table as he passed.

"We couldn't get to her," the chairman muttered, seething. "She's a Neteru, and protected by prayers and a team of guardians. She is at the core of a trinity of formidable forces. A ring of guardians, the Templars, the warrior angels." The chairman's eyes had narrowed at the mention of angels and he'd growled, shaking his head.

Carlos looked up and held the red glowing eyes in a lethal stare. "And Nuit?"

The members at the council table shook their heads.

"The only one who can get to her in thought projection, or close enough for an abduction, is someone she wants . . . someone she trusts, someone that can make her drop her guard and come to him," the attorney retorted, drawing a series of threatening hisses from the table.

"But even with an abduction," the chairman warned, "when she gives herself, it must be of her own free will, or the vampire seed might not take root in her womb. That is the only way Neteru souls are kidnapped. Her will must be in alignment with the ritual. This is what Nuit never knew. We discovered his plan before he fully dredged our knowledge chambers. Unless she is seduced, the vampire seed within her won't harvest. The Neteru physiology, combined with an iron will and a strong spiritual nature, fights off an unwanted inhabitant or possession like a virus. This is why they are impervious to a bite, once fully mature. We must get to her before she crosses over."

The attorney's eyes searched Carlos's with desperation. "We need someone to get to her whom she will freely surrender to— someone who can corrupt her so that she will subject herself to the ritual. If she refuses . . . we'll need someone to kill her. We cannot allow a Neteru, young enough to cross both millennia, to begin to produce more Neterus. It's a chance we get only once every thousand years, but the realms of Heaven haven't made females in a very long time. And there's *never* been any huntress to bridge a millennium like this . . . so dangerous with the Armageddon so near."

"Hmmm. . . ." Carlos nodded. "I have seen her in my dreams recently." He watched the seated council erupt in excitement, communicating in the foreign language that he was starting to understand. He knew he had to get them to a point of trust, frenzy for the product, in order to buy him leverage, room to maneuver.

"Her scent is intoxicating," Carlos murmured, teasing them with the description—and using their own wiles against them. He closed his eyes and brought Damali to his mind, and deeply inhaled and shivered, sending a collective shiver through the group.

"We haven't had a female Neteru grace the blue planet in the gray zone of choice in more than three thousand years," the chairman breathed out. "Not since Kemetian times in what is now referred to as Egypt. Prior to that, we located one in the Nubian empire. These female Neterus were so strong we had to literally destroy human empires to eradicate their lines, which still flourish! The recessive gene is so strong that it floats amongst the human population, hiding in human bloodlines, waiting for an anointment above to be released. None of us ever know exactly when a Neteru might be created by *them*."

Carlos opened his eyes and snatched the vision from them. "Talk to me, *hombre*. What's in it for me, and what assurances do I have that if I deliver her, I won't get whacked?"

The group fell silent.

"It's in your contract," the attorney said coolly, and then collected the papers and pushed them forward again, laying a quill pen dipped in blood from his goblet beside it.

Carlos shook his head. "It's written in a language I can't yet understand—and it's got a lot of fine print."

"You have three days to bring her to us, or we take away your immediate turn!" Again, the chairman was on his feet. "Let him feel our withdrawal of protection, since he apparently doesn't appreciate our offering!"

Instantly, hunger tore through Carlos's abdomen, and the pain of Nuit's bite began to sizzle and burn. The agony made him cry out and drop to his knees.

"Let him hear his master's call—which we have cloaked from him!"

An earsplitting decibel sounded inside Carlos's head that made him yell and hold the sides of his head. He could see Nuit's eyes behind his lids, and the urge to go to him was so great that it made him stand. Then, just as quickly, it was gone.

"Do you see what we have spared you from?" the attorney murmured in an even tone. "In three moonlights, or less I believe, your brother, your cousin, and your best friends will be under Nuit's siren call. They will go home, first, to feed—to their mothers, dear Juanita . . . an old lover of yours . . . and to your mother, your grandmother, and all your friends."

Satisfied that Carlos had been duly reprimanded, the chairman sighed, his tone weary. "This feeding will fan out to consume all in your immediate family until it is exhausted, and then it will continue in concentric rings. While the dilution of the fourth-generation bite will not produce more vampires, it will produce madness, and human family members that are predators, cannibals, serial killers, and the like. This is the nature of the fourth and weaker vampire generations, which will beget a fifth, and then a sixth, and so on—we populate with an exponential fury, unless we self-contain. Think about it. This is what Nuit has visited upon your human family, as well as upon your new vampire family. All we ask for is one human girl to stop this carnage."

Breathing hard, Carlos held on to the edge of the council table for support and then wiped his brow. "I want to cut a deal."

"We have already given you extreme latitude before this council table," the chairman said in a bored voice, the threat fully disclosed in it.

"You want this Neteru, you talk to me. I can get you in, or you can let another thousand years pass. I could go to Nuit, kill off my family to save their souls before he does them, and suffer the consequences until he's pissed off enough to stake me him-self—or we can cut a deal."

The group exchanged nervous glances with each other and then the chairman spoke. "Your proposal?"

"Number one," Carlos huffed, slowly regaining his compo-sure as the pain abated. "I need to be able to move between Nuit's camp and this one undetected. Keep his monitoring blind to my activities. Let me project only those images I want him to see, undetected."

The chairman nodded. "This makes sense, and is of value to our council."

"Okay," Carlos said, his voice gaining strength. "I want to put my brother and my boys down. And I want the rest of my undead family marked as off-limits."

The seated members again erupted with dissention at the re-quest.

"Order, order," the Parliamentarian shouted. "A seal of off-limits for unclaimed humans is easy. But we do not easily put down second or third generations, unless you want your own lieutenants? That is understandable, but your closest allies in life not coming under you, once Nuit is terminated, gives us pause. Why?"

Carlos glanced around nervously. He could not divulge that he wanted his brother's and his friend's souls saved. But a lie came to his lips quickly. "I don't want anyone in my inner circle possessed by an Amanthra."

"You propose to wipe out all of Nuit's made vampires, his Minion, too?" The attorney glanced at the group. "Ambitious. Very ambitious. We may have made a correct choice." He returned his attention to Carlos. "We generally never leave territory open—which is also why we didn't eliminate Nuit until we had a replacement. But you make a valid point. The entire Nuit line, the Minion, has been polluted. We can give you blank lines within his registry to fill. As you kill one of his, you can replace it with one of yours, until the line is purged. Feed well."

"Ruthless. Ambitious. I like it." The chairman nodded. "So be it. If you come with us, you take Nuit's territory, rebuild at will, and you will also get one-sixth of the Neteru vessel heritage. If we are able to compromise the Neteru, her heir will be a daywalker—which will produce more daywalkers. One-sixth of that number will come under your leadership."

"She's beautiful," Carlos murmured, using the mere mention of the Neteru to buy time. "And I owe Nuit. He'll pay."

"Yes. Vengeance is such a driving force."

Carlos nodded.

"Then, you're with us?"

He picked up the papers, but left the pen, and skimmed the documents he couldn't read. "I want a translation. I want to see my requests in blood—especially the part about me being the one to enter the slayer for the group. I also want to sign it just before my delivery of her to you, and after I have had a chance to peruse the fine print. I want amnesty from the agony pit—if Nuit does me first. But know that I will hunt that bastard down for the return of the double-cross . . . it's personal, and it ain't business between him and me. I want to be the one to take him out. And this discussion will be considered a verbal contract."

The attorney leaned in to the chairman. A low murmur ensued and then both beasts parted.

"We don't like verbal commitments—but given the pressure of time, and the unusual circumstances of all of this, plus your palpable hatred of Nuit—a wondrous emotion—we are willing to seal the bond the old-fashioned way." The attorney accepted the papers back from Carlos. "I will have new documents drawn up in human blood, forthwith."

Carlos nodded. "I'll need a layout of his lair and the demon realms so I can know how he moves."

"We'll send it by messenger," the chairman said with an uneasy smile. "You ask for difficult information, however. We know some of it, but not all. But we will give you a tour of Hell before you go."

"Send what you have then," Carlos said, turning to leave. "And I'll need an escort to the topside."

The chairman nodded. "Then, we have an agreement?"

Without turning fully around, Carlos cut a sharp glance at the group. "I will off Nuit, and I will find the Neteru," he intoned flatly.

The group hissed its acceptance.

THE LEGENDS CONTINUE WITH

The AWAKENING

A VAMPIRE HUNTRESS LEGEND

TAKE A SNEAK PEEK

In order to cause the enemy to come of their own volition, extend some [apparent] profit. In order to prevent the enemy from coming forth, show them [the potential] harm.

—Sun-tzu, *The Art of War*

TIME WAS of the essence. He stood outside Damali's compound on the dark side of the road and willed the phone inside to ring. A male voice answered, and sounded weary.

"It's Carlos. I need to speak to Damali."

In the background, beyond the mute option that had been engaged, he could hear mild pandemonium break out as she came to the phone.

"Carlos, where are you?"

He looked down at his T-shirt and sealed the gunshot hole in it, then glanced at his hand, dissolving the image of Nuit's ring. "Close by. I want to take you up on that invitation to come in. There's a lot going on, and I have some info."

"We can come get you . . . uh . . ."

"Tell the team I am not being followed—but I do need you to kill the exterior lights for a minute so I can come in."

She'd put her hand over the receiver, and then had hit the mute button again. An argument was underway. He let out his breath hard. Time was ticking, and tonight would be the last night he could really help her. He called her in his head. Get back on the phone.

"We don't turn off the lights," she said quietly.

282 L. A. BANKS

His mind wrestled with the obstacle, trying to work around her team's resistance. "Tell them to lower their guard—a knight of Templar visited me, and left the newspaper. I need to get info to the group for tomorrow. He gave me some maps that I didn't understand."

She paused, and then began a flurry of words back to her group. Good.

"Just ten minutes, then I'm out—I have other pressing business going on in the streets. Tell them, okay?"

Her hand covered the phone and he could hear her battle for him. She didn't even hit the mute this time. Real good. The knight hadn't lied.

He closed his eyes, already invited, just blocked by the damned contraptions they had everywhere. He was not going through the door's double-lock process—he'd fry. He hoped that nobody would panic and hit the hall sprinklers. This was bullshit. But on the other hand, he was glad she was so well fortified . . . it just bothered him that, at the moment, he was on the other side of her world.

"Tell them," he added, slowly, "not to blast me when I come through the door. I've got maps that will burn in the ultraviolet light, the knight said—now I don't know what the hell he was talking about, but—"

"Bring them in. We won't flash you."

He could hear the team murmur agreement, and he relaxed as the lights around the compound went out. But he hesitated for a moment, scanning the terrain to be sure he'd be the only guest, while another part of him became mildly concerned. *Baby, do not panic and toast a brother—cool? Everybody just chill, no lights, crossbows down, everybody just take it easy.*

Carlos kept the mantra in his mind as he crossed the road, hoping that the lights wouldn't suddenly come up. But when he reached the door, Damali and two of her male crew were there. She was unarmed; they weren't. But he crossed the threshold nonetheless, received a quick hug from her in the dark, and immediately she pulled away from him and led him to the inner rooms with two henchmen at his back.

The hug had destabilized him a bit, but he shook it off. Had to stay focused. This was business. It was about her safety. But in the dark . . . wow. Okay. Think.

Slightly taken aback, he surveyed the extensive weapons room as an Asian guy at the computer panels flipped a master switch and he could feel the entire compound heat up like it was a tin can in a microwave. This, he hadn't anticipated.

"Shabazz—"

"Save the intro, Damali. Me and Carlos know each other, or should I say, we remember each other. Lotta guys in the neighborhood did time for workin' with him, or got shot."

Carlos nodded to Shabazz. What could he say? There was no defense. It was what it was.

Damali let her breath out hard and extended her arm, moving it slowly as it swept the room. "Rider, J.L., Dan, Big Mike, Marlene, Jose is sick—but will recover. There. You met everybody, everybody, meet Carlos—or re-meet him, whateva. The man came to help. So chill."

"Speak," the one pointed out as Big Mike said. "Now."

"Wait," the tall guy with spiked hair interjected. "A formality. My name's Rider," he added, picking up a crossbow. "They call me the Nose. And, while I can't put my finger on it, the scent ain't right. So . . . how the hell did you know where we were? I don't like it."

"He saved me, guys, remember?" Dan said fast. "This guy put everything on the line, fellas. Seriously." Standing, Dan's expression held an apology.

"Rider, stop. Put the weapon down, okay?" Damali shook her head and stood in front of Carlos. Although fatigue had dimmed her sensory awareness, common sense still prevailed. If Carlos were a vampire, or vamp helper, no religious guy would have let him know their location. The Templars weren't that sloppy.

"If a Templar sent you," Marlene said suspiciously. "Then?" But Marlene pulled back a bit and folded her arms. "How about if you stay on that side of the room, and Damali comes this way and stands with us . . . just till we get comfortable. We don't get many visitors at night around here—none that don't bear fangs."

"You know, Mar, now that you mention it, the hair is standing up on my arms." Shabazz bristled and picked up a weapon—glancing at Big Mike and J.L., who gave him nods and flanked him. "Damali, come on over to this side of the room."

"No! Would you guys stop? Carlos, show them whatever it is you came to show us."

"Thanks, D," Carlos murmured. The fact that she had remained on his side of the room was not lost on him at all. The Templar had made good on both parts of his agreement; he'd get him into the compound and would try to surround him with enough mercy that the guardians wouldn't sense his vampire status. But he only had a few minutes. Damali and her team, although weary, had keen sensory ability. He had to talk fast and get out.

"I got a newspaper shoved through my front mail slot, and inside of it were some drawings I couldn't understand at first . . . until this guy came and told me to choose wisely—then rolled. It was the weirdest thing. Said something about New Orleans, and bullshit going down at the big international concert. I figured one or two things—either the guy was whack and could pose a threat, so you should know, or, it had something to do with all this bizarre shit we've seen lately."

One by one the stances before him relaxed, and Carlos kept his attention roving over their expressions. It was a definite standoff, and the monitor behind J.L disturbed him. It was flashing like wild, but he'd been able to mute the sound. His attention was divided between many things at once. It was sapping him to project, cover the hole on his shirt, conceal the ring, keep the alarms from sounding, and stand away from any unusual lights on the table. The smell of holy water and incense was wearing him out, as was Damali's fragrance. The joint was a freakin' oven. He had to materialize maps and hope the guardians would heed the tunnel layouts before daylight came and the illusion of the maps torched. The big guy named Mike kept tilting his head like a bloodhound, like he could hear something, and the hunger was beginning to come back—the energy drain, kickin' his ass. He'd need to feed again after all this.

"Look," Carlos said, tossing the maps out for the guy named Mike to catch. "I don't know why I bothered. Turn off the lights, and I'm out. No need in jeopardizing you all—I have a lot of people looking for me. Dig? I want to slide out of here cool like, and not get sprayed when I roll."

The attention of Damali's palace guards went to the maps, and the blinking monitor no longer made the huge brother keep tilting his head. They descended upon the information like vultures, but he was curious—Damali hung back, near him. Deep.

"Where did you really get that, Carlos?" She'd whispered the question so quietly that she'd almost mouthed it instead of speaking.

The complexity of her question, and the way her voice had murmured, made him step closer to her than was advisable. The nearness was working on the wrong side of his brain, gnawing it away from cool logic.

"Now is not the time, but you have to trust me."

She nodded, and put her hand on his arm. He stood there glancing at her team as they absorbed the information, trying his best not to breathe in too much of her. The heat of her hand was melting his common sense. He needed to get out of there. Now.

"Do you know what this is, dude?" Rider walked around the table and saluted.

Shabazz and Big Mike gave a grudging nod.

"Looks like these things can open up a portal at will—big change," Shabazz muttered. "Not good."

"Apparently, there was an alliance formed," Carlos began with caution. "We're in the last days, the knight said, and key sectors of the demon realms have joined with a major sector of the vampire empire. Evil is concentrating, gaining force."

"A vampire-Amanthra hybrid . . ." Marlene whispered, making the group stare at her. "I didn't think it was possible, because the two species are enemies. But now it all makes sense."

"That's what the superstitious guy said." Carlos allowed his statement to sink into the wary team around him, and just pointed toward the maps without crossing the invisible boundary that had been drawn between the sides.

"He went on and on about how it used to be that the vampires could only come up through lair sites—burial sites, where they kept their coffins—and had to have human helpers move their coffins from place to place. But, under Fallon Nuit, he made a pact with the demons, and can use demon transpo levels to move underground without human support—like high-speed train zones through the third and fourth layers of Hell. Like I said, do what you want with the info. He was talking some crazy shit. I need to go."

"Man, you mean these things can just take a Concorde up from Hell and exit at any demon portal? Or they can jet underground and come up through any of Nuit's or his vampire line's lairs without aboveground movement?"

"Gone are the days of having Igor move a vamp's coffin in a horse and buggy and stow it in a basement, I guess," J.L. said with sarcasm. "This is the era of the global economy, brothers."

Carlos nodded to confirm the answer to Rider's question and to add weight to J.L.'s statement. Things had changed, and it was better that Damali's squad knew that, didn't underestimate what they were dealing with.

"That's what happened in Philly—it was like sound got sucked right out of the air in a vacuum, then vamps came up. We'd seen 'em manifest before, but not with the total absence of sound." Mike let his breath out and just shook his head. "This is problematic."

"Understatement," Rider muttered.

"The absence of sound is a result of the speed and the matter displacement. Demons move in silence—as do ghosts, but the vampires have more density, which is why they hold their form . . . unless they will a transformation into something else." Marlene shook her head. "It's all so clear. But I don't know how to block a moving target."

The team passed nervous glances among them. Carlos struggled as much with his desire to tell them more in order to give them a fighting chance, as he did with the oppressive environment they had him now trapped within. But he needed to get them to understand before he got out of there.

"Other master vampires cannot use the tunnels—Nuit was the

only one who formed an alliance . . . the religious guy said."
Carlos shrugged, trying to seem blasé about the whole thing, but
they were staring at him hard. "He said those zones are heavily
guarded by very militant elementals that were marginalized by
the vampire empire. The shit is getting ready to hit the fan, from
what I understand. You have the old vampire guard who can't
maintain unilateral power for business as usual, you have the new
guard that doesn't know how to utilize their power without
running amuck—and neither side can keep a lid on the chaos.
There are side deals and pacts being made everywhere."

"You seem very well versed—if not intimate—with the
whole issue at hand," Shabazz said in an even tone as he slowly
looked up from a map.

"I ought to be," Carlos admitted, shaking his head. He had
to think fast on his feet. He'd fucked up, had told them way
too much in his urgency to protect Damali. He and Shabazz
were from the same badlands in the past, and the bottom line
was that a brother from the hood could smell bullshit a mile
away—sensory gift or not. Shabazz wasn't even one of the noses,
but he could feel shit.

Carlos passed his line of vision over the group in a slow,
serious rove. "They did my brother, my cousin, my two best
friends—you read how they found them—their mothers
couldn't even bury them right. So, maybe that's why the Templar dude, being of the cloth and all, had some mercy, and filled
me in. That was cool of him, given that I was on a rampage to
find out who did it. Maybe they just didn't want me to snuff
somebody innocent and start a damned war."

"You're starting to believe this stuff, aren't you?"

Damali's question hacked at him. If she only knew. Believe?
He'd seen both sides; a slice of Heaven and a whole lotta Hell.
If he could just draw her into his arms and explain how this

crazy bullshit had gone down—and why it was now so important for her to trust him—if it was the last thing she did—even
if he was mixing truth with the evasions and lies now—it was
coming from a correct place in his heart. He tried to send it by
thought, but gave up, afraid to chance it. Not now. He was
already spread too thin.

"I'm starting to see things that I never understood before,"
he told her truthfully. "I don't know what to think, or what to
do, so I came here. That's all I can tell you."

"I know exactly where you are," she whispered, and briefly
looked away.

When her line of vision broke its hold on his, the absence of
those deep, brown orbs of understanding made his chest cavity
constrict from the loss. *I never want to hurt you, baby . . . that's
why I can't stay much longer.* He had to get it together. Pull out
of his own thoughts. He'd lapsed, trying to talk to her from his
mind. But that was pushing the envelope—he had to focus to
keep all illusions intact.

"What's in this level-three tunnel, man? Or on level four? A
demon grabbed at Damali today, and I'd like to know what we're
up against if we have to go after it." Rider had set down his
weapon to hold an edge of the map, but kept sniffing, and then
appeared to shake off a disturbing scent.

Carlos glanced at her. "You all right, baby?" He could feel
possessiveness riddle him. Who'd touched her!

She nodded, and he looked up at the team.

"I'm okay," she murmured, and came closer to him, burning
his shoulder where her touch landed. "Don't worry."

Carlos remained very, very still. He had to. He simply looked
at her as she touched him. It had seemed like she'd extended her
arm in slow motion, and he could see her pulse beat in the
delicate inside of her elbow, right where the forearm connected

to the upper arm, and beneath her bronze skin a faint blue-green vein hid . . . moving life through her. The motion was mesmerizing, as was the scent that the shifted air carried when she'd reached for him. And she wanted him to stay tonight for his own safety . . . to sleep in her room, love her hard and fast then tender so she didn't have to think about tomorrow. Had she any idea?

"I know you got a torch for my baby sis and all, brother, but you need to check them heat-seeking looks toward her while she's got six Glocked-up brothers and a momma who can fight staring you in the face," Mike said.

Whoa, bad slip. Way out of order. The big brother had bristled, rightfully so. All Carlos could do was nod and wait for the ruffled feathers to settle. Shit, he had to get out of there. Damali was a telepath—even if he wasn't sending, he was receiving, and it was messing with his cool. *Baby, please stop.*

"Mike, please," Damali whispered. "Can we stick to the matter at hand?"

This situation was getting confusing, and way too tense. Carlos let out his breath hard and raked his fingers through his hair.

"Listen, man, here's the deal—all bullshit aside. On level one, you have your average, run-of-the-mill ghosts, haints, souls that died with a grudge in their hearts, issues, and whateva. Level two, they get a little more trippy—like the poltergeists and the kind of mess that can possess somebody to make them do some whack shit in one second, then make them all of a sudden wake up from the daze, and not know anything about the three bodies in the room with them."

"Keep talking," Rider said. "The man is making sense here."

"All right," Carlos pressed. "I'ma say this one time like the guy told me, then I'm out. I've got things to do. He said, the further down you go, the less ghostlike the demon becomes, and the more solid it becomes as the density gets thicker—it compresses the soul-weight and creates these hideous deformities, and the souls that were once within those things are jacked and stored to be fed on within the levels, twisted like the demon's bodies are. The third level is where vengeance creatures come from and their territory is so wide it overlaps a part of the fourth level. So you've got your recipe for the garden-variety demon. By the time you get all the way down, though, now you are in a very sophisticated space. These are the things that take on the original form of man. The longer the being can hold its human form, the more sophisticated—like the difference between werewolves, at level five, and vamps—level six."

J.L. nodded, appraising the maps. "It's like a deconstruction/reconstruction pattern. First the body dies, the soul leaves—if it goes down to level one, it remains this floating, unformed negative energy. The further it gets pushed down, based on the weight of the sins on its back, depends on what level it clocks in at. Then there's the crossover zone," he added, pointing on the map that three people held.

"Yeah," Carlos said, pleased. "Level four. From there the physical matter starts trying to come back into its original form for reentry into the world. As above, so below. From above it is a very cool process—that's where babies come from."

Carlos chuckled, and Shabazz and Big Mike gave him a lopsided smile along with Rider.

"But," Marlene said in a quiet voice, "coming from the other direction, the birth process is backward. It spews up fully formed horrible entities, already corrupted, and at the end of their lives—instead of innocent, beautiful entities, not fully formed, growing, at the start of life."

The group fell quiet for a moment, and Carlos studied them, remembering Marlene's loss, and his own. He could have sworn that Damali visibly cringed as Marlene had spoken. It was as though her hand had mentally reached out to touch his face, but then retreated. Maybe it was just the bitter agony of hearing himself described as a creature of the night that had made him believe such a foolish thing. Maybe it was simply knowing that a mother stood in the room, remembering what her baby was like before it had been turned. Although they were blind to him, he could pull from them, and both seers barraged him with truths that hurt too bad to think about. Now all of those emotions crushed in on him. But he could still swear that Damali had reached out in her mind to stop the pain.

"What's on level seven?" Dan murmured.

"The exact opposite of what's in seventh Heaven," Damali said softly, "and we don't even name it in this compound."

"Okay," Rider said on a long breath. "So. If Nuit's gang can use the demon high-speed line, and won't have traditional aboveground coffins, how do we find them?"

Carlos put his hands behind his back and began to pace to keep from touching Damali. "His spot in New Orleans has a door."

"Been there, seen it, done it, not going back," Rider said emphatically, shaking his head.

"It's light sensitive," Mike added. "Breaks up illusion."

"Thought projection," Carlos replied, and then caught himself as the group stared at him. "The church guy said to bring down the light or let the light shine, some shit like that to dispel the illusion. Truth works the same way—all that religious rhetoric—the truth shall set you free. Makes as much sense as the rest of the stuff he said."

Again, he could feel the group relax, one by one. Another close call. Damn.

"Nuit has a mansion in Beverly Hills under an assumed

name—that's a possibility, and he owns a significant share of the high-rise that the Blood Music offices occupy, and we could place a safe bet that he'll open a channel in each of these five concert locations. If I was a betting man, and believed all the hype some sword-carrying priest told me, then I'd put my money on that as a sure thing."

"So," Damali said, going over to Carlos to touch his arm again, "if time wasn't so tight till the international thing, we could have tried to get invited to perform at one of his major concert locations. That way we could have gripped up and blasted it with light, hit 'em with some serious spoken word of truth, and we would have been able to open up one of his holes—then could find the coffin, and stake this bastard. We're already locked in to do your club as a venue, so I don't think we can get to do the big stadium portions at this late juncture. But we know all the locations of where major sections of their concert will be held, so at least we can go back later."

"We only need to take out the head to get to all the seconds that need to be eliminated, which takes out the thirds, and the fourths, and so on. We can cover everyone under Nuit with a salvation prayer, and when we take the head of the hydra, the rest of them will perish," Marlene said with a strong voice. "I've gotta do it for Raven."

Carlos didn't say a word. They didn't understand. One had to *individually* name each soul one wanted to claim back. Not to mention, the only reason it seemed that the seconds and below got dusted, had much to do with territorial realignments. If there was a master to step in, those lower levels weren't going any-where—unless that master wanted to build from the ground up. But that was way too much detail to drop on an already wary group. So, rather than further indict himself, he just nodded. Later, maybe, he'd explain to Damali.

"It's like an implosion bomb, the empire starts collapsing from the outside in until a whole line dies with one stake to the master's heart." Big Mike folded his arms over his chest. "Judged you wrong, Carlos. My bad. Was serious science you dropped."

"It's cool," Carlos said quietly.

Just listening to the way they described the wipeout, he wasn't sure why it tugged on him, but it did. Plus, what that big brother was talking about were fairy tales . . . unless a territorial harvest was turned down—which just didn't happen. And Damali's second touch was still seriously messing with his cool. His equilibrium was off by a long shot. His ten minutes were closing in on him. Marlene was looking at him real strange now, and Damali had come up to him—he could feel a hug pending and that was not the thing for her to do right now. It was time to jet.

"Look, I told you as much as I know, and I know you guys think I'm crazy. But I figured I'd pass on the message. However, right now, I need to handle some business in the streets. Hit the lights, and I'm out." He was babbling, and realized that he wasn't making sense. The temperature had kicked up, and that UV border . . . with Damali calling him from deep inside her head. *Oh come on, baby, cut it out.*

She filled his arms and hugged him, closing her eyes as her head found the center of his chest where it had been the night before. He could feel tears inside her heart as it thudded in anxiety against the cavity that held his dead one. She breathed life into him by sheer force of will, her grip tightening as her mind tried to get him to understand.

Magnificent, glorious warmth entered him and radiated out. Didn't she know that she was trying to use her body as a human shield to protect him from outside harm, and yet he was the very harm that she was grasping so tightly against her breasts?

Still she held him, her eyes siphoning a decision as she looked up, slaying him where he stood, in front of others who would never comprehend. Beautiful vision, they had named her correctly . . . still believing in him so much—and he couldn't promise not to manifest everything she abhorred.

"I wish you would just stay and be on our side."

"I can't. Baby . . . listen—"

"It's so crazy out there and I keep seeing you hurt bad in my head. Don't leave; please . . . don't go back out into that madness. If a Templar of the Covenant came to you, then it's not too late."

She closed her eyes and tilted her chin up and breathed deeply while shaking her head no, don't go. He raised his chin higher than hers and tried to fight the urge to close his eyes, too, and lost. Her protective squad had every right to just waste him on the spot; he knew it, but didn't care. Because at that moment, he couldn't resist breathing in her hair, and there was no force on the planet that could have stopped the tremor that she'd sent down his spine with her hand. He'd take a silver bullet for her— or whatever else they had for him, as long as it put him out of his misery.

"I gotta go," he whispered to her, ignoring the very concerned team in his peripheral vision. They were becoming further and further away in his mind as her face tilted up toward his again and her lips parted.

"Why, Carlos? Has it always been like this? You know you have been dancing on the edge of disaster all your life, and this time, I think you're in too deep. Didn't you see the maps of Hell? Or if you don't believe, then look at what's in the newspapers. Isn't that alone enough? Where does all this lead?"

He couldn't answer her, as a power within Damali that was greater than fear, greater than self-preservation, greater than caring what others might say, exuded from her and began seeping into his pores, and it was this thing called righteous conviction. She'd held her ground against him for five years on the point, and yet here he couldn't last five minutes in her arms . . . not with her team looking anxious and holding weapons. She had him trapped by her spoken words—truth. And he was bound by every other gift she'd been blessed with, and it began unraveling his instinct for survival, right at the foundation level . . . and replaced it with the next one up on the primal rung.

He'd opened his mouth to urge her to let him go, and she'd filled it with her own. Just like that. Right there. No argument. Her brethren were left dumbfounded. The lady that was like her mom stood paralyzed, wringing her hands. It happened so fast, a split-second reflex. Had been a long time coming—but still blew him away.

That's when his inner foundation snapped, discipline uprooted, logic vanished, and his fingers became tangled in her hair, despite the throats that cleared in the background, while his hand slid down the center of her back, and they hit a wall by the door with force, the seal between them unbroken. He had thought he'd crushed her spine, somehow, until she gasped, and that had only made him kiss her harder, swallowing the sound, her desire in his throat, his lungs, sending back his own deep reply, fueling a double-edged hunger which she answered with a hard rake down his back. Right then and there, as her nails scored his flesh, he felt himself lose it. He pulled back when his gums began to rip too fast. He took out the frustration on the cinder-block wall next to her. His cover was blown.